MAKE YOU FEEL MY LOVE

A SMALL TOWN ROMANTIC SUSPENSE

KAIT NOLAN

Make You Feel My Love

Written and published by Kait Nolan

Copyright 2016 Kait Nolan

Cover design by Lori Jackson

AUTHOR'S NOTE: The following is a work of fiction. All people, places, and events are purely products of the author's imagination. Any resemblance to actual people, places, or events is entirely coincidental.

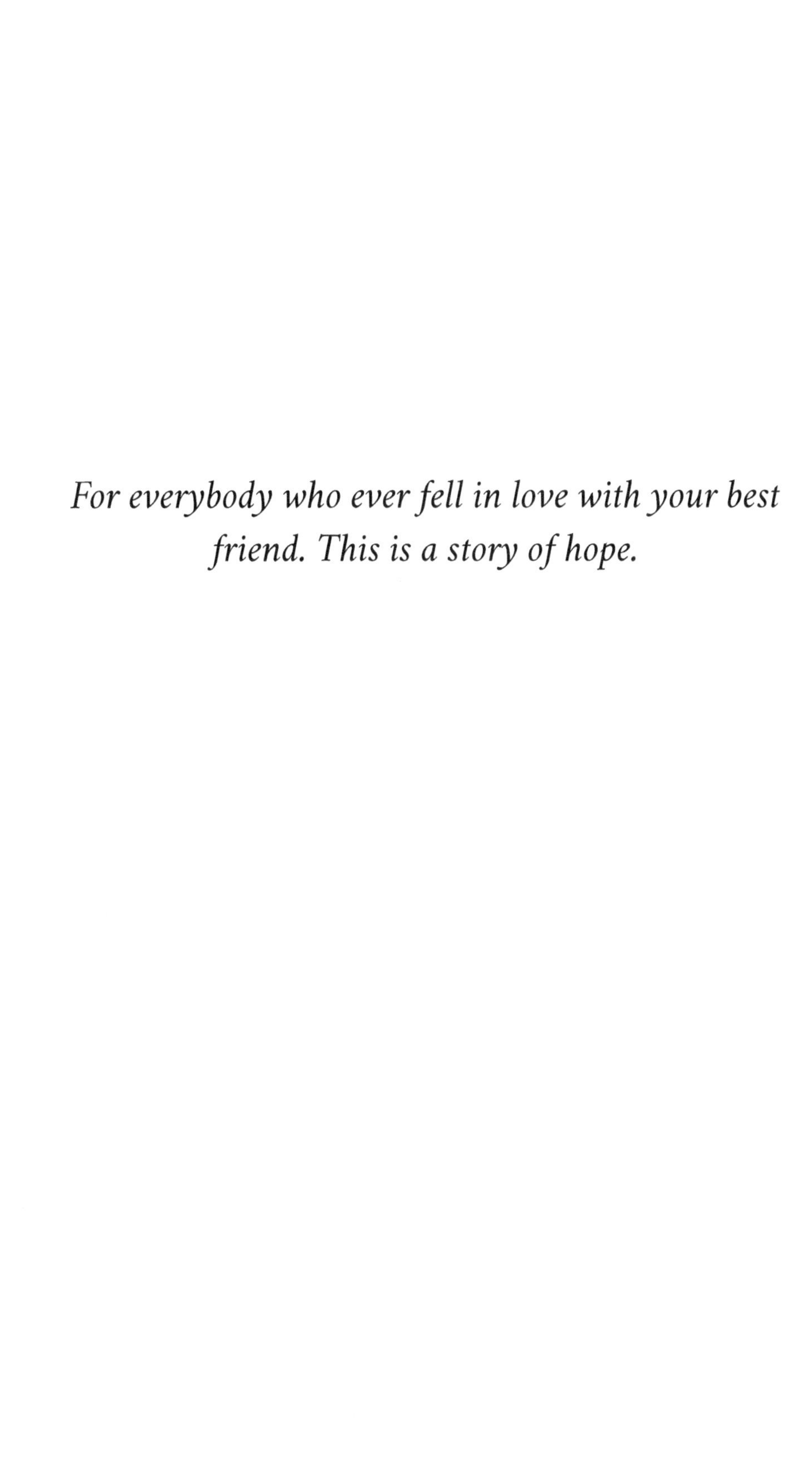

For everybody who ever fell in love with your best friend. This is a story of hope.

A LETTER TO READERS

Dear Reader,

A few points of note:

The original version of this book, *If I Didn't Care,* came out in 2016. At that point, I had already been waiting what felt like FOREVER to get to Autumn and Judd's story because a lot of stuff had to happen in Wishful to get to that point. I rushed through the book—the fastest one I've ever written—and put it out. The vast majority of readers were happy. And so was I— for a while. But there were certain elements of the story that just kept niggling at me. Points that just burrowed under my skin because they'd been poorly thought out and I *knew I could do better.* That's one of the greatest blessings and joys of being an indie published author. I CAN fix the things that bother me. It took me four years to figure out how but *Make You Feel My Love* is the culmination of my true vision for what Autumn and Judd's story could be. Nearly half the book has been rewritten, doing a better job of setting up for the series that follows, and all of it has been tightened up and smoothed over. As such I've chosen to release it as a brand new book with a new title and remove the original version from sale.

This book is set in the Deep South. As such, it contains a great deal of colorful, colloquial, and occasionally grammatically incorrect language. This is a deliberate choice on my part as an author to most accurately represent the region where I have lived my entire life. This book also contains swearing and pre-marital sex between the lead couple, as those things are part of the realistic lives of characters of this generation, and of many of my readers.

If any of these things are not your cup of tea, please consider that you may not be the right audience for this book. There are scores of other books out there that are written with you in mind. In fact, I've got a list of some of my favorite authors who write on the sweeter side on my website at https://kaitnolan.com/on-the-sweeter-side/

If you choose to stick with me, I hope you enjoy!

Happy reading!

Kait

CHAPTER 1

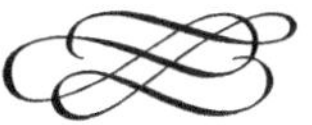

Dear God, if I'd wanted to break up elementary school fights, I would've become a teacher.

Headed into the second leg of a double shift, Officer Judd Hamilton tried his best to clamp down on the irritation. He had, after all, volunteered to organize FountainFest safety for the police department. And if that meant keeping Jim Vernon and Neil Faber from coming to blows over who got to kick off the 1-mile Fun Run, then that's what he'd do.

Beyond the two geezers, he caught a glimpse

of his girlfriend, Mary Alice, smiling at him. Her group of third graders was obviously excited about the race but behaved themselves. Unlike these two. He really wished he could put the pair of them in time out.

Instead, he tried his best to channel the calm, reasonable tone he'd heard Mary Alice use on her class. "Look, gentleman, I respect the fact that you were both told you could fire the starter pistol. I know it's a big honor—" *for the three seconds it will take for everyone to forget you were ever there,* "and neither of you wants to be disappointed, but let's have a little bit of perspective and festival goodwill, okay?"

"I'm not giving up my place!" Jim bounced like a banty rooster.

Neil's age-spotted hands curled to fists. "Why you old—"

Judd inserted himself bodily between them. "Y'all simmer down, or neither of you is doing anything." His over-tired mind raced, looking for a solution that didn't involve him plunking both of them in a cell for the duration of the festival. Somebody somewhere had to have some more blanks. "Look, if we can come up with a second starter pistol, you could both take the shot starting the race simultaneously. Equals. Is that acceptable?"

"I don't know…" Jim waffled.

Recognizing an opening when he saw one, Judd pushed. "Wouldn't it look good to the townspeople to see the presidents of the Kiwanis and Rotary Clubs joint officiating?"

Neil crossed his arms, rocking back on orthopedic-sneakered feet. "Well, I suppose that might be okay."

"As long as we both get to have our banners," Jim insisted.

"One on each side of the starting line," Judd promised.

"I can live with that," Neil allowed.

"Good. Great. Y'all do that. Banners in place on those barricades, and y'all get in position. The race should be starting in fifteen minutes."

Lord have mercy. Was all this extra crap *really*

worth enduring for the chance to be Chief of Police?

Of course it was. Because being Chief wasn't the end goal. It was just a means to an end.

He waited until the combatants scurried off to their respective civic groups, then radioed to find some blanks. Couldn't very well have civilians firing actual shots, when town was crawling with pedestrians for the first annual Wishful FountainFest. Looking at the throngs of people, Judd couldn't help but wish their city planner wasn't quite so good at her job. The department didn't have the manpower to adequately police this many people.

Should've called in some of the off-duty deputies from the county.

But the departmental budget couldn't afford that either. Still, he'd seen at least two of the deputies in the crowd. Men he trusted, who could handle themselves. If anything went down, they'd lend a hand. Not that anything was *likely* to happen, but Judd had plenty of personal experience that made him less com-placent than most.

As soon as the starter pistol situation was taken care of, Judd walked over to Mary Alice. Her sunny hair was pulled through the back of a FountainFest ball cap, and she was dressed to run in a t-shirt and shorts that showed off her toned legs. The sight gave him a bit of a jolt. He was so used to her conservative, elementary school attire, he often forgot what was under-neath. Which was a terrifying sign of exactly how much he'd been working these last few months.

Need to rectify that.

"Kyle, pull your shorts up. Does anybody have to go to the bathroom before we get started?"

"Everything under control here?" Judd asked.

She looked up, blue eyes twinkling. "As in control as it ever is."

"At least they're better behaved than the race officials," he observed.

"You get whatever that was sorted?" Her gaze slipped past his shoulder. "Danielle, stop picking your nose."

"Barely. Race will be starting in just a bit." A jaw-splitting yawn interrupted the statement.

She gave his arm a sympathetic squeeze. "Hang in there. Once this double is over, you'll be off for four whole days."

"Thank God." The prospect of eight straight on a horizontal surface was more appealing than Venus herself.

With a quick glance at her charges, Mary Alice stepped into him, rising on her toes. Judd still had to lean down so she could whisper in his ear. "Maybe after you've slept, we could spend some quality time together. Do a little catching up."

He hummed a noncommittal noise, wondering why he couldn't drum up any enthusiasm about getting reacquainted with those legs of hers. It was the double shift. Had to be. A flash of red hair distracted him from the suggestion of what they could do with some of that quality time.

Autumn Buchanan, his oldest, dearest friend, cut through the crowd with Boudreaux, Judd's massive bloodhound-mastiff mix, trotting beside her on a leash. While he'd been on nights the last week, she'd been dogsitting. Livia Applewhite, the children's librarian and one of her closest girlfriends, trailed in her wake. Judd straightened, eyes zeroing in on the number pinned to Autumn's chest.

"Good morning, y'all!" She immediately launched into cheery greetings to the children she and Livia knew from the library, introducing them to Boudreaux. The dog sat, patiently enduring the kids' adoration, his big tail slowly sweeping the sidewalk.

"Are y'all looking forward to the race?" Livia asked.

As she drew the children into excited conversation, Autumn stepped forward, extending the to-go cup in her hand. "I come on a mission of mercy. A Zombie Killer from The Grind.

Extra shot of caramel, just how you like it. Figured you'd be dragging about now. Plus, Boudreaux's missing his daddy."

Judd automatically took the cup in one hand, and gave his dog a head rub with the other, but he couldn't tear his eyes off of Autumn. "Thanks. What are you wearing?"

She glanced down at her shorts and fitted tank top, which displayed miles of lean, toned legs and arms that he forced himself to ignore. "I realize you're on a double, but if you're so tired you don't recognize running gear, I'm not sure you should be on duty."

"I'm talking about the race number."

She deliberately widened her green eyes at him. "It's called *participation*."

"You're not running." With a struggle, he managed to make it a question rather than an order.

"I am, actually. Livia, Riley, and I are doing it together."

Frustration whipped through him. "You

aren't supposed to exert yourself. Dr. Webb said—"

"That exercise is *good* for my heart."

"He meant yoga or swimming." Hadn't he? Nice non-competitive stuff that wouldn't get her heart rate or blood pressure up. Nothing that might aggravate her heart condition.

"It's a one mile *fun run,* not a triathlon. Besides, Boudreaux is looking forward to some exercise. Aren't you, boy?" She scratched behind his ears, and Boudreaux pressed into her touch, eyes rolling back in bliss.

Missing his daddy, my ass.

"Boudreaux's idea of exercise is walking from the sofa down to the end of my dock."

"Which should be proof enough that I won't be over exerting myself. Stop worrying, Grandpa."

That was like ordering him not to breathe. He couldn't just turn off twenty-five years of protective instincts. Not when he could still so clearly see her lying in that hospital bed, hooked up to half a dozen monitors and machines.

Someone's voice boomed over a bullhorn. "Everybody participating in the Fun Run please take your position behind the starting line. The race will begin in five minutes."

Livia craned her neck to look over the crowd. "We should go find Riley."

"Gotta go." Autumn was already turning away before he could think of any other rational arguments against her running in this race. "Drink the coffee, Judd. You'll feel better. Bye, Mary Alice!"

Beside him, Mary Alice lifted her hand in a wave. "She'll be fine."

Judd grunted a response and scanned the course to see what medical personnel were on duty, in case something went wrong. The First Aid tent was about thirty yards away, on one corner of the town green. They were more expecting scraped knees and sprains, but a defibrillator would be there. And he had his own EMT training to fall back on in an emergency.

None of it made him feel any better, but short of bodily stopping her from participating, it was the best he could do. Not that she'd had any incidents in years, and her last check-up with her cardiologist, three months before, had given her an all clear.

Judd blinked, realizing Mary Alice had been talking to him. "Sorry. What?"

A flicker of exasperation passed over her pretty face. "I asked if you'd be up in time tomorrow for us to go to your family's Sunday brunch?"

"Yeah, sure. Mom's been fussing she hasn't seen me." It'd be good to see his family. Plus, he needed to firm up plans to go shopping with Autumn for his brothers' birthday. No one was better at coming up with the best gag gifts for the twins than she was.

"No one outside the department has seen you since you went on nights a month ago."

"Part of the job." He shrugged. "Race is about to start. Y'all have fun and be careful."

He bent to give her an absent kiss and hit her cheek when she turned at the last moment.

Okay, so she was annoyed. He'd work on smoothing that over once this shift was done and he'd slept. He headed further up the street, judging the best spot to keep an eye out for Autumn. Just in case. The race course ran the length of the green, down Main Street, onto Franklin Street before looping back on Market Street to finish on the opposite side of the green. If she had issues, it would be on the tail end of the course. He positioned himself on the far corner of the green at Main and Spring Streets to watch the start.

At 6'3", Judd could see over most of the crowd, so when the starter pistols went off—in tandem, thank God—he kept an eagle eye on the surge of people flowing down Main Street. With her bright flash of hair, Autumn was easy to pick out. She, Riley, and Livia were in a tight cluster, with Boudreaux trotting ahead. None of them was going faster than a jog. He could tell Autumn was even talking and laughing as they went. The tightness in his chest eased a fraction.

Mitch Campbell, one of Judd's poker buddies, stepped up to the curb to watch the girls. "I don't think Boudreaux quite knows what to think about all these people."

"We both know he'd follow Autumn anywhere."

"Didn't know she was running."

"Neither did I," Judd grumbled. But at least she was being smart about it. No outright sprinting. And honestly, Autumn was never reckless with her health. She just seemed to worry about it a lot less than he did.

"Not sure you can call what they're doing running," Mitch observed as they disappeared from view.

Judd turned to make his way to the opposite corner, across from Sweet Magnolias Bakery, aware of Mitch falling into step beside him.

"Man, you look like warmed over death this morning."

"Thanks for that. Coffee hasn't kicked in."

He drained it on the walk, feeling a rush of gratitude that Autumn had thought of it. With all his herding of people this morning, there hadn't been time to go by The Daily Grind himself.

"You gonna make it to poker night next week, now you're finally off nights?"

"That's the plan. But I've gotta work on digging myself out of the doghouse with Mary Alice. I've been working my ass off and neglecting her lately." Longer than lately, if he was honest with himself.

"Man, buy her something shiny. Never met a woman who couldn't be appeased with jewelry and flowers."

"Jewelry's never been my style."

"Even better," Mitch declared, thumping him on the back. "She won't expect it and it'll be a surprise."

"You sure?" Didn't gifts of jewelry come with certain expectations?

"Absolutely. Go by Sanderson's and ask

Rosanna about the doghouse special. She's got a good selection of options."

Judd spared Mitch a glance. "You sound like you have a lot of experience with this."

"Well, I'm still friends with all my exes."

There.

Autumn came into view, moving with the same unhurried jog she'd had at the start. Boudreaux trotted obediently beside her, periodically looking up at her in complete adoration. Her cheeks were flushed from exertion, but not alarmingly so. She was okay, exactly as she'd said she'd be. The tension in his muscles drained out, and Judd could practically hear her in his head, *See there, Grandpa.*

Turning back to Mitch, he picked up the thread of conversation. "But they're exes."

"Only because I got out before any of them got too serious. Talk to Rosanna. She won't steer you wrong."

What the hell? It couldn't hurt.

"WE NEED A PLAN OF ATTACK."

Autumn looked with affectionate forbearance across the table at her best friend and thought of how many times in the past twenty-five years he'd said exactly that. "It's shopping for birthday presents, Judd, not a war."

"Same difference. There are *people*." His sharp blue eyes narrowed on the word.

She smiled into her coffee. "You're just grumpy because you haven't recovered from FountainFest and all those extra shifts you've been pulling."

"Hell yes. Ergo, I want to get through this whole process as quickly as possible." He inhaled a quarter of his tall stack of pancakes in about three bites, as if to prove the point.

"We *could* have done this sooner if you weren't working all the time," she chided.

"Couldn't be helped. Chief Curry's been leaning on me pretty heavy lately."

"Which is exactly what you wanted."

Judd shrugged. "I figured the decision about the replacement Chief would've been made by now. Nobody thought this would drag on for over a year. Either way, this is the time we've got, and gag gifts must be procured. It's tradition."

Curmudgeon or not, Judd Hamilton was reliable as the rising sun. Since the pair of them were old enough to ride their bikes downtown, they'd established an annual tradition of finding the best possible gag gifts for his twin brothers. As she'd been an honorary Hamilton for more than a decade, she took great pleasure in punking Leo and Eli.

As they polished off their breakfast and Judd wrote out a list of stops like he was planning a tactical assault, Mama Pearl brought their check. Autumn started to reach for it, but Judd's hand shot out and snagged it.

"What are you doing?"

He was already digging out his wallet. "Buying breakfast."

Autumn bristled. "I can buy my own breakfast."

"You've been working on half-time hours

since spring. I've been working overtime. I'm buying breakfast."

"Don't be an ass."

"I'm an ass for buying my oldest friend breakfast?" He fixed her with that cop stare that was meant to intimidate but instead heated things that had no business heating.

Autumn shifted in her seat, crossing her legs to get more comfortable and bumping his instead. A zing of awareness shot from her kneecap further north, and she repressed the urge to curse, focusing instead on keeping every nuance of her expression dialed to annoyed rather than attracted. God knew, she had plenty of practice.

Before she could come up with an answer that wasn't some shade of "I don't need you to take care of me"—which would just piss him off —Mama Pearl came back.

She gave a hmmph that conveyed a wealth of opinion over their stalemate before handing Autumn a thick envelope. "Omar sent this out. You won the pool on Tucker and Corinne."

Judd tossed down his napkin. "Of course you did. How many does this make?"

"Seventeen," Autumn said sweetly, plucking the check from his hand and pulling three fives from the envelope to pass back to Mama Pearl.

He stared at her. "Seriously?"

"What can I say? I'm lucky when it comes to betting on love." Which was an enormous crock of shit. She'd never been brave enough to gamble with him. Until today.

"She is the reigning champion," Mama Pearl confirmed, before ambling off to get her change.

"What's your secret?" Judd asked.

"Secret?"

"Why is it you're so good at picking who's going to end up with who and when?"

He absolutely wouldn't like the answer to that. Reminding Judd that she was adept at reading people's body language because she'd grown up in a household where understanding that meant the difference between surviving her father's crazy pseudo-religious delusions and getting the belt—or worse—would ruin the mood of the day. He'd gotten her out years ago. That was the important thing. Besides, it was a lot more fun using her skills for love instead of survival.

Now her brain was occupied with broaching a far more terrifying topic. How exactly *did* you tell your best friend you're in love with him?

"Maybe it's all those romance novels. It's made me extra sensitive to spotting the signs. And anyway, betting on love sure as hell beats editing dissertations for foreign students in terms of supplementing my income."

His lips quirked in that rare devil-may-care grin that made her heart stutter. "You've actually made enough on this to supplement your income?"

It wasn't the only supplement to her income, but it was the only one he needed to know about. She made a show of fanning the remaining cash in the envelope. "I just got handed all my shopping money. For the twins and for a splurge."

"Then I guess we'd better go spend it."

Per tradition, stop number one was the fountain in the middle of the town green. Constructed just after the Civil War, the fountain had earned some local notoriety over the past century and a half. It was, after all, why the town was named Wishful. Usually Autumn tossed in her coin and made a less selfish wish—there were plenty of other people who could use a little bit of magic. But if she was really going through with this, she needed all the help she could get. She'd even saved a silver dollar specially for the occasion. The coin lay against her sweaty palm. She stared down at the smooth surface of the water, trying to slow her heart and think of the right way to phrase the wish.

"You okay, Firefly?"

The childhood nickname pulled her back to the past, to the first time they'd stood here and the wish she'd made then. The casual stroke down her back kept her in the now.

"You know, when we were twelve and you brought me here that first time, I didn't believe in wishes. Didn't see the point. But you gave me a quarter and told me to make a wish anyway. For anything I wanted. Do you know what I wished for?"

"What?"

She lifted her gaze to his face. "I wished for a new family. And you gave me yours. I can never repay you for that."

"We're not keeping a balance sheet, Autumn. It's not something you owe us for."

No. That had been a gift without price. And if she did this. If she changed things, his friendship wasn't the only thing she risked.

Be brave. Be like the strong heroines you write about.

Eyes on his, she fisted the silver dollar and made her wish. *I wish for the courage and strength of heart to do what needs to be done, say what needs to be said.*

She didn't look as she tossed the coin. Didn't even glance over at the solid *thunk* in the water. She could only watch him. For twenty-five years, he'd been her strength, her shield, her confidant. And she was about to see if he'd be more.

"Judd, there's something I need to—"

"Autumn!"

The sound of her name had the words clogging like a logjam in her throat as she turned to see who had such craptastic timing.

"Mark?"

A history professor at Wachoxee County Community College, Mark Caulfield had been stopping in at the library once or twice a week for a couple of years. He was charming, erudite, and a little shy. Lanky, with a penchant for tweed—a less attractive Jude Law type. Livia had been making bets for months about when Mark would get up the nerve to ask Autumn out. He always seemed to stop just short of crossing the line from flirtation to action. Which was perfectly fine with Autumn. She enjoyed their flirtation, enjoyed the lack of pressure to actually commit to anything else. And here he was with flowers in his hand when she was about to confess her love to Judd.

Crap on a cracker.

"Good morning, lovely lady." With a sheepish smile, he held a bouquet of bright yellow tulips out.

Autumn reached to take the flowers automatically, though a part of her instinctively recoiled. She couldn't stop the flinch as her hand curled around the stems. "What's this?"

"I saw these and they made me think of you. A little spot of sunshine. I went by the library to deliver them. Livia told me you were out shopping, so I took a chance that I could catch you."

Autumn made a mental note to murder her friend. She forced a smile and focused on the gesture rather than the flowers themselves. There was no possible way Mark could've known she loathed yellow tulips. They'd been her mother's favorite flower. "They're lovely."

She waited, watching splotches of color rise

to Mark's cheeks as he shifted from foot to foot. *Please don't let today be the day he finally asks.*

Mark finally seemed to register Judd's presence, which said a lot about the man's focus on her, as Judd had been looming behind her like a guard dog since the moment Mark had shown up.

"Hi. Mark Caulfield." He offered his hand.

Judd stepped forward to take it. "Judd Hamilton."

"And you're—"

"The best friend," Judd supplied. His gaze swept Mark from head to toe and clearly found him lacking. Not that anyone who wasn't well-versed in the microexpressions of Judd would notice.

"Ah," Mark said.

The silence spun out. One beat, then two.

Ordinarily, Autumn would've jumped into the breach, tried to put Mark more at ease with the scripted niceties used by all women in the South. But she wanted—needed—him to go away. So she said nothing, employing the same tactics she knew Judd used in interrogation, hoping Mark would be so acutely uncomfortable, he'd lose his nerve.

"Well, I—you're in the middle of something. I just wanted to give you the flowers. I'll let you get back to your shopping now."

"Thanks."

"I guess I'll see you when those interlibrary loans come in."

"I'll be sure to let you know," she promised.

Mark gave a little wave and shrugged his messenger bag higher on his shoulder, heading back across the green.

Autumn turned back toward Judd. She felt the weight of his gaze—those eyes that always saw too much and not enough.

"Do you want me to take them?" He knew. Of course, he knew what these would mean to her. It was just one of the many reasons she loved him.

"No. They're just…flowers. I can deal. Just… just tell me when he's gone so I can find somewhere to dispose of them."

Mark's interruption had seriously thrown Autumn off her game. Because the moment to speak had passed, she didn't resist when Judd took her arm. "C'mon. Let's walk."

"Let's swing by Brides and Belles. I'll give them to Babette. Someone might as well enjoy them."

"Sure. I've got something to pick up in that area anyway."

Dimly, Autumn wondered where, but was too rattled to ask. She'd find out soon enough.

She felt better once the flowers were out of her hands. Steadier. She joined Judd back out on the sidewalk. "Okay, List Master, where is our first stop? You said you had something to pick up over here."

"This way." He headed down the block. As she fell into step beside him, he said, "Hey what was it you were going to say earlier? Before we were interrupted. You seemed pretty serious."

"I was. I…" Autumn trailed off, staring blankly at the display window he'd stopped in front of. "What are we doing here?"

"Oh, I've just got to run in and pick up something for Mary Alice."

"Here?" They were standing outside Sanderson's Jewelers.

"Yeah, I've got something on order. Want to come in and see?"

Autumn's mind ground to a screeching halt, as everything she'd been about to say simply blanked. Judd Hamilton did not buy jewelry. At no point in their twenty-five years of friendship had he ever given something sparkly to one of his girlfriends. He'd never even gotten any cheesetastic jewelry for his mom on Mother's Day. And he had something on order for Mary Alice.

There was only one thing it could possibly be.

Something burst inside her, a white hot nova of shock sweeping through her body, reverberating through her chest. For long seconds, she waited for the pain to take her to her knees. But there was no physical pain. She wasn't dying this time, even though she was losing him now as surely as she'd nearly lost him years ago to a bullet meant for her. And for a moment she regretted that the surgeons had repaired her heart. Because that meant she had to live through this, watching him build a life with someone else, knowing she'd never even been in the running.

She drew on every shred of control she had to smile at him. Because she loved him and she wanted him to be happy.

"No. That's what I wanted to tell you. I'm going to have to bail on our tradition. I'm supposed to meet Mitzi to help finish up a grant for the library. With all the budget cuts, I really can't afford to tell her no, even though it's technically my day off. There's a deadline." The lie rolled off her tongue with surprising ease.

His expression clouded. "Well shit. Why didn't you say something earlier?"

"She just emailed me this morning, and I thought we could at least do breakfast. But I need to get on. You go ahead and finish your shopping. I'll see you later, okay?"

Worry was written all over his face as he studied her.

Please. Please let me go right now.

"Yeah, okay."

Because she felt the weight of his gaze on her, she didn't run, though every instinct urged her to flee. She kept her strides even and unhurried, though she was starting to shake. She kept her head held high, though she wanted to scream. She'd survived more than her fair share over the years. She'd find a way to survive this.

But as she passed the cursed fountain, she wondered how she'd survive it without him.

CHAPTER 2

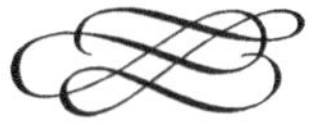

$\mathcal{A}$utumn was lying.

That fact didn't concern Judd nearly as much as the why behind it. She was a lot more upset about the flowers than she wanted to admit. He'd seen her face, seen that subtle loss of color in her cheeks as she'd accepted them. The poor bastard couldn't have known the dark associations she had with yellow tulips. Caulfield had effectively killed any shot he might've had with Autumn—if he'd had a shot to begin with. She hadn't looked thrilled to see him.

Was she having the nightmare again? And what the hell could Judd do about it if she was?

The question circled his brain as he stepped back out of Sanderson's. Had she looked more anxious the last few weeks? Shown any signs of being less rested than usual? Had she seemed off somehow? He didn't know and that pissed him off. He was her best friend. He ought to know these things. But he'd been working so damned much, he'd barely seen her. He'd seen Mary Alice even less—hence the apology bracelet he'd just picked up. He hoped Mitch was right and it would take him out of the running for world's worst boyfriend. The fact was, his relationships had been taking a backseat to the job lately, and that needed to change.

Birthday shopping without Autumn held absolutely no appeal. Who else was going to help him find the most embarrassing gifts for his brothers? So he blew off the rest of his carefully constructed list and headed for the offices of *The Wishful Observer*. Maybe his mom knew what was going on.

She was just emerging from the conference room as Judd stepped into the newspaper. "Judd!"

"Hey Mom." He gave her a squeeze.

"I wasn't expecting to see you twice in two days. Where's Autumn? Weren't you two headed out to shop for the twins?"

"We were but she bailed on me."

Patty frowned. "That's not like her."

"I know. We had a bit of an incident."

Over another cup of coffee, Judd filled her in on Mark Caulfield and the flowers. "She tried to play it off like it was no big deal, but ten minutes later she outright lied to my face and left. She hasn't missed this tradition in eighteen years."

"It's been a long time since she got that rattled. Is something else going on?"

"I was hoping you could tell me. I haven't exactly been on the same wavelength as everybody else the last few weeks. Did something happen while I was working nights? Has she seemed off to you? Worried at all?"

"No. I mean, you saw her at brunch yesterday. She was completely herself—irreverent as ever, teasing Leo and Eli."

"Not even concerned about being down to half hours at work?"

"Not at all. Although, I admit that worries me some. It's not as if head librarian was ever a job that paid big bucks that would've given her the chance to save much. But she insists she's fine financially every time your father and I ask if we can help."

"You and I both know she won't take financial help. We may all consider her part of the family, and she'll accept everything that goes along with that until it comes to paying her own way."

After her mother split town and her father went to prison, there'd been no question that Autumn was moving in with them. She'd finished the last year and a half of high school living as an honorary Hamilton. He'd never understood why his parents didn't just adopt her and formally make her the daughter she'd always been.

"Do you think she's really okay, money-wise?" his mom asked.

"She's been cleaning up on all the pools at Dinner Belles. Got a fat envelope at breakfast this morning for Tucker and Corinne. But I have a hard time imagining she's making so much there that it's really alleviating the strain." Which left him wondering if she'd cut everything back to bare bones without telling him. Was that what today had been about? Was she finally going to ask for help? "I wish she'd just move out to Hope Springs with me and save on the rent money until she's in a better place financially."

His mother arched a brow.

"What's wrong with that? She loves being able to look out over the lake."

"Well, apart from the fact that Autumn likes having her own space, I expect Mary Alice would take issue with it."

"How is it any different from my making Leo or Eli the same offer?"

Even as she stared at him in disbelief, Judd told himself it wasn't justified.

"Because as much as we love her, Autumn isn't your sister. Nobody else can possibly understand the closeness you two share. That's hard to compete with."

He and Autumn were bound by blood in ways so much thicker than family. The truth was, he'd never had a girlfriend who wasn't threatened by their relationship. But there was no reason for it. Things weren't romantic between him and Autumn. They never had been and never could be.

"Mary Alice gets along with Autumn just fine."

"Or she's too hung up on you to say otherwise for fear you'll dump her."

Judd scowled. "I wouldn't do that."

She looked askance at him. "Really? If she put her foot down and gave you an ultimatum, her or Autumn, you'd be okay with that?"

"You know I don't do ultimatums. But I could certainly have a discussion about it like a rational guy to explain how things are."

The truth of it was that he had a responsibility to protect Autumn, so she'd always be a big part of his life. Any woman he was with had to be okay with that. And why shouldn't she be? Autumn always went out of her way to be friendly and inclusive when he dated somebody. Well, except for one or two girls in college, but they'd been all wrong for him, so Judd wasn't about to complain.

Patty was still looking at him like he had a few screws loose. Before he could open his mouth to explain—or dig that hole any deeper—his cell phone rang. Checking the screen, he recognized the number for dispatch. "Hamilton."

"Judd, where are you?" Inez Barlow, who'd served as both dispatch and admin for the department for nearly twenty years before he'd joined it, sounded shaken. And she was never shaken.

Judd snapped into go mode. "At the paper. What's wrong?"

"You need to come in. It's Chief Curry. He's had a heart attack."

THE CAVALRY WAS COMING in hot. A cloud of dust boiled up behind the two cars barreling down the drive to Applewhite Farms. Autumn rose from the swing, shifting her death grip from the chain to the porch rail because her legs weren't exactly stable.

As soon as she was parked, Livia charged up the stairs, pale blonde hair caught up in a princess tiara that said she'd come straight from storytime. Riley was right behind, lab coat flapping in the breeze. Bless them. Autumn hadn't said what the emergency was. They'd both just made arrangements and dropped everything because she needed them.

Because that's what friends did.

"What's wrong?" Livia demanded. "And why are we meeting way out here? Not that I mind offering up my house to the cause, but if we need to hide a body, I've gotta change clothes first."

"We're here because I'm a lousy liar, and if both of you showed up at my place, Judd would know something is wrong. And I just…can't, right now."

Riley slid an arm around her shoulders and the simple touch made Autumn want to crumple. "Honey, what happened?"

"Fucking Mark." Except, no, that wasn't fair. This wasn't Mark's fault. He'd just been in the wrong place at the wrong time.

Livia cringed. "Oh God. He looked so cute and hopeful with his flowers and so disappointed when you weren't working. I didn't think it was a big deal that I told him where you were."

"He had either the best timing or the worst. I don't know which. He stopped me from making a complete fool of myself."

Riley and Livia exchanged a look. "With Judd?"

Autumn nodded once, her throat constricting with the effort of everything she was holding back. "I was going to tell him."

Riley's arm tightened. "Tell him what?"

"Everything. That I'm in love with him. That I always have been. That I want to be with him. I was going to lay it all on the line." She shook her head in futility as the tears spilled over. "God, I'm so stupid. I should never have paid attention to that letter."

Livia closed ranks, wrapping an arm around her waist, as if she knew Autumn couldn't keep standing on her own. "What letter?"

There was no explaining it. Not without coming clean entirely. But why else had she called her friends? Wasn't it time to tell *someone* the secret?

"It's a lot to explain."

"Then let's go inside. We'll make you some tea, and you can take your time."

They bundled her through the door,

nudging her onto the sofa in the living room. Autumn hadn't realized she was cold until Livia draped a throw around her shoulders. Nearly ninety degrees outside and she was freezing. Clutching the blanket tighter, she cuddled the box of tissues Riley retrieved from the powder room and cried harder in gratitude for the comfort of other women.

By the time Livia came in with a tea tray and a plate of cookies, she'd managed to get herself somewhat under control. As her friends arranged themselves on either side of her, she slipped off her shoes and curled her feet up beneath the throw. "Thank you."

Riley handed her a mug. "You take all the time you need, sweetie."

There was no easy way to do this, so she'd just rip the Band-aid off. "Livia, get your laptop."

She brought it, tapping in the password and handing it over.

"No one knows what I'm about to tell you

both. And I want to keep it that way for reasons that will be rapidly apparent. Your word."

Riley's blue eyes went wide with suspense. "Of course."

Livia drew an X in the air over her chest. "Cross my heart and may I never get another pedicure as long as I live."

Autumn rested her hands on the keyboard, her fingers drumming a light tattoo on the keys, though not hard enough to actually type anything. "Okay, so when they cut our hours at the library the first time, I was looking around for some alternate ways to bring in extra income."

"Sure. We both were. I, at least, had income from the farm to fall back on. I've been wondering how you were doing with all those dissertations."

"I haven't been editing dissertations. I mean, I did to begin with, but it was enough to make me want to stab someone. I avoided going into academia for a reason. So I kind of did a thing. A potentially crazy thing, as an experiment. I didn't actually expect anything to come of it."

"Have you been selling sex toys on the side?" Riley asked.

Autumn sputtered a laugh. "What?"

"It was the first potentially crazy thing I could think of that you might do."

"I am not selling sex toys." Although given the lengths she'd gone to in order to meet her own needs in that department, it might not be the worst idea in the world. "I wrote a book."

Livia bounced on the sofa. "I didn't know you wrote!"

"I don't. Didn't. The book started out as therapy, way back in college. Something to exorcise my demons. I scrapped it forever ago. No one was ever supposed to see it. There was too much thinly veiled reality and wish fulfillment in the original plot. It was just a vehicle for all my fantasies." Of which she'd had plenty. "But with the boom in self publishing, I thought I might as well pull it back out and see if I could do something with it. I decided to take the core concept and hone it into something…else. Romantic suspense with a kick ass shero, who takes no shit and goes after what she wants. And I self-published it under a pseudonym."

As she brought up Amazon and typed in her pen name, Autumn felt more exposed than if she'd been standing naked on a table in front of a roomful of people. Was it too late to run away to Timbuktu?

"Harper Jackson?" Riley asked, peering over her shoulder.

"Yeah."

"Great name. But why a pen name? I'd want to tell everybody I know."

"We live in the buckle of the Bible Belt. You've seen the reactions of some people to the romance section at the library. Hell, our boss is one of them. If Mitzi had her way, she'd axe the section entirely. Given the heat level in what I write, I don't want to open that can of worms."

"That's totally fair." Livia leaned over her shoulder. "How many books are there?"

"Three, so far. The first two are standalones because I didn't know if they'd do anything. I just had fun writing the first one, so I wrote another. But people liked them. So then I started a series, since those sell better. I'm writing the second book in that right now."

"I need to borrow that for a minute." Livia yanked the laptop away. "Need to exercise my one-click buy finger."

"Me too!" Riley's fingers were flying over the face of her phone.

It was both a thrill and a terror to watch her friends buy all three books. To know that someone she knew—more than one someone— would be reading them.

"Holy crap," Livia broke in. "These are doing really, really well."

No one had been more surprised about that than Autumn. "Yeah, it's picked up since I re-leased my latest book. Enough that I've been able to stay afloat and keep my apartment, even though we're down to half-time hours. I'm about half-way through the next book in the *Redemption Ridge* series. Income should get a nice boost when that's out and there's more there for people to buy."

"This is all wonderful," Riley said. "But I don't understand what this has to do with Judd."

"Cooper—the hero of *Forged in Blood*—is Judd in almost every way that matters. The book was...a way to give myself the fantasy. Lilah is this amazing, take no prisoners woman, and almost from the first, I started getting fan mail. Emails from these women who loved Cooper as a hero, but more, who absolutely adored my heroine. With every book I get more of them."

Autumn shrugged and began shredding one of the tissues. "Anyway, last week I got this email from a woman who read my books and really identified with Lilah's situation. I don't know what the backstory was—she didn't say —but she was so inspired by Lilah that she took charge in her own life and went after this guy she's been pining after for years. And it turned out he feels the same and they're getting married in May. I'm invited to the wedding."

Riley clutched a hand to her heart. "Awww. That's so sweet!"

"It is. It's so awesome. And I kept rereading this letter. I mean, here is this woman, this complete stranger, who's braver than I am, who went after what she wanted and had it pay off in a big way. Lilah is supposed to be based on me. How can I keep writing books about women like her, if I'm not willing to do the same? To put myself out there?"

"So you decided to tell Judd the truth," Riley prompted.

"I did. I mean…I know it was selfish of me and completely unfair to him. He's not free. But I just…it's been fourteen years and I thought, if not now, then when?"

"And Mark had the craptastic timing to interrupt." Livia groaned. "I'm sorry. That sucks. But just because it didn't work today, doesn't mean you can't try again."

"Yes, it does." Autumn's throat ached with the truth of it.

"Why?"

Another sob broke free. "Because Judd bought an engagement ring."

"Oh honey." Riley tugged her close.

"I bailed on him at Sanderson's. I just couldn't…"

"Well, of course not!" Livia frowned. "But are you *sure?* Did he *say* that's what he was buying?"

Autumn sniffed and wiped at her tears. "No, but Judd doesn't buy jewelry. Ever. He never has."

"Then maybe you're wrong."

At the sound of an incoming text, Autumn pulled her phone out of her coat pocket to find a message from Judd.

Family meeting at Mom and Dad's. 7 tonight. Got news.

The words slid through her ribs like a knife. She handed the phone to Livia. "No, I'm not."

Livia swore.

"And now I have to go over there and face him and Mary Alice and his entire family and pretend that I'm fine. That I'm happy for them.

All because I've never been brave enough to say anything until it was too late." Regret pressed so heavily, Autumn wondered she didn't just sink through the floor. "I don't know if I'm that good an actress."

Riley stroked her hair. "I hate this. I can't tell you how much I hate this. And I wish to God we could fix it for you."

"It helps that you're both here. It helps that at least somebody knows now."

"Well, we can't fix his stupidity. But we can get you ready for tonight," Livia declared.

"How's that?" Autumn asked.

"You're going to finish having your cry, because you totally deserve it. Then you're going to guzzle some water and take some headache medicine and have a nap. And when you wake up, we're going to whip out the Visine and some cucumber slices to erase all the signs of your crying jag. After that, you're going to go home and put on your bitch boots and redo your make up. Then you're going to go over there and hold your head up high, because you are Autumn Freaking Buchanan, and you are awesome, and if he doesn't see that, then he's an idiot you're better off without."

Autumn flashed a watery smile because she knew it was what Livia wanted. But as she took comfort from her friends, she couldn't help but think that the only idiot here was her.

CHAPTER 3

Interim Chief of Police.

The idea of it zinged around his brain like a pinball. Judd had been working for this position for years, but he'd never in a million years wanted to get it like this.

The scent of antiseptic coated the back of his throat and made him twitchy. He despised hospitals. It was all too easy to remember lying in that bed, seventeen years old, hooked up to machines and in agony as his body healed, knowing that taking that bullet hadn't been enough, because the heart defect no one knew about had still nearly killed her. Autumn had lain in the next room over, pale as death, with an uncertain prognosis after emergency heart surgery. He'd made so many deals with God, promising to do anything and everything necessary to protect her, if only she'd wake up again. Being back here, waiting for news on Chief Curry's condition, brought back that same sense of impotent frustration, of being able to do nothing to help.

He'd already been formally sworn in by the City Council. Whether Robert liked it or not, his retirement started today. But there were dozens of things Judd needed to talk to the other man about before he truly took the helm of Wishful PD. Given he'd already been here for six hours, that might not be happening today.

"Hey, sweetie."

Judd looked up to find Mary Alice striding across the waiting room, a Styrofoam box in hand.

"I thought you could use something to eat."

He accepted the box and set it in the next

chair so he could pull her in for a hug. Her arms wrapped tight around him, and he buried his face in her hair, letting the scent of her lavender shampoo block out the hospital smells that had him wanting to crawl out of his skin. After a long minute, he pressed a kiss to the top of her head. "Thanks."

They sat. Judd opened the box and dug into the chicken strips inside.

"Has there been any news?"

"He came through surgery fine. Double bypass. Woke up a couple of hours ago, but I haven't seen him." Other officers from the department had been in and out, but for the moment, he was up here alone.

Mary Alice laid a hand on his knee. The small weight of it was a comfort. "I know cardiac stuff is particularly upsetting for you. But I'm sure he'll be fine."

"Doc was optimistic. His great niece came in from Texas to take care of him and make sure he follows orders. As long as he does that, he'll be fine." Judd had to believe that was true. "But he's done with work."

"So who's going to run the department?"

"For right now, me."

"They're appointing you Chief?"

Judd held up his hand for quiet, though the news would be getting out soon enough. "Interim."

Mary Alice tipped her head against his shoulder. "It seems wrong to congratulate you, even though this is what you've been working for."

"I know. But it is what it is. I'll do whatever has to be done."

"You always do."

They lapsed into silence as he finished the food she'd brought.

"Officer Hamilton?"

Judd tensed and rose as a nurse approached. "Yes?"

"Chief Curry is ready to see you now."

"Is he—"

"He's tired but alert. Already had some visitors. We can give you half an hour to sort some things out, then he needs his rest."

Judd looked back at Mary Alice.

She waved him off. "Go ahead. I'll catch up with you later. I know you've got a lot to take care of."

A familiar face was stepping out of the room as Judd strode down the hall. Nash Brewer, a former Air Force pilot turned reserve officer for Wishful PD, was herding a compact brunette into the hall. "Come on. You can ride herd on him all you want when he gets home."

The woman's jaw set with a mulish stubbornness Judd recognized from Chief Curry himself. "But—"

"No buts, Rowan." Nash shut the door behind them and lowered his voice. "You're no good to him if you drop yourself."

Judd noted she didn't step back when Nash stepped into her space. Instead she swayed toward him, just for a moment, as if she wanted to lean. Then she caught sight of Judd and straightened.

Nash's gaze lingered on Curry's great niece for a beat too long before he turned and offered a hand to Judd. "Chief."

As Rowan scowled, Judd winced. "Too soon, man."

Nash offered an easy shrug. "Somebody's gotta start. Robert's been ready for retirement for a long damned time now. Glad it was you instead of an outsider."

"You and me both." He turned to Rowan. "We've not met, but I've heard a lot about you." Robert bragged every chance he got on his great niece, who was a cop in Houston. The two were tight. "I'm Judd Hamilton."

"Rowan Beale. I'm here to browbeat my uncle into slowing down."

"Might take more than a browbeating," Judd observed.

"I'll tie him to a damned chair, if I have to."

Nash's lips twitched. "Can I sell tickets to that?"

Rowan elbowed him in the ribs, but a smile

flickered at the corner of her mouth. "Don't be an ass."

"C'mon. Let's go to the cafeteria, get some coffee and sandwiches or something and let Robert say whatever he needs to say to Judd."

"Fine. But I'm not leaving the hospital tonight."

The sound of their quiet bickering carried down the hall until they turned the corner. Judd waited another minute, taking the time to ground himself and shut away his instinctive discomfort at being back in a hospital. But that minute was for naught as he slipped into the room and caught sight of the gray pallor of Chief Curry's face.

"Well, don't hover at the door, Hamilton. Come in."

"Sir." Judd did as ordered, moving to stand at the foot of the bed, even as his gut clenched. "How are you feeling?"

"Like I got hit by a semi. But I'm alive, so I'll take it. Sit down, son. We've got things to talk about."

Judd sat in the chair beside the bed.

"Sandra said you're already sworn in."

"Yes, sir. I'm sorry it happened like this."

"Been telling them I wanted to retire for over a year now. If I hadn't been so damned picky about my replacement, this might not have happened." Robert sighed. "Well, what's done is done. You're in it now."

"So I am."

"I know you're wondering why I didn't just pick you."

"The thought had crossed my mind, sir."

He was the obvious candidate. Veteran of the department, solid record, love of the community.

"That has a lot to do with the phone call I got before I had the goddamned heart attack this morning."

"From who?"

"Department of Corrections."

It could be anything. As Chief, Robert had regular contact with the Mississippi Department of Corrections. But Judd's blood turned to ice.

"Jebediah Buchanan is being released."

Hands curling to fists, Judd's heart kicked into to a gallop. "How can fourteen years be sufficient time served for attempted murder?" He and Autumn had given testimony for Jebediah's most recent hearing, and he'd known on some level it was possible, but he just hadn't imagined…

"Good behavior, overcrowding," Robert continued, interrupting his thoughts, "and he's managed to convince the Parole Board that he's turned over a new leaf. I didn't get through all the details before I keeled over."

Judd popped out of the chair and swore, long and vicious, as he paced the small room.

"That. That right there is why I can't support your candidacy for Chief a hundred percent. Because Autumn is your Achilles heel. You're not out for this job for the town. Not completely. You want it because you think it'll help you keep her safe."

As it was true, Judd saw no sense in denying it, but after everything he'd given the department, the lack of total faith stung. "I've never shirked my duties because of Autumn."

"No. If anything, you're the best trained man I've got. You never got complacent about living in a small town and thinking bad things don't happen here. You know better than most that they absolutely do. But I've got serious concerns with how you'll deal with this situation, Judd."

"I'll do whatever's necessary."

"You'll do whatever's within the law."

Bristling, Judd glared at him. "You think I'd do anything else?"

"I think if push came to shove, you've proved you'll do anything for that girl." Robert settled back against his pillow, looking suddenly ten years older. "I was there that day, Judd. I remember. I remember both of you nearly dying. I remember wanting to kill him myself. It was the worst fucking case I dealt with my entire career. So I get that this is an emotionally charged situation. But I want to remind you that you'll be working for this city. You'll answer to the Mayor and City Council. The good of the entire town is now in your hands, and you can't be showing favoritism to her, no matter the circumstances."

"I'm aware of that," Judd gritted out.

"Fact is, you're the best candidate we've got, and your performance over the next few months will determine whether or not you keep the job. Don't blow it."

"I don't intend to."

"Well, don't you look cute tonight?"

Autumn's smile felt brittle as Patty ushered her into the house. "Thanks."

She'd taken Riley and Livia's advice, managing to erase all signs of her crying jag. Under any other circumstances, she'd feel great about the new jeans she was wearing, since she knew they did amazing things for her ass. The sleek, sleeveless sweater she'd been saving for her campaign to impress Judd had a scooped neckline that displayed other assets, and bitch boots were usually a confidence-boosting accessory. But the outfit didn't really feel like the armor it was intended to be. It certainly hadn't stopped her from lingering in her car for fifteen minutes, trying to think of an excuse to get out of this.

"Have you eaten? We've got leftover pot roast from dinner."

"I'm fine, Patty, thanks." No way could she actually eat anything with her stomach tied in knots. Everything was about to change, and she didn't know how she'd survive it.

"Go on through then. Everybody's in the living room. I'll be right along with the coffee."

Autumn hung back, not wanting to see the happy couple. "Why don't I help you with that?"

"Nonsense. I'm just waiting on the pot to finish brewing. You go ahead."

Deprived of her last delay tactic, and not quite enough of a coward to go hide in the bathroom, Autumn pasted on the best impression of cheerful and relaxed she could manage so as to greet Judd and Mary Alice with a smile.

Judd wasn't smiling when Autumn came into the living room, and Mary Alice was nowhere in sight.

But no, that wasn't right. Surely if he was about to announce his engagement he'd actually look *happy* about it. Unless maybe he and Mary Alice had already had some sort of fight? What if this wasn't the happy, planned engagement she'd imagined? What if Mary Alice was pregnant? Judd was absolutely the type who'd insist on doing "the right thing." And he'd have no qualms about breaking the news by himself to allow her to save whatever face she could.

Gripped in the horror of that scenario, she almost missed when Judd asked, "Did y'all get the grant done?"

Grant? Oh right, the lie she'd told him this morning. "Sure did."

Judd was eyeing her in that way that said he probably knew she was lying but wasn't going to call her on it. At least not now. She'd have to think of some better excuse to cover her ass when he did.

Patty came in and set a coffee tray on the table. Her husband, Owen, leaned forward to grab a cup. "Well son, out with it. What's this news of yours?"

Autumn tensed, fighting not to knit her hands together as she adopted what she hoped was a neutral expression.

"Chief Curry had a heart attack this morning."

As exclamations of alarm circled the room, she could only blink. Well, that explained his grim demeanor. He and the chief were pretty tight. Judd thought the world of him. But...why would he start there if this was about his engagement?

"He's okay, but he won't be working again. I was sworn in as interim Chief of Police this morning."

"Interim?" his father asked.

"It's not how the City Council wanted to do

things. Basically, I'm on a probationary period until they decide whether I'll keep the job permanently."

"A job?" Autumn didn't realize she'd spoken until everyone turned to look at her. "This whole family meeting is all about a job?" Her voice came out a little choked, but there was nothing she could do about it. What control she'd managed to cobble together this afternoon was fraying with every second of this conversation.

Judd studied her, concern etched across his brow, and she wondered what he could see. "Partly."

Partly. Which meant there was more. The job was just the warmup to the rest of the story.

Her shoulders wanted to curl in, her hands ached to lace together, but she held herself straight and proud. "Congratulations. I know you've been busting your ass for this."

He was going to hate it. The politics, dealing with the department budget, and all the other things that went along with being Chief that weren't the actual police work he loved. But Autumn voiced none of those concerns. He'd been dead set on this path for the last few years, and he'd have to figure that out for himself.

"It's not how I wanted to get the position."

Patty shoved up from the sofa. "Well, I hate it for Robert, but I'd say this calls for something stronger than coffee. I'll go dig out the champagne!"

"Mom, wait. Hold the champagne. There's something else."

She hesitated at the seriousness of his tone, brows drawing together in concern.

But Judd wasn't looking at his mother. "I need to talk to Autumn first. Privately."

There was absolutely no way she could keep up this facade that everything was fine if he got her alone. She needed the burden of keeping up the mask in front of all of them.

"I don't see why you can't just tell everyone at once." Autumn aimed for breezy and fell a few steps above wheezy. God, she couldn't breathe.

Judd frowned, then crossed the room to take her hand.

No. Oh, no. He'd gotten the job he was gunning for and now he planned to move on with the rest of his life. Was he really going to announce his engagement like this? Holding *her* hand for some kind of moral support? Did he know how she felt after all? Know that this was going to crush her to bits?

She braced herself, wondering how he'd say it. *Mary Alice and I are getting married. I've asked Mary Alice to be my wife and she said yes. We want you to be godmother to our future children.*

"Jebediah's being released from prison."

Her thoughts careened to a stop like the screech of a record. "What?"

"The Parole Board met and approved his release. They called Chief Curry this morning, just before his heart attack. He gets out on Saturday."

Autumn jerked her hand free to cover her mouth, as if that would stop the scream welling up inside her.

It couldn't be true.

"No. We delivered our victim impact statements two months ago, just like every year. The Parole Board can't just change their minds. Not on something like this."

Except they had. She could see the truth of it in Judd's eyes.

"I'll make you pay. Faithless, disobedient whore. One of these days, I'll make you pay." The words her father had hurled at her as the bailiffs hauled him out of the courtroom the last time she'd ever seen him echoed through her mind.

Autumn couldn't breathe. Blindly, she reached out for something to hang on to as her world tipped hopelessly out of balance. And Judd was there, as he was always there.

"Breathe," he ordered.

"I can't...I can't..." A mountain sat on her chest. Dimly, she knew her blood pressure had sky-rocketed and she had to get it down, but she couldn't think past the panic. Because her own personal boogeyman was being released from Hell.

Judd pressed her hand over his heart so she could feel the beat of it, strong and steady. Not out of control like hers. His other hand slid beneath her hair to cup her nape, tipping her face to his. "Look at me. Match your breath to mine. C'mon now. In and out."

Her vision grayed at the edges, but she focused on the feel of his hands, warm and solid. An anchor in a world gone mad. His eyes filled her vision, a deep cerulean blue, shot through with streaks of silver in a burst around the iris. The broad chest beneath her palm rose and fell with careful, modulated breaths. Something loosened in her rib cage. On his next inhale, she took a ragged breath of her own.

"Good girl. In and out."

The mind-numbing panic began to recede and, with it, what strength was left in her legs. Autumn crumpled into him, closing her eyes as his arms locked around her.

"Why couldn't he be dead?" she whispered.

"We're not that lucky, I guess."

"This is crazy," Patty burst out. "How could they possibly let him out after what he did?"

"I don't have all the details yet. Robert had his heart attack in the middle of the call. By the time I found out about it, it was after business hours. I'll call in the morning to get the full details."

"I can't face him," Autumn rasped.

"You won't have to." He tightened his hold on her. "He won't get near you. I'll make sure of it."

"We all will," Eli growled.

He and Leo closed in, a matched pair of willing guard dogs. They almost made her smile. Almost.

The feel of Judd's heartbeat soothed her. Proof of life and survival. She'd do anything to ensure he stayed that way.

"It's a small town, Judd. If he comes back, I'm bound to run into him eventually."

"My town, my rules. Whatever can be done, I'll do it."

She took in the set of his jaw and another

truth sank in. "This is why you went for Chief. Because you knew this was coming."

He didn't even try to deny it. "Am I supposed to apologize for that? I've been expecting this for a while. The Parole Board was divided at his hearing last year. He's been a model prisoner. I knew it was only a matter of time, so I've been taking steps."

She pulled away to pace. "I don't even know what to say to that." How could he do this for her and be with someone else?

Did Mary Alice know about any of this? This was the ugly truth of Autumn's life. Being with Judd, it would eventually touch Mary Alice, too. No matter how much Autumn hated that he was with her, the woman didn't deserve this.

"You can say anything you like about it. It's done."

But it couldn't be done. She wouldn't let the cancer of her past keep spreading. The answer to this entire horrible situation was staring her in the face. She just had to be brave enough to actually do it.

Anything to keep him safe.

Autumn turned, wishing she could deaden the ache inside. "I already know how to deal with this, Judd."

"Good. I'm glad we're in agreement," he said.

"I'm leaving Wishful."

"You're moving in with me."

Their words overlapped, and she saw the moment hers registered. He physically flinched back, as if her statement had slammed into him like her father's bullet. The sight of that look on his face again had her stomach pitching.

"*No!*"

"Judd—"

"Move back in with us," Owen urged.

Autumn appreciated the offer of an escape from close quarters with Judd. "I won't put you and Patty at risk."

Judd grabbed her by the shoulders. "You can't just run. There's no need for that. I can keep you safe. I *will* keep you safe."

Gently, because she recognized that, for once, he was the fragile one, Autumn pushed away. "This isn't about my father."

"Then what the hell is it about?"

Finding a life without you. Maybe Judd hadn't proposed to Mary Alice yet, but he would. And Autumn didn't want to be around for that. But she wasn't about to admit it. Not now.

"My job's been in the toilet for over a year. It's just time." And as she faced him in the house where they'd shared so many memories, inspiration struck. "I tried to tell you this morning."

His face went gray. "This? *This* is what you were going to tell me?"

She wanted to take it back, to do anything to erase that look of utter betrayal. But there was no way out of this situation without hurting them both. Miserable, she just nodded.

His hands curled to fists and a muscle twitched in his jaw as he tried to hold on to his temper. "Where will you go? What will you do? Do you already have a job lined up?"

The answer to that was easier than it might've been. "My mother's in Denver."

Judd stared. "Your mother? When did you find her?"

And the shocks were just gonna keep on coming. "I've always known where she was."

"Why didn't you say anything?" Patty leaned into Owen, as if she, too, felt the sting of Autumn's betrayal.

"At first it was to protect her. Until the trial was done, I didn't want to risk that he'd be set free and go after her. And then...I was afraid you'd send me away."

"Oh honey." Autumn heard the tears in Patty's voice. "We'd never have sent you away. Not then and not now."

She knew that. Knew that this family was so much more hers than the one she had by blood. And she'd do anything to protect them. "You're not sending me away. I'm choosing."

"How can you possibly go to her?" Judd demanded. "She *left* you."

She'd let him think it all these years because

it was easier than the truth. "No, she didn't. We were both supposed to leave that day."

"What?"

"She had a plan to get us away from Wishful, away from my father." But going meant walking away from Judd. No goodbye, no contact. She'd been more afraid of a life without him than she'd been of her father. "I made a choice. I chose you. And because I did, you nearly died. I won't do that again. I won't use you as my shield."

"Fuck that. I'm not some untrained kid anymore."

"It doesn't matter. If I stay, it paints a target on your back because you'll be my shield. You will stand between him and me because it's what you do, it's who you are. You've been my protector since that playground in first grade." Autumn reached out, unerringly laying her hand over the scar on his chest she could find blindfolded and in the dark. The phantom taste of his blood coated the back of her throat and with it, shades of the abject terror that had haunted her for fourteen years. Ruthlessly, she fought it back. "Less than a centimeter, Judd. I won't go through that again. I can't."

She stepped back. "You're Chief of Police now. You've got more than me to worry about."

CHAPTER 4

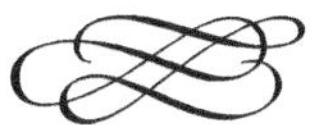

Judd hadn't slept for shit. Too many bombs had been dropped yesterday. He had a feeling they'd be dealing with the fallout for a long time to come.

But life wasn't going to slow down and give him a chance to adjust to the fact that his whole world had irrevocably shifted on its axis. Jebediah was still being released at the end of the week. On a medical release, as it turned out. After all this time, the son of a bitch really was dying. Judd wondered how fast. Either way, formalities had to be observed. So here he was in Lawley for a meeting with the Wachoxee County Sheriff and Jebediah's parole officer, going over the particulars. If he was lucky, he might have time to swing by and see his grandparents on the way home. Maybe Nanna could come up with a way to convince Autumn to stay.

Sheriff Bill Riggs, a balding man with just a bit of a paunch straining the buttons of his uniform, leaned back in the chair behind his big metal desk. The surface was littered with stacks of files, proving that he was still very much active in his department. "I know this is an unusual situation, what with your personal involvement, but trust that we've got your back on this."

Judd hadn't expected anything less, but having the sentiment confirmed made him feel an iota better. "I appreciate that, Sheriff."

"Oh now, none of that. You're Chief of Police now. Call me Bill."

Judd nodded. "Thanks. I feel better knowing you were here when all this went down the first time. You know what we're dealing with."

"Ugly business," Riggs agreed.

In the other guest chair, Tyrell Weller, Jebediah's parole officer, leaned forward. "How's his daughter taking it? I assume she's been notified."

Judd couldn't stop the clench of his jaw. "She's leaving Wishful."

"Damn." Weller shook his head. "Shame she feels like she has to do that. But can't blame her."

"She'd already been making plans before this."

"Oh, well, good timing then, I guess."

There was nothing good about any of this.

Nobody was happy with Autumn's decision, leastwise Autumn herself. She could say anything she wanted about the practicalities, but he knew her. She didn't want to leave. But no amount of discussion by him or his parents would sway her. He wanted to believe she'd get past this, that she was just scared. But he couldn't escape the fact that she'd already decided this before she even knew about Jebediah.

How could she not have told him about her mother? They'd never lied to each other.

Really? You're going to harp on honesty?

Okay, so he'd lied to her about the *one* thing. But it had been for her own good, so he could continue to keep her safe. Everything he'd done had been to keep her safe.

How's that working out for you? She's leaving.

It was hard not to take that as a slap in the face.

And yet, what right did he have to try and keep her here? Just because he'd made her the compass of his life didn't mean she had to do the same. He had no hold over her other than friendship. He'd made sure of that, hadn't he?

Impatient to be finished, Judd rose. "I need to be getting back. There are a lot of details to be sorted with Robert still in the hospital."

"Of course." Bill rose, too. "Give him my regards. And good luck with the new position."

"I will. Thanks."

"It's a real pity things worked out like this. I'd been hoping to sweet talk you into coming to join my investigative unit."

Judd paused. "You wanted me for detective?"

"You'd make a damned fine one. Good instincts. That work you did on the Fornell case was top notch. Another day or two and her daddy would've gotten away with her."

Instead, the girl was safely with her mother, out of state, and her father had gone to prison for kidnapping. Judd had been proud of his work on that case, proud of the outcome. It was the sort of thing that made up for all the other shit he dealt with as a cop.

"I'm just glad it turned out all right."

"You decide you're tired of running things, you give me a call," Riggs told him.

"I'll keep that in mind. Tyrell, I'm sure we'll be in touch."

Judd shook hands with both men and headed out.

Detective.

The idea of it circled around his brain as he

climbed into his cruiser and headed toward his grandparents' farm.

Like so many other areas of his life, Judd had become a cop to protect Autumn. Even at eighteen, he'd known Jebediah would get out someday, and he'd wanted the authority and training to do something about it when the time came. That he'd stumbled into his passion had been happy coincidence. Investigation was his favorite part of the job. It fired his mind, kept him on his toes, and, most importantly, fed his deep-seated need to put away the bad guys. The idea of doing *just* that for a career was beyond appealing. If things had been different, he'd have been all over that.

But things are different. Autumn's leaving. Your reasons for becoming Chief aren't valid anymore.

No. He wasn't willing to accept that. Autumn wasn't gone yet, and for better or worse, he was Wishful's Chief of Police. He wouldn't be shirking that duty.

Pop's truck wasn't in the drive when Judd pulled up to the house, but he could see Nanna kneeling in her vegetable patch, a broad brimmed hat shading her eyes.

She sat back on her heels as he approached. "What a lovely surprise!"

Despite his foul mood, he worked up a smile for her. "Hey, beautiful."

"Help me up. These knees are a mite creakier than they used to be."

Judd took her extended hand and pulled her to her feet and on into a tight hug.

She gave him a solid squeeze. "You want to talk. Come on and let's get some tea."

Because the morning hadn't yet warmed up past comfortable, they settled on the back porch with tall glasses of sweet tea.

"Your mama called."

"She told you then."

"About Jebediah. About Autumn leaving," Nanna said.

Well, that saved him some time. "She can't leave."

"You don't want her to leave."

To his mind, it was the same thing. Judd

rolled the cold glass between his palms. "She doesn't want to leave either. I know she doesn't. She just doesn't think she has a choice."

Nanna pinned him with a gimlet stare. "So give her a choice."

His heart began to pound. The same thought had been circling beneath the surface of his brain just waiting to rise to consciousness. He didn't know if he was strong enough to lock it away again.

"It's not that simple."

"Sure it is. You have the power to make her stay. You always have."

Autumn's voice echoed in his head, cutting him to the quick yet again.

I made a choice. I chose you.

She'd chosen him and because she had, she'd been home that day when Jebediah discovered his wife had left him. She'd been home to be a target for his rage. Jebediah had taken one look at the two of them together and seen nothing innocent. An hour later and he might've been right. They'd been on the cusp of changing everything.

Instead, it had ended in blood.

Judd had known then that he could never risk being with Autumn. He could never risk it not working out and leaving her unprotected. That was more important now than ever. His memories of that day were the only thing he'd ever lied to Autumn about.

"We're her family. How can she walk away from that?"

"Maybe because it hurts her too much to stay."

Judd dropped his gaze to his tea.

"Did you really think she'd forever be okay watching you with somebody else?"

Maybe he had thought that, at one time. He'd thought they could stay the friends they'd always been and develop relationships with other people. He'd wanted her to have some normal. She deserved someone who'd love and adore her, who'd put her first. He'd thought that if he led by example, thrown himself into other relationships, that she'd feel comfortable enough to do the same. And he'd thought maybe, eventually, he'd find a woman who'd fill that void for him, make him truly feel, deep down, that he'd done the right thing. Autumn had always been supportive of his relationships, and it'd taken a while for him to realize she'd stopped trying to find one herself. The small, selfish part of him had been glad of that, and he knew that made him a right bastard.

"You're not pulling any punches today."

"You don't come to me for coddling, sweetheart. You come to me for sense. You're a good man, Judd. I know you want to do the best for everybody, and you don't want anybody to get hurt. But I think maybe it's time you considered that Autumn has the right idea in running away from home."

"Running doesn't solve anything," he insisted.

Nanna tipped back the last of her tea. "Might if you ran with her." With that parting shot, she rose. "It was good to see you, baby. Give everybody my love."

THE DAY her father got out of prison, Autumn gave serious thought to hiding out in her house. She hadn't seen anything in the news about Jebediah, but it was only a matter of time before the media caught wind of his release and the vultures descended again. He'd find her, like a scavenger stalking carrion birds to find an easy meal. And then…she didn't want to think about what he'd do. Judd had told her about the medical release, but no matter what Jebediah had, he was too damned mean to just conveniently keel over and stop being a problem. In the end, she went to work because the impulse to hide smacked too much of the scared little girl she'd been, and she'd worked far too hard to overcome those early years to go back there now.

But as she went through the soothing, methodical process of reshelving books, she was starting to reconsider.

"Who's the author again?"

"Harper Jackson. I'm telling you, you've *got* to read them. They're outstanding."

Twin spurts of excitement and paranoia shot through her at the sound of her pen name. Dear God. Someone local had read them. She resisted the urge to peer around the shelf to see who.

"Romantic suspense, you said?"

"Yeah. They're, like, Nora Roberts but hotter. I tell you, that Cooper about made my panties burst into flame."

Dear *God.* Someone local had *read them.* Had Livia or Riley spilled the beans? Or had this been a fluke?

A decided sense of dread settled in Autumn's gut. She'd changed the names and settings and masked the most obvious similarities to reality, but there was so much of her in there. So much of Judd and the rest of Wishful. What if people recognized them? What the hell had she been thinking, putting her most prurient fantasies out there for public consumption?

"You look like you swallowed bad sushi."

Autumn jolted, the book in her hand flying up as she spun toward Judd. "God!"

Of course, he just reached out and snagged it as easily as the footballs he'd caught in high school. One brow lifted.

Had she shrieked? A quick glance around said yes as she noted several pairs of eyes aimed in their direction. Consciously lowering her voice, she glared at him. "What is the matter with you? You know not to sneak up on me!"

Judd handed the book back and stepped close enough to run a hand down her arm. "Sorry. I thought you saw me coming."

Since when had she ever seen him coming?

"Why are you even here today?" he asked.

"Where else would I be? I'm not going to hide from him." Not anymore.

"But you have no problem running."

Oh, so they were still in this fight? Autumn hadn't been sure. Judd had been largely MIA the last several days as he leapt feet first into his new job as Chief of Police. She wasn't sure how much of that was him taking time to cool off and how much was legitimately being busy. Seeing him now, the strain of little sleep etched on his face, she felt guilty for being the cause of any of that.

She shoved the book onto the correct shelf. "I told you this has nothing to do with him."

"You really expect me to believe that?"

"What do you want me to say, Judd? That I hate this? I do. That I don't want to go? I don't. But look around. My reasons for staying have been dwindling. I have to be able to support myself."

"There are other jobs. And there's bound to be something closer than Colorado."

Undoubtedly that was true. She hadn't actually looked yet. But if she was really going through with this, having a complete, fresh start seemed the only way to go.

"I'm not a hundred percent set on Denver. I

just feel the need to try and reconcile with my mother."

"She left you," he said again. "Whether you were supposed to go or not, she didn't ever come back for you after he was put away. She could have and she didn't."

"She couldn't come back here. I lived through all of it with her, so I completely understand the memories this place holds for her. I could've gone to her at any point, and I chose not to. I survived because of you and your family. She never had that kind of support."

"And yet you're going to just walk away from yours?"

Temper leapt like a caged beast. How dare he act like this was some thoughtless, casual decision. Did he not understand how codependent and dysfunctional their relationship was for two people who weren't romantically entangled? No, of course he didn't. He'd spent his life putting her first in every way but the one she wanted most. She couldn't live like that anymore.

But neither could she hurt him with the truth.

"I don't make this decision lightly." *I don't walk away from you lightly.* She wasn't a hundred percent certain she could walk away from him at all. But she knew beyond the shadow of a doubt that he'd never be the one to walk away from her, so she had to be strong enough for them both.

She turned away, heading for the reference desk and hoping to put an end to this discussion. Her steps faltered as she saw Mark patiently waiting.

Crap. Caught between a rock and an awkward place.

Before she could decide whether to try and hide, Mark turned and saw her. He shoved his glasses up the bridge of his nose and grinned broadly, offering a little wave.

Straightening her shoulders, Autumn went to do her librarian duty. "Hi Mark. Here for those interlibrary loan books?"

"Partly." He slung his omnipresent messenger bag and a small camera bag on the counter.

Her gaze drawn to the latter, she asked, "Picking up a new interest in photography?"

"Oh, it's not new. I like taking pictures of historic sites and the like. Just got an upgraded model, so I've been testing it out."

"Cool." She moved to the shelf of interlibrary loan books and pulled the ones labeled with Mark's name. Aware of Judd propping himself on one elbow on the side counter, Autumn kept her attention on her patron. "You said there was something else I could help you with? More of your genealogy research?"

"Dinner," he said.

Was he looking for cookbook recs? "Beg your pardon?"

"I came to ask you out for dinner."

Well, crap, she'd just walked right into that one.

For about half a second she considered it. He was sweet, if a little nervous, and certainly intelligent, and she did want to move on. But in no universe was he ever going to compete with Judd. No one was ever going to compete with Judd. Which left her with finding some way to gently reject Mark without embarrassing him.

"What she's trying to find a way to tell you, Mark, old buddy, is that she's fixin' to be moving."

Autumn resisted the urge to slap Judd upside the back of his head.

Mark blinked owlishly. "Moving?"

Judd just fixed that implacable cop stare on her, daring her to confirm it. He didn't think she would.

"Not that I don't appreciate the thought, but I'm afraid he's right."

"When?"

"I'm still firming up my plans." Damn it. Now it sounded like she was just giving him the brushoff. "But with my hours having been cut at the library, I've been looking for a while now."

"I see." Mark took off his glasses and polished them with the front of his polo shirt.

"Well, guess I waited too long to make my move."

Autumn gave him a sympathetic smile. "I'm really sorry, Mark."

"No problem. I'll see you around as long as you're still around, I guess. Best of luck."

He'd already turned and high-tailed it out before she realized he'd left his books.

Autumn popped Judd on the arm, which had about as much impact as a mouse kicking an elephant. "You didn't have to be an asshole just because you're mad at me."

"No reason to get the guy's hopes up if you're really going."

Autumn pinched the bridge of her nose and struggled for patience. She'd sprung this on him out of nowhere. He had a right to be upset.

"I don't want to fight with you, Judd."

"I don't want to fight with you either." He leaned both elbows on the counter. "Listen, why don't we just table this for now? There are bigger things going on today. I thought tonight we could grab a pizza and have a marathon of your favorite 80s movies. *Sixteen Candles. Pretty in Pink. The Breakfast Club.*"

He was pissed off and hurt and still willing to watch cheesy, romantic movies with her. God, she loved him so much. "I appreciate your attempts at distraction, but I already have plans with the girls. Besides, you need to go spend some time with Mary Alice. You've been spending all your time with me, with your new position as Chief. Go do damage control." Look at her being the consummate best friend.

"You're sure?"

"I'm sure." She forced far more certainty into her voice than she actually felt.

He stared at her for a long moment, and she recognized him wrestling with whether to say something. Evidently deciding against it, he tapped the counter. "Okay then. But I'll call to check in later, okay? And if you see anything, hear anything, sense anything that feels off, you call me."

"I will."

Livia passed him as he was stalking out. She

cranked her head to look over her shoulder at him as she came the rest of the way to the desk.

"What was that all about?"

"We're in a fight," Autumn said, which was easier than getting into the details.

"You two never fight."

"We do. It's just really, really rare."

"What are you fighting about?"

"I'll tell you about it tonight. I've got some prospective news." Maybe if she actually told her other friends about moving she'd be more committed to actually going through with it.

Livia cast a quick look around and lowered her voice. "About your dad?"

"No. Something else. We'll talk about it later. In any event, let me just say that I'm looking forward getting together with you and Riley for *Outlander* tonight. I could do with some distraction."

"You can count on us."

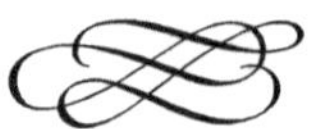

CHAPTER 5

"I'm so glad we're finally able to do this." Mary Alice sank into the chair Judd pulled out for her.

"We definitely need some one-on-one time. I'm sorry I didn't get the chance to pick you up. I had some things I needed to take care of at the station."

"It's fine."

"No, it's really not," he said. "It's not fair to you that I've been so consumed with work."

"You're driven. It's one of the characteristics I admire about you. And I know your level of busy isn't likely to change now that you're Chief." She accepted the menu offered by the server. "Thank you."

"Well, that's part of what tonight's about. It's true that I've got a lot more responsibility with the job, and you know well enough that it's not an eight-to-five kind of thing. But I really want to make our relationship a priority."

She brightened at the words, and he had to give Autumn props for pushing him into doing this.

"I'd really like that, too."

Over appetizers, Judd made an effort to prove that he could still be charming. By the entree, he remembered all the reasons he'd stayed with Mary Alice. She was sweet and funny and genuinely *good*. He spent so much time facing the darker side of society, being with her was like a breath of fresh air, reminding him that there were still good people in the world. By the time the waiter cleared their entrees, Judd was feeling more mellow than he had in weeks. As they waited on their shared dessert—the caramel cake The Spring House was famous for—Judd decided it was a good time to give her the gift he'd picked up.

"You're one of the best parts of my life, you know that?"

Arching one brow, she gave a sassy smile. "Am I now?"

He reached across the table to twine his fingers with hers. "You're really special to me."

"You're special to me, too, Judd."

"There's something I want to—well, I'm not great with words. I've never done this before."

Mary Alice flexed her hand in his, her cheeks going pink, her eyes wide. "Doesn't have to be pretty. Just say it."

God, had he been so wrapped up in work that trying to give their relationship the priority it deserved was tantamount to announcing he thought they should use his cuffs for more than just work? The thought derailed his poorly planned speech. "How about I just show you?"

"Okay," she breathed.

He reached into his suit pocket and brought out the long, slim jewel case, setting it in front of her. A trace of confusion flickered over her face.

"Go ahead, open it."

She released his hand and opened the box.

Judd knew the moment she laid eyes on the thing that Mitch had been wrong. This bracelet was absolutely not going to get him out of the doghouse. It had, in fact, maybe lodged him there more firmly. This is what he got for taking relationship advice from one of the most notorious players in Wishful. Damn it, he knew he shouldn't be buying jewelry for a woman. He resisted the urge to squirm in his seat as she stared at the bracelet, clearly wishing it would turn into something else.

The arrival of their dessert prolonged the awkward silence as they both waited for the server to leave again.

"What's wrong?" Judd asked.

"It's...a bracelet."

"Not your style? What was I thinking? You

work with little kids. A bracelet would probably be in the way. I'm sorry, I'm sure I can return it." He knew no such thing, but it seemed the thing to say.

"It's not that."

"What then? Wrong size?"

"No. The size is fine. I just thought…"

"What?"

"With the fancy dinner, and the talk about making our relationship a priority, and how I'm one of the best parts of your life, I just thought…"

"What?" he asked again.

She finally lifted her gaze in exasperation. "For an incredibly astute cop, you're an amazingly dense man. I thought you were proposing."

Judd's mouth fell open. "I…" What the hell did he say to that? Proposing? That was the last thing he was thinking about. He wasn't in a position to take on a wife.

"Oh my God. Why are you so surprised? We've been together for two years. We're not getting any younger. It's the natural progression of a relationship."

"Well, I know, but I…we hadn't even talked about…" Sweat broke out between his shoulder blades.

Mary Alice shook her head, eyes going suspiciously shiny. "I was so stupid."

Oh shit. Oh no. Don't cry. "No. No you weren't." It was his instinct to comfort, even when he didn't entirely know what to say.

"They warned me you'd never actually commit. That no one else would ever come first for you."

"Who? What are you talking about?"

"You're a serial monogamist, Judd. But you're a commitmentphobe."

Embarrassment slid into defensiveness. He knew how to commit. "How is that even a thing?"

"You'll go so far. No further. Because there's always Autumn."

"She's my best friend. That's it."

"Is it? Is it really? Is it normal to drop everything for your best friend, no matter what's going on or who you're with?"

"Her father just got out of prison. She needed support." No way could Mary Alice understand how much. She, with her upper middle class upbringing so much like his, couldn't possibly fathom the hell Autumn had lived through, never knowing what to expect, never knowing what Jebediah's God would tell him to do next.

Mary Alice waved her hand, like that was nothing. "And that's awful—for both of you. I get that."

No, she really didn't. But Judd hadn't invited her to the family meeting the other night because he hadn't wanted this to touch her any more than it had to. Maybe it had been a mistake to try to shield her. Maybe he should've let her see.

She rolled on. "But if it isn't that, it would be something else. You always, always choose her."

"It's not about choosing," he bit out.

At the edge of the table, his phone began to

vibrate. Of course, it was Autumn. Because why shouldn't Mary Alice have more ammunition for this conversation? Judd reached for it automatically, but she laid her hand over his.

"Whatever it is, let someone else handle it for once."

Under other circumstances, maybe he could've done it. But with Jebediah a free man, there was no way he could just let her go to voicemail. With an apologetic wince at Mary Alice, he slid the phone free.

"Hey Autumn. What's up?"

Her hysteria practically reached through the phone to grab him by the throat.

He shoved back his own panic. "Wait, wait, what? Slow down. Tell me what's wrong."

Through another hiccupping sort of sob she managed to force out, "My house is on fire!"

A thousand scenarios, each one worst than the last, unfolded in his brain. And he wasn't there.

"Are you all right? Where are you? Are you outside? Have you called 911?"

"The fire department is on the way. I wasn't inside. Riley and I just got home and found it like this. It's my side. She managed to get into her unit to get the cat."

"Both of you stay back. Lock yourselves in a vehicle until somebody gets there. Have Riley call Liam." Riley's former-Marine fiancé would keep them both safe.

"He's on his way."

"So am I. Just hang tight." He'd hung up the phone and shoved back from the table before he looked at Mary Alice.

She shook her head, her pretty face a mask of regret. "I can't live like this anymore, Judd. I can't play second fiddle. Just go."

Miserable, hating that he'd hurt her, Judd stood, pulling several bills out of his wallet to cover the check. "I'm so sorry."

"So am I."

Then he bolted without looking back.

~

Lock yourselves in a vehicle. Judd's order ricocheted through Autumn's brain. He didn't think this was an accident.

Fresh terror had her dragging Riley and Valium back toward the car, searching the darkness for shadows that didn't belong. Was he out there, watching her as her life burned? Had he spent the last fourteen years planning this in revenge?

"The fire department is on its way and Liam's coming."

"Get in the car, Riley."

"But why?"

Because it would at least provide some modicum of cover if her father was lying in wait to snipe them. But she didn't want to infect her friend with the fear running rampant in her blood. "Judd said so."

They climbed back into Riley's sedan and backed up to make room for the fire trucks that were en route. Then they sat, saying nothing. Riley watched the fire spread, Valium clinging to her like a yowling burr. Autumn looked everywhere else, trying to find the thing that was out of place. But she saw nothing. No threat, save the fire itself. Panic began to ebb, replaced with helpless rage.

Everything she'd worked for, everything she'd built was inside that duplex apartment. This would ruin her. One of the first things to go when her hours got cut had been renter's insurance. Her paltry savings would barely be enough to replace the bare essentials. But nothing could replace the memories turned to cinder and ash. The photographs, the lifelong collection of notes from Judd, the mementos and trinkets. All gone.

Worse, this didn't just impact her. Riley had been through so much last year when the pharmacy flooded. The financial burden had nearly crippled her. Now, to have her home destroyed, too…

Autumn wanted to crumple and weep. But she refused to give him the satisfaction. If he'd been foolish enough to make this declaration of war, there'd be proof. Judd would find it. And Jebediah would be put away again.

Sirens sounded in the distance as a vintage Mustang tore into the drive. Liam leapt out of the car, and Riley scrambled out, flying into his arms. The sight of those strong arms closing around her, the instant, unwavering support made Autumn's throat ache. She wanted that with Judd. In truth, she had it. But he'd only go so far and no further. For tonight, she'd have to make do with scraps.

By the time Judd made it, Wishful's finest were working to salvage Riley's side of the duplex. Autumn knew without being told that her own was a total loss. She couldn't think about that yet. Couldn't face the overwhelming task of recovering from this disaster. So she focused on the fury, using it to straighten her spine and hang on to the last vestiges of control as she climbed out of the car.

"Autumn!" Judd caught her up, wrapping her tight in his embrace. And for that moment, she didn't care that he belonged to someone else; she didn't care that this could never be more than it was, because with his body pressed to hers, she felt safe for the first time since this ordeal began. He was her shelter, always.

Cursing her weakness, she clung to him and broke.

Judd held her as she wept, pouring out all the grief, all the fear, as the firefighters struggled to salvage what they could. A second engine arrived, one of the volunteer departments from nearby Chapel Creek lending their backs to the cause. Judd shifted to block her view of the house. Not that it mattered. She already knew it was lost. But his hold on her never slackened, even as his own men arrived and took orders to begin a search of the surrounding area.

At last the fire was reduced to sodden, smoking coals. Autumn had run out of tears, and she felt as hollowed out as the half of the duplex that had been her home. Riley's side still stood, more or less intact. There'd be smoke and water damage, but maybe she wouldn't lose everything. Autumn couldn't bear the idea that more of her friends were collateral damage to her father's hatred.

"I'm taking Riley back to my place. She's wiped out, and there's nothing else we can do here," Liam said.

"I'll let you know when it's clear to enter the structure again so she can assess damages and see what can be salvaged," Judd promised.

If there'd been a drop of moisture left in Autumn's body, she might've started crying again. "I'm so sorry, Riley."

Riley gave her a tight squeeze. "Honey, it's not your fault. And I've got renter's insurance. After what happened with the pharmacy, I've learned to be prepared. I'm safe. Valium's safe. That's the important thing. It'll be fine."

Autumn wished she could believe that.

Liam's car inched through the crowd of vehicles, as the fire department began coiling up hoses.

"They'll start winding things up here

shortly. Things will have to cool more before the fire marshal can do his thing to determine the cause of the blaze. You'll come home with me." It wasn't a question.

Since she had nowhere else to go, Autumn didn't argue. There was nowhere else she'd rather be anyway. She nodded, rubbing at eyes gritty from crying and smoke. For the first time, she focused on what Judd was wearing.

"You're wearing your date suit."

He glanced down and shrugged.

"I pulled you away from time with Mary Alice. Of course I did. I'm the one who told you to go do damage control in the first place." She scrubbed both hands over her face. "God, what must she think of me?"

"It doesn't matter. I'm exactly where I'm supposed to be right now. You're not in this alone."

But she'd just gotten a stark reminder of the status quo, so when he reached for her again, she just shook her head. No matter how much she wanted to lean on him, she had to learn to stand on her own two feet.

Darius Greeley strode up.

"Report," Judd ordered.

"Nothing yet. We've combed a mile in all directions. But we don't have the manpower to do a tight grid. Could be we'll find something once it's daylight."

"See that it's done."

"Yes, sir." He shifted a sympathetic gaze to Autumn. "If there's anything to find, we'll find it."

"Thank you, Darius."

As he strode away to confer with the rest of his team, one of the firefighters approached. Beneath the soot and sweat, Autumn recognized Ben Rawlings. The set of his mouth was grim.

"Real sorry about all this, Autumn."

"Thanks."

"Any idea when the fire marshal will be here?" Judd asked.

"Early morning, I expect. It won't be cool

enough to properly investigate until then. But I can already tell you it was arson. Clear signs of accelerant. And it looked like the whole place had been tossed."

Autumn's blood ran cold. "Judd, has someone checked your house?"

He stroked a hand down her back. "I sent a patrol. It's fine."

Ben studied them. "Neither of you seems surprised. You have an idea who might do this to you?"

"Yeah." Judd's expression was grim. "Look, Autumn's about dead on her feet. I'm gonna take her home. Have the fire marshal call me as soon as he hits the scene. I want this investigation opened as quickly as possible so we can catch this son of a bitch."

"You got it, Chief."

CHAPTER 6

Autumn said nothing as Judd ushered her into his house. Boudreaux barked and jumped with joy that his favorite human had come to visit. At her absent pat, he began to whine and pace. The shock was setting in and, with it, a healthy dose of fear that made Judd want to slam his fist through a wall. The son of a bitch had fucked with the wrong man. He'd find Jebediah and put him away for good this time.

He opened his mouth to say he'd take her bag upstairs. But, of course, she had no bag. Because she'd just lost everything she owned. A fresh wave of rage washed through him.

"Why don't you get a shower, wash off the smoke?" he suggested. "I'll round up something for you to sleep in."

Autumn just nodded and went upstairs, Boudreaux on her heels.

With nowhere to redirect his fury, Judd scrubbed both hands over his face. His team had found nothing on their search. They'd be out again at first light. Any evidence from the fire itself would come from the fire marshal, and he'd proceed with the investigation from there. Tyrell Weller was already trying to track down Jebediah, who hadn't yet checked in. He'd be a fucking idiot if he checked in after this, so, chances were, they'd be orchestrating a man hunt tomorrow. Autumn shouldn't be left alone while he dealt with that. The whole family had been notified and were ready to circle the wagons.

He heard the shower cut on.

Tomorrow. All the rest of this would have to wait until tomorrow.

Grabbing a bottle of water from the fridge, he trudged up the stairs, pulling out his phone as he went.

He found a text from Mary Alice.

Is Autumn okay? I heard about the fire.

He'd walked out on her, all but thrown her ultimatum in her face, and she was still checking up on the woman she saw as competition. Because Mary Alice Reed was, down to the bone, a good woman. And he'd been an asshole. Not that he wouldn't do it again under the circumstances, but he owed her an apology. He owed her a lot more than that.

It was way past a decent hour to call, so he shrugged out of his suit jacket and thumbed back a reply. **Physically, yes. But she lost everything.**

An answer came almost immediately. **God, I'm so sorry.**

So she was still up. Judd didn't hesitate before making the call. As soon as she picked up he said, "I'm the one who's sorry. I shouldn't have walked out on you like that."

Mary Alice sighed. "Your friend was in trouble. You kind of rock the white knight routine, Judd. It's part of the appeal. If you'd stayed, you wouldn't be the man I fell in love with."

Judd winced.

Before he could figure out what to say, she continued. "How's Autumn?"

"In shock. Once that wears off—well, she's got a tough road ahead."

"She's staying with you." It wasn't a question.

"Yeah. Safer here." As he said it, he keyed in the code to set the alarm.

Her silence spoke volumes.

"Look, you weren't wrong about anything you said. I've been a shitty boyfriend, especially the last several months. There were reasons, but none of them were fair to you. I'm sorry for that. I honestly never intended to hurt you."

"I know. And I get it. Autumn will always come first for you. I guess I've known it for a while now. After what the two of you went through together, that's really not surprising. You are such a good man, Judd, and I wanted you to be the right one for me. But I deserve more than good intentions, and at the end of the day, that's all you really have to give."

The accusation, delivered in her soft, kind voice, hit him low in the gut, like a punch slipping under his guard. Had all his girlfriends felt like this? Had he really done this to all of them?

"So…that's really it, then?"

"Yeah, I think it's for the best."

What more was there to say? "Okay. Good night, Mary Alice."

"Good night. And Judd? I really am sorry this happened to Autumn. She didn't deserve this kind of bad luck."

He didn't bother to mention that it had nothing to do with luck. "I'll let her know."

After he hung up, he sat on the edge of his bed, waiting for some sense of devastation or anger that his girlfriend of two years had truly dumped his ass. But he felt only remorse for not having treated her better. She was right. She did deserve more than he had to give.

The shower down the hall cut off. The sound spurred him into motion. He still needed to find Autumn something to sleep in. Disappearing into the closet, he snagged one of his soft chambray button downs. She tended toward cold, so the long sleeves ought to keep her warm until they could pick up something more suitable.

When he came back out, she was standing just inside the bedroom door, wrapped in a towel, her hair slicked back. And it didn't matter that her eyes were bloodshot or that the skin beneath them was bruised with exhaustion. His mouth went bone dry at the sight of all that creamy skin.

Say something, asshole.

He dropped his gaze to the floor. "I'm sorry, I meant to get something before you got finished, but I got caught on the phone."

"Not like it's anything you haven't seen before."

But it'd been more than a decade since he'd seen this much bare skin outside the context of swimming. And then they'd been under his parents' roof.

She crossed the room and plucked the shirt from his numb fingers. "Close your eyes."

He obediently slammed them shut, turning around for good measure. He heard the towel drop and couldn't stop his mind from painting a picture of her, still rosy from the shower, sliding into his shirt. His hands itched to touch and he went hard.

No fucking way.

"All done. Which room am I in?"

He almost said, *Mine.* Because once upon a time, it wouldn't have been a question. But a lot of years had passed since then. Things weren't simple.

Readjusting his pants, he turned back around, keeping his gaze firmly fixed on her face, though he could tell well enough that the shirt hit her mid-thigh. "The blue one." He'd earmarked that one for her when he'd bought the house, because including her in long-term plans was simply instinctive, no matter how irrational.

He handed over the bottle of water and some headache medicine. "You'll want to drink that down before you go to sleep."

She took them without argument, following him to the room next door.

Judd turned back the covers. "I got some of those foam pillows you like. You want an extra blanket?"

She crawled in the opposite side. "No."

He wanted to stroke the lines of tension away. "Are you gonna be okay in here by yourself?"

She rolled over, giving him her back, saying something that sounded an awful lot like, "I don't have a choice."

Boudreaux leapt onto the bed, curling up in the crook of her legs.

Judd pressed a hand to the bed but didn't touch her. He didn't know the right thing to do and that left him uneasy. Moving across to the dresser, he opened the top drawer and pulled out a night light. He didn't know if she still used one or not. When she'd been a child, her father's most frequent punishment that didn't involve a beating was to lock her in a closet. She'd been terrified of the dark. He didn't want to leave her in it now. Plugging it in, he straightened.

"Thank you," she said softly, eyes fixed on the light.

At least he'd done something right. "I'll be just next door if you need anything."

"Night, Judd."

"Goodnight, Firefly."

AUTUMN WATCHED THE CLOCK, seeing the minutes tick slowly away, and with it, her chance for escape. There was no way she'd make the meeting point now. Mama would go without her. She'd made that perfectly clear when they went over the plan. If Autumn didn't come, Mama couldn't afford to wait. She was leaving Wishful today, come hell or high water, to start a new life far away from Daddy and his rage.

Maybe, if it had been a normal day, Autumn would've gone with her. But Judd had asked to meet her after school to talk. He'd been so serious and nervous. Judd was never nervous. And she knew they were finally going to talk about it. How things were changing between them.

She loved him. It seemed she'd always loved him, the serious, blue-eyed boy, who'd protected her from the day they'd met. Some would say family mattered more, but Autumn had a lifetime of bruises that said otherwise. If the choice was leaving the physical pain and leaving him or staying for the chance of something better when they turned eighteen in a little over a year—well, there was no question in her mind.

Here they sat, hands clasped, on the sagging, slipcovered sofa in her living room. In and of itself, that wasn't unusual. Judd was a touchy, affectionate sort of guy. It had been important to him to show her that not all touch was in anger. He was one of the very few people who didn't make her flinch at sudden movements. But his palm had never sweated holding hers before. She didn't even mind because this was Judd, *her* Judd, trying to find the words. She prayed they were the ones she wanted to hear.

"What did you want to talk about?" she asked.

"I've been doing a lot of thinking."

"What about?" *Please say us.*

"You and me."

Giddy nerves bubbled in her blood. She struggled to keep her voice normal. "Yeah?"

"We've been best friends since we were six."

"And we'll be best friends until we're a hundred and six." She knew this down to her very marrow.

"Absolutely." The conviction in his voice never wavered. "But I've just been… Have you ever thought about us as…something else?" He lifted his gaze to hers and his eyes were so intense, they pinned her to the spot. Not that she wanted to move away from him.

"What kind of something else?" She knew what she wanted with him. Everything. But his friendship was too precious to her to risk it without being absolutely clear what he meant.

"You and me. Like, together. In a relationship."

"More than friends?" she asked softly.

Judd hesitated, stroking a thumb over the back of her hand. Autumn felt the touch through her whole body.

"Yeah. I mean, it's not an ultimatum or pressure or anything. And if you don't want—"

Autumn laid her free hand over his mouth to stop the flow of words. The inadvertent press of his lips against her fingers sent a fire down her arm. "All the time," she whispered.

"What?"

"I think about it all the time."

His gaze sharpened. Of course, he wouldn't

be that guy who got a goofy grin at finding out they were on the same page. "Yeah?"

Autumn nodded, thinking that the time for awkward words was past. If only he'd kiss her, they could clear the rest of this up in a hurry. Or not a hurry. Not a hurry would be even better.

Judd shifted toward her on the sofa, his knee bumping into hers. Everything in her wanted to leap into his arms, close the distance between them, and finally, *finally* explore this heat that sparked every time he was near. But that wasn't his way. Judd was all about the slow and careful, especially when it came to her. He treated her as someone of value. Someone he treasured. She'd never get enough of that.

He reached up, skimming a hand along her cheek. She turned into his touch, her eyes half-closing to better focus on the sensation. Slowly, his hands slid beneath the heavy fall of her hair, stroking along her nape. The whole time, his eyes stayed on hers, watching, assessing her reaction to every touch.

She'd go mad if he didn't kiss her.

"I won't break, Judd," she whispered.

One corner of that serious mouth curved up. The sofa dipped between them as he leaned in.

"What the hell is going on here?"

Autumn's eyes flew open. Crushing disappointment mixed with panic as she scrambled back from Judd. "Daddy." How had she not heard him get home?

He stood in the doorway, a bunch of yellow tulips crushed in his hand, his eyes cold as ice as he stared at them on the sofa. "I said, what the hell is going on here?" His voice held that carefully measured tone that said he'd been drinking and was trying to hide it.

"Nothing's going on. Nothing happened." She was stumbling over her words because she'd wanted something to happen. And in Jebediah Buchanan's mind, thoughts were as good as deeds when it came to sins.

"I got eyes in my head to see otherwise, girl."

He shifted his icy stare to Judd. "How long you been fucking my daughter?"

Temper cut through Judd's shock, straightening his spine. "I'm not. We're not. It's not like that! I swear."

"Then, after desire has conceived, it gives birth to sin; and sin, when it is full grown, gives birth to death. Get outta my house, boy." Jebediah swung his attention back to Autumn. "Where's your mama?"

"I don't know." It was the truth. She wasn't about to say her mother was gone.

Her father moved toward the back of the house.

Judd hadn't budged.

Autumn risked moving closer to nudge him toward the door. "You should go," she said in a low voice.

"I'm not leaving you with him like this."

"If you stay it'll only make it worse." She'd pay for her sins tonight. Jebediah would take it out of her hide. "Just go."

She managed to herd Judd into the kitchen

before he dug in his heels. "Don't stay here. Leave with me."

Autumn cast an agonized glance back at the living room. Her father would be coming any minute, and Judd needed to be gone. "I can't. You know I can't."

"Autumn—"

"Please, you need to go."

Something crashed from the back of the house. "Sidda!" Jebediah roared.

He knew. Oh God, he knew.

"Go, go, go. Go now." Autumn shoved at Judd, which had zero effect.

"Not without you." He was pulling her toward the door, and it was her turn to dig in her heels.

"Bitch! Faithless whore! Painted Jezebel!"

"Come on, Autumn."

Jebediah lurched into the kitchen, the flowers still in his hand. "Gone." He took in Judd and Autumn, halfway out the door. "No other woman of mine's gonna leave me."

Autumn saw the gun as if in a dream. It rose slowly, in a perfect arc to point at her chest.

Judd swept her feet out from under her, and as she fell, time sped up again. He dove toward her father. The gun echoed like cannon-fire. Judd crashed to the floor, still managing to catch Jebediah around the ankles. Her father toppled.

Autumn scrambled to her feet, terror a live wire in her blood. Judd wasn't moving. The tulips lay scattered around his prone body, their petals crushed, stems broken. Jebediah was trying to get up. She grabbed up her mother's cast iron skillet and ran at him, swinging with all her might. It connected with a solid *thunk*, the impact reverberating up her arms. Jebediah dropped like stone.

Autumn kicked the gun away and crouched by Judd, in the spreading pool of red.

"Judd. Judd!" She rolled him over. Blood. So much blood. The shot had hit him in the right side of his chest. No exit wound, which meant the bullet was lodged inside somewhere.

He took a gurgling breath.

"Hang on. You have to hang on," she ordered, grabbing a couple of kitchen towels and the phone from the wall.

She pressed the towels against the wound and leaned. Judd groaned.

"I'm sorry. I'm sorry, I have to stop the bleeding."

With one blood-smeared hand, she managed to dial 911. She didn't understand a word the operator said, she just started speaking. "This is Autumn Buchanan at 117 Cedarwood Road. Send an ambulance and the police. He's been shot. Oh God, he's been shot. Please hurry."

The operator was saying something, but she couldn't hold the phone and keep pressure on the wound.

"Autumn," Judd wheezed.

"I'm here." An awful pressure was building in her chest, like a balloon being inflated in her rib cage.

"Something…something…need to…"

"Don't talk. Save your strength. An ambulance is coming." *Please God, let it be coming.*

"Tell you…"

"You tell me on the other side of this. You're going to be okay. You're going to be okay, damn it."

But his blood continued to pulse, hot and wet through her fingers.

Autumn's face was wet with sweat and tears. "Don't leave me. Don't you dare leave me, Judd Hamilton." Her vision was going black around the edges, and the pressure in her chest turned to pain. She had to hold on. Had to keep him from bleeding out before the paramedics arrived. In the distance, sirens wailed.

"Autumn—" His eyes closed.

"No. *No.* NO! Judd! Wake up. Wake up!" She risked reaching for his throat, trying to find a pulse. But there was nothing.

She was screaming now, sobbing as she knelt in his blood and watched the only good thing in her life fade away. Something in her chest burst, a brilliant fountain of pain that had her slumping over his body. Dimly, she thought she'd escaped her father anyway.

"Autumn, wake up!"

She broke from the nightmare on a gasp, as if surfacing from a deep swim. And for the first time since they were teenagers under his parents' roof, Judd was there to pull her free of the night terrors.

"It's okay. It's okay. I'm here. I'm safe." He hauled her into his lap, dragging her hand and pressing it to his bare chest so she could feel the thump of his heart. Not slow. Not steady. She'd scared him.

Autumn curled into him, not yet able to speak. Sweat slicked her skin and chills of old grief and terror wracked her body. The taste of his blood still coated her mouth, and her throat was raw from screaming. Boudreaux laid his head on her knee, whining. She pressed her face into the hollow of Judd's throat, breathing him in until both their hearts began to slow. He smelled of good, clean male and sleep, that indefinable trace scent she recognized on an instinctive level, though it had been years since they'd shared a bed.

"I should've realized you'd have the nightmare again after tonight."

She didn't tell him she'd never stopped having the nightmare. It had gotten less frequent over the years, and sometimes she was able to pull herself out before getting to the end. But the only easy sleep she'd had since he'd been shot had been the year she'd spent in his arms. After she'd moved in with the Hamiltons, her night terrors had woken the entire household. Judd would comfort her, and they'd fall asleep together on the living room sofa, her hand over his heart, as it was now.

After her heart surgery, keeping her blood pressure down had been paramount. Recovery from aortic valve replacement was no easy business. Eventually, he'd just spent the night in her bed. His parents and brothers knew, but no one said anything. Nothing improper had ever happened, and eventually they'd both started to heal from that horrible day.

Judd's fingers massaged the tension in her nape and shoulders. "Okay?"

"Yeah."

God she'd missed this. The comfort, the closeness. Having him to turn to in the night, just to touch him, to reassure herself he was alive and safe. She'd never trusted any of her handful of lovers enough to actually sleep with them.

She had no right to sleep with Judd now. He wasn't hers. She should kick him out and just accept the fact that she'd be staring at the ceiling until dawn. But the idea of letting go of him when the scent of his blood was still fresh in her mind had her wanting to curl in and hang on tighter.

"Think you can sleep now?"

No. "Probably."

"Okay." He stood and strode toward the door, her still in his arms.

"What are you doing?"

"Taking you to my bed. You need rest, and we'll both sleep better this way."

How many times had she dreamed of him doing this? But no, not this. Not comfort after the nightmare. He wasn't choosing her. Not how she wanted.

She should say no. Just curl up with Boudreaux on the sofa downstairs. But she was so damned tired. Every inch of her felt flayed and raw, aching, and Judd was the balm. Guilt held no power over her when she was like this. So she didn't protest. Not when he pulled back the covers and laid her in his big king-size bed. Not when he crawled in beside her, wrapping her tight in the embrace that would keep the nightmares at bay. And listening to his strong, steady heartbeat, she slid into thick, dreamless sleep.

CHAPTER 7

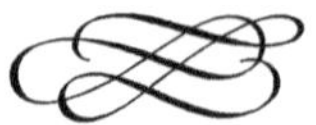

Wisps of smoke still curled from the wreckage of Autumn's apartment, as Judd stood with Fire Marshal Charlie Hammond. The acrid stench of smoke, burnt chemicals, and melted plastic hung in the air, a strange counterpoint to the bright blue morning.

"Preliminary results confirm Ben's assessment. It's absolutely arson. On first inspection, it seems the perp splashed accelerant all over the far wall of the structure."

"Opposite the other side of the duplex?"

"Yeah. Origin was definitely Miss Buchanan's side. Burn pattern suggests it started downstairs. So he came in, did whatever he was going to do, splashed accelerant on the wall, and lit it from the back door."

Judd locked away the rage and tried to ignore his personal connection. He had an investigation to conduct, and he needed a cool head. "Why just the one wall?"

Charlie shrugged. "A half-assed attempt to protect the other half of the duplex? Don't know yet."

"Ben mentioned he thought the place had been tossed before it was lit up."

"Less to see at this point that would verify that, but it's common enough. Arson is often someone's attempt to cover up a robbery."

Autumn was a librarian. What did she have to steal? And why wouldn't a perpetrator toss Riley's place, too? Harder to get into somehow? No, this wasn't a crime of convenience. Typical burglars didn't travel with accelerants. Taking the time to light the place up added to the time for the overall job. The idea of a robbery just didn't play for Judd. This kind of destruction felt personal and not just because that was the most obvious answer.

"What about just straight up vandalism and maliciousness?"

"Sure, sometimes. I'll know more after I've been through. I'm waiting on my backup to arrive before I attempt to enter the structure."

"I need everything you can find. I've got a personal stake in putting this son of a bitch away."

"Soon as I know anything conclusive, you'll be the first to know."

The radio on Judd's belt squawked. He pressed the button on the handset at his shoulder. "This is Hamilton. Go ahead."

"Tyrell Weller is here with the suspect, Chief."

"Copy. I'm on my way."

"Got one on the hook already?" Charlie asked. Being out of Lawley, he didn't know the history at play here.

"The victim's father just got out of prison yesterday."

Charlie whistled. "Damn. Stupid and spiteful bastard if the first thing he did was come here to torch her place."

"She's the one who put him away. If stupid and spiteful will get him locked away permanently, I'll take it. Anything you can find, Charlie," Judd called, and climbed into his cruiser as the fire marshal gave a two-fingered salute.

He checked the dash clock on the drive. Autumn and his mother were meeting Nanna in Lawley to shop for essentials. Despite the fact that he'd rather have splinters shoved under his nails, Eli was tagging along. Not that any of them really thought Jebediah would make a move on her in broad daylight, but there was safety in numbers. Even secure in the knowledge that Jebediah was presently in custody, Judd felt better knowing his brother was with them.

Autumn had been annoyed with him this morning. He'd refused to leave her alone at his place until his mother could swing by. Instead, he'd hand-delivered Autumn to his parents' house, with firm instructions that she not be left alone. He needn't have worried. Patty had full Mama Bear mode engaged. Autumn hadn't raised any protests about his mother's fussing.

Neither of them had said a word about last night—at least not the part of it spent in his bed. He'd woken first, still tangled up with her. With any of his girlfriends, he would've been itching to climb out of bed, get his space, get started on his day. But he didn't move a muscle, not wanting to disturb Autumn, despite the fact that his arm and shoulder were completely numb.

He'd never been able to actually sleep with anyone but her. Maybe because he was afraid of what might come out of his mouth. He had no idea if he still talked in his sleep, but he dreamed of Autumn so often he didn't want to risk it. His girlfriends had been threatened enough about her. He'd never wanted to try to explain how they'd shared a bed for a year. Not one of them would've believed it had only been platonic.

It hadn't felt platonic this morning. It had felt like coming home.

Guilt prickled at that. Less than twenty-four hours ago, he'd been together with Mary Alice. And yet, in two years together, he'd never shared this intimacy with her. He'd never been content just to watch her sleep and memorize the lines of her face.

As he pulled up to the long, low brick building that housed the Police Department, Judd locked all those thoughts away. The last thing he needed to have in his mind when going head-to-head with Jebediah Buchanan was how his daughter had looked in his bed.

Tyrell rose from his perch on the edge of Darius's desk. "Didn't think I'd be seeing you so soon again."

Judd shook the other man's hand. "Where is he?"

"In interrogation," Darius replied.

"What's his demeanor?" Judd asked.

"Cooperative."

"Look, Chief, there's something you need to know before you go in there. I know you like him for this arson, but he's got an alibi," Tyrell said.

Judd fixed him with an expectant stare.

"He didn't even get into the county until this morning. Most of yesterday was spent purchasing a car. He checked into a fleabag motel in Greenwood at 5:30 yesterday and was seen eating at the truck stop across the street at 7:00."

"Witnesses?"

"Spoke to the guy he bought the car off of. Just an ad in the paper. And there's video footage of him at the truck stop. Time-stamped."

"Where'd he buy the car?"

"Indianola. Another former inmate picked him up and dropped him there," Tyrell explained.

Charlie hadn't reported an estimated time for when the fire started but it'd been 8:00

when Autumn called him. Not enough time to set the blaze and get back to Greenwood, seventy-five miles away, to be caught on camera at 7:00. Unless Charlie found some evidence of a remote starter, Jebediah hadn't been here.

"All that means is he wasn't the one to directly strike the match." Judd strode toward interrogation.

He'd only seen Jebediah Buchanan once since the trial. Because of Autumn's PTSD, their annual testimony to the parole board was made without his presence. But when Judd had graduated police academy, he'd made the trek to Parchman to look the bastard in the eye and make it clear that if he ever got out of the hole, Judd would be there to stop him from getting anywhere near his daughter.

That had been a brief visit. Jebediah had sat across from him in his orange prison jumpsuit, shackled to the metal table, his lean form gone mostly to fat from years of a prison diet. Judd had said his piece and waited for the pseudo-religious babble and invective. But Jebediah had said nothing, merely taking in Judd's full police uniform before staring off into space somewhere over Judd's left shoulder.

As he stepped into interrogation, Judd's first thought was that this man bore no resemblance to the Jebediah he'd last seen. The full head of hair had gone to dirty gray and thinned until a speckled pate showed through. The puffy, pallid skin was shrunken now, as if he were being slowly mummified. The gnarled, knobby hands were liver spotted and curled with arthritis where they lay on the table. But the eyes—the same vivid green as Autumn's—were clear as they flicked up to meet him. Even from across the room, Judd could see the deep grooves in his face, dug from pain.

"What is it? Cancer? ALS?"

"Why do you care? It's terminal."

And it couldn't have done its worst any faster?

Judd took a seat across from him, something niggling him about the other man's appearance. "You know why you're here?"

"Figure you've got to make your point and harass me now I'm on the outside."

"That was my original plan. See, I'm Chief of Police now, and this is my town. I'm not happy you're here, as you might expect."

Jebediah looked neither impressed nor afraid. "The Lord says, if I confess out loud and seek forgiveness from others, then I'll be cleansed of all unrighteousness. I just want to make things right with my daughter before I go."

He doesn't look crazy, Judd realized. He didn't believe for a minute that Jebediah was actually better. That kind of delusion just didn't up and go away, even when the alcohol dried up. But apparently, in all these years, he'd learned to hide it. Maybe that was how he'd finessed the parole board.

"Cleansed of all unrighteousness," Judd repeated, struggling to keep the incredulity from his tone. "Well now, I guess you're really pushing the envelope on that one, what with wiping out all her worldly possessions. As I recall, you weren't big on worldly possessions."

The old Jebediah would've gone off on a rant about the evils of material things or some shit. This one just sat, surprise flickering over his face, along with a dawning realization that this was why he'd been dragged in. On the heels of that came the anger. "I haven't been anywhere near Autumn, and I don't know where she lives."

Judd wanted to poke at that anger, add fuel to the fire to get him to incriminate himself. "Bet you could've found out. Maybe tagged one of your prison buddies, who already got out, to drive up here and set her place on fire, while you were conveniently caught on camera, eating dinner, calm as you please, more than an hour away."

"Autumn's house burned?" Jebediah blinked in apparent confusion, understanding that this wasn't a hypothetical question.

"Yeah. Last night. Curious thing that should happen the day you got out."

"I had nothing to do with that."

Like he was gonna say anything else.

"Right. And you want to make amends. With the daughter whose welfare you haven't even asked after."

"If she were dead or hurt, you wouldn't be sitting calmly in that chair."

Calm was the very last thing Judd was feeling. But he had years of experience hiding his emotions in stressful situations. He didn't like the casual way Jebediah made the statement. As if Judd were of no concern.

Jebediah leaned forward. "You think I don't know you want to take me apart? You're looking for the first excuse to put me back inside. But I have news for you, *Chief.* I'm not going to give you the satisfaction. I was a model prisoner, and I'll be a model parolee for as long as God allows me to grace this earth. So whatever it is you think you have on me, keep looking. There's nothing there."

"I'll be the judge of that," Judd said. "Let's talk about your day yesterday."

"I REALLY WISH you had let me buy you those boots," Patty complained as they hauled purchases in from the car.

"You've done plenty," Autumn assured her. "I feel bad enough I couldn't rein Nanna in." As it was, Judd's grandmother had bought her a work week's worth of dresses, two new pair of dress shoes, and a pair of completely unnecessary but gorgeous earrings.

"That just proves you're human." Eli dumped his load of bags in the living room floor. "Trying to stop Nanna from doing anything she wants to do is like trying to lasso a runaway train."

"That is the absolute truth," Patty agreed.

Autumn looked over at her little brother, who'd let them drag him all over Lawley, for everything from clothes to underwear to toiletries, without complaint or even so much as an eyeroll. Stepping over the bags, she rose on tiptoe to kiss his cheek. "Thanks for coming with us."

Eli flashed his crooked grin, a mirror image of Leo's. "Clearly someone had to haul all this booty."

They'd all worked hard to pretend this was just a big shopping spree instead of the first step in Autumn starting over. She'd let them have the thin illusion because they thought it made her feel better and their support meant more than she could say. But her own mind had been occupied running numbers, sorting out how much she could afford to spend on necessities, what had to be bought now and what had to wait.

The vast majority of the clothes had come from the Goodwill and Salvation Army thrift stores, as well as a trendy little consignment shop she and Riley had found on a previous trip to Lawley. The used clothes didn't bother Autumn. Most of her wardrobe had been secured in a similar fashion growing up, so she had ample experience with how to stretch a buck. She still wanted to make a pilgrimage to Starkville and Oxford to hit up the thrift stores there—college towns tended toward high turnover and a lot of nice brands—but she wanted to go on her own, so it'd have to wait until she got her car back. Still, the day's haul was a good start to a long road.

"I wish we could've just gone straight to Judd's to drop all this off. Then I could at least get things put away instead of taking over your living room." And she could have some much needed alone time to have a good cry over all the things no amount of money could replace. The loss of those mementos, gifts, and memories had been hovering at the back of her mind all day, a heavy weight on her heart.

"He was clear about you not being left alone, and I'm not going to cross him on this," Patty said.

Autumn sighed. "I know."

Patty wrapped an arm around her shoulders. "I know you'd like to get settled."

Settled. Because she was living with Judd

now. The thing she'd been trying to avoid for years because proximity made hiding her feelings all the harder. She gave brief thought to asking Patty if she could stay here. The offer hadn't been retracted, but Autumn knew absolutely no one was willing to cross Judd on the best way to protect her. Autumn had no desire to paint targets on Patty or Owen's backs either, so she didn't ask. And a tiny part of her could admit that she wanted to be close to Judd, which just reinforced that she needed to get the hell out of town.

She'd email her mother tonight. Start making plans. She couldn't go right away. Even though she'd been frugal, between all the must-haves and the new laptop, she wouldn't be able to move now. Deposits on a new place, utilities, first and last month's rent all added up to an out of reach total. But maybe she could get that ball rolling by planting the seed with her mother. Then after another couple of months of royalties…maybe.

She needed to get her new laptop set up and

finish the next book in *Redemption Ridge*. Fans were primed for the next installment about the Oliver family, and God knew she was going to need whatever boost in income it could provide. Thank God for cloud storage. The backup of everything ought to be on the servers, so she shouldn't have lost anything there.

"Can I borrow a couple of suitcases so it's at least easier to haul in?"

"Of course. Eli, you want to grab some from the attic?"

"On it."

As Eli disappeared down the hall, the kitchen door swung open. "Mom? Y'all back?" Leo called.

"In here!"

He came in, Boudreaux trotting at his heels. The dog broke away and came straight for Autumn, giving her a thorough sniff from breast to toe.

"Who's a good boy?" She gave him a good rubdown. "What's he doing with you?"

"Picked him up this morning. Judd said you

were worried about leaving him alone out at the house."

This family was just racking up the brownie points. There was a guard posted on Judd's place, but even so, she'd been worried that someone might try the same treatment on his house. It was bad enough she'd lost all her things. If anything happened to Boudreaux… she couldn't even think about it.

"Did you finish?" Patty asked him.

"Just. Thought I'd come straight over with it."

"Straight over with what?" Autumn asked. Because they all had that look that said they'd been up to something.

Leo produced a thumb drive from his pocket. "Why don't you fire up that new laptop there and see?" He picked up the box and examined it. "Nice specs."

"If I had to get a new one, might as well upgrade to one that will last for a while." Especially since one of her major sources of income depended upon it.

She pulled the new machine out and began the process of setting it up as Boudreaux stretched out at her feet. "Has anyone heard from Judd since this morning?"

Eli returned with the suitcases. "Not about the investigation. Just to check on you."

Autumn knew he'd be bringing her father in for questioning. Whether he'd yet found enough evidence to charge him with anything was another matter. If it was there to find, she had faith Judd would find it. His entire career as a cop had proven him thorough and dogged. He always got his man.

She wished she knew what was going on.

"Okay, hand it over and let's see what you've been up to." Autumn plugged the flash drive into the side and opened the folder. The whole thing was full of JPEGs. She toggled the view to extra large thumbnails and watched her screen fill with pictures. Pictures of her and Judd. Her with the rest of their family. Going back *years.* Lifting a hand to cover her trembling mouth, she scrolled through, feeling her throat tighten with every row. Her history with Judd was right here. Not all of it, but a huge chunk. Even quite a few she hadn't seen herself. All memories she thought she'd lost to the fire.

"I pulled out all the old albums before we left this morning and had Leo scan everything. I'd been meaning to have it done anyway, and I thought you'd like copies," Patty said gently.

Autumn had to swallow several times before she could speak. "I don't know what to say."

"I put a call out to all your friends, too," Leo said. "Everybody's rounding up stuff from high school and college. I'll put those together as they come in. And if you'll let me know which ones you want, I'll have prints made for you to frame."

The tears spilled over then, cascading down her cheeks in a hot flood. She set the laptop aside and headed for Leo, who took one panicked step back before opening his arms.

"You gave me the best thing ever, so you're going to have to deal with the ugly cry." And it felt so good to be crying with relief instead of the tearing grief. She knew she wasn't through with the grief yet—not by a long shot—but this gift was a balm to her ravaged heart.

Oh, who was she kidding? She could never leave this family. Any of them. And it would kill her when Judd married Mary Alice.

Leo wrapped his arms around her. "Oh, well, it was no big deal. Just a few hours with a scanner."

"It's a huge deal to me." She gave him a tight hug and a watery kiss on the cheek before turning to Patty. "Thank you. I can't tell you what this means to me."

Patty stroked her hair back. "You don't have to, sweetheart."

Part of her wanted to curl up in one corner of the big leather sofa and cuddle the laptop as she looked over all the pictures and lost herself in memories. Instead, she managed to pull herself together. She washed her face and set to neatly folding and consolidating her purchases into the two suitcases Eli had brought down from the attic, while her cloud drives synced to the new hard drive. The small progress left her feeling mostly human again by the time Judd showed up for dinner.

He took one look at her and crossed the room in two strides, reaching out to stroke a thumb over her cheek. "You've been crying."

Everything in her wanted to lean into his touch, to recapture the intimacy of his bed this morning. But the desire was chased by a frisson of guilt. He didn't belong to her, and she didn't have trauma to fall back on as an excuse for infringing on Mary Alice's territory just now. She stepped back and reached for the laptop.

"Happy tears, actually." While the rest of the family finished prepping dinner, she showed him the collection of pictures.

"I've got more at the house. I'll dig them out for you."

"Later. What I really want to know is what happened today." Was her boogeyman still out there?

Judd rubbed a hand across the back of his neck and dragged it over the tension in his shoulders, something he only did when things hadn't gone the way he wanted on a case. "I had your father brought in for questioning. He's got a solid alibi for the time frame of the fire."

Autumn frowned. "But how can that be?"

"Just means he didn't physically set it. It doesn't rule out that he had someone else do it. I'm still waiting on the fire marshal to get back to me with the evidence he collected at the scene today."

"But you didn't have enough to hold him," she concluded.

"No. His parole officer is keeping him on a tight leash, while we conduct the investigation. For now, he's staying at the Mockingbird Motel. He's got a car. Piece of shit Taurus in maroon. Same vintage Mitch used to drive back in high school."

That would be easy enough to look out for.

"There's something else." He tugged her to sit on the sofa, tangling his fingers in hers.

Autumn's stomach knotted. "What?"

"Jebediah's dying. Don't know what of.

Cancer probably. He looks like shit. I'm guessing he doesn't have a whole helluva long time."

She waited to feel…something. Any pang of sorrow. But she felt only relief. "He's too mean to just up and die."

"Probably. He says he wants to make amends with you."

"Amends?" Autumn couldn't stop her voice from shooting an octave higher in disbelief. "Is he out of his mind?"

"That was pretty much my reaction, too. But I just wanted to warn you. He'll likely try to seek you out. I've already got Tucker McGee filing a restraining order. We'll get a temporary one in place and then go before the judge as soon as we can get on his schedule to make it permanent. But I don't know how much Jebediah will give a damn about that. If he's really dying—and I'm pretty sure he's not lying about that—he may decide whatever version of making amends is worth more than his freedom for whatever time he's got left."

"Supper, you two!" Patty called.

Autumn rose, disentangling their hands. "I'll be on my guard."

"See that you are. And I'll see that you've got someone on you for the foreseeable future until we determine how much of a threat he is."

She didn't relish the idea of a 24/7 bodyguard. But they'd have to talk about that later. For now, there was poppyseed chicken to eat.

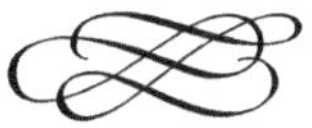

CHAPTER 8

"Dinner was great, Mom. Can I help with dishes?" Judd asked.

Patty waved him off. "You get Autumn home. She's had a long day, and I know you have, too."

Home. Judd chose not to analyze exactly how much he liked the idea of Autumn being included as part of that.

Autumn stacked plates beside the sink. "I want to swing by my place and pick up my car. I don't like being dependent on everybody else to get around, and I've got at least a few things in it."

Judd hesitated. He had multiple reasons for not wanting to head over there, not the least of which was that the sight of what was left of her duplex would probably be a serious emotional sucker punch.

"I don't know if that's such a good idea."

"Why? Is my car considered evidence?"

"No. I'm just not sure you're ready to go back there yet. It's pretty rough."

"I don't think there is a right time to go see the burned-out shell of my home, Judd. I'd rather get it over with. Besides, I'm headed back to work tomorrow, and I want to drive myself."

His brain was already reviewing the security of the library. It was minimal, with multiple points of access. He didn't like it. "Should you be going back so soon?"

"Doesn't matter. I need the hours. I can't afford *not* to work as many as Mitzi will give me."

Of course, she'd need to recoup her losses however she could. Judd understood that. But the practical side warred with the personal as he tried to find some other rational reason to say no instead of admitting the real reason he didn't want her mobile.

His silence stretched on too long and Autumn's eyes narrowed. "You think if I have my car, I'll bolt."

Sometimes Judd really hated how easily they read each other. "You were pretty hell bent on leaving, and I can't imagine this has exactly been a motivation to stay." She was the victim, not a material witness, so he couldn't order her not to leave town.

Autumn took a breath, clearly trying to find the right words. "Putting aside the money, which I no longer have to put into moving, I'd never leave without saying something first. I couldn't walk away without saying goodbye when I was seventeen, and I can't do it now. Am I scared? Yeah. I'd be stupid not to be. And I know that right now, I'm safer with you than anywhere else. I swear I won't do anything foolish. I just want my car."

He hadn't truly realized how much he'd believed she'd leave until the threat of it loosened its fist around his heart. "Alright. We'll go pick it up."

They loaded the suitcases with her new stuff into the trunk of the cruiser and put Boudreaux in the backseat. On the drive over to her place, he asked, "Is there anything you want me to pick up for the house? Some girl thing for the bathroom? Some particular groceries? I haven't even looked at the fridge." He wanted her to be comfortable. More, he wanted her to accept that it was her home now and embrace it.

"We'll figure it out. Listen, Judd, why don't I talk to Mary Alice and explain this? She's bound to be uncomfortable with the idea of me living with you, even under these circumstances."

Shit. "That's not necessary."

"Really. I don't want to cause any more problems between you two."

"You can't."

"I'm not trying to get all up in your business.

If you think it'll do more harm than good, I won't talk to her."

Judd sighed. "No, I mean you can't cause any problems between us. We broke up."

He could feel her staring at him. "Broke up. When?"

"Last night."

"Before or after I called you?"

"It doesn't matter, it's done."

"It matters to me. Which was it, Judd?"

This was the last thing he wanted to talk about, but he knew she'd never let it go. "After."

Her head thunked back against the seat. "God, Judd, I'm sorry. This is all my fault."

"No," he snapped. "This is not your fault."

"But if I hadn't called—"

"You did exactly what you were supposed to do. If you hadn't called me directly, dispatch would have. And if it had been dispatch that called instead of you, I'd have been beyond pissed, not to mention worried. We broke up because I took her for granted. That's not on you."

Whatever she might've said died on her tongue as they pulled into the empty drive of the duplex.

"Oh my God. It's worse than I remember from last night."

Judd reached across to take her hand, but she was already climbing out of the car. Well, at least she'd dropped the subject of Mary Alice.

Autumn took half a dozen steps toward the house then stopped and wrapped both arms around her middle. What little color she'd had faded from her cheeks. Judd let Boudreaux out with a firm order to heel and joined her, resting a hand on her shoulder in silent support. She didn't turn into him, and he didn't know what to think about it.

"How bad is Riley's side?"

"There's smoke and water damage, but most of it is fine. She'll have to move, obviously, but Liam's nearly finished renovating their new place."

"Good. That's good. After everything she went through with the pharmacy flooding last year, I couldn't bear to cause more problems for her."

"This isn't on you either. It's on whoever lit the place up. You being a target doesn't make this your fault."

"It still feels like my fault."

Boudreaux barked a quick warning yip as a truck pulled up to the curb. Judd bit back his next argument as Charlie climbed out.

"What're you doing back here?" Judd called.

"Wanted to double check something before I called you." He strode over. "Since you're here, I'll show you directly. I've got extra turnout gear in my truck. Keep you from getting ash all over your uniform."

"Charlie, let me introduce you. This is Autumn Buchanan. Autumn, Fire Marshal Charlie Hammond."

The two shook hands. "Real sorry about this, Miss Buchanan."

"Thank you." She took a step away and Judd dropped his hand. "I don't suppose by some miracle my laptop survived?"

"Afraid not," Charlie said.

Autumn's shoulders slumped. She looked back to Judd. "I'm just going to go. Unless you need me for something?" This she addressed to Charlie.

"No ma'am."

"Judd, if you'll pop the trunk so I can get my stuff, I'll get out of the way."

He transferred her suitcases to her car. "Why don't you take Boudreaux on home? I don't know how long I'll be here."

"Sure."

"There's an officer on duty out there if you need anything. I'll see you back at the house, okay?"

"Yeah. C'mon, Boudreaux."

His dog leapt into her car. Judd watched them drive away.

"So it's that kinda personal, is it?" Charlie asked.

Judd turned his attention back to the other man. "Excuse me?"

Charlie cocked a brow. "Got the vic staying at your place?"

"We've been best friends since we were six." If he'd been from Wishful, that's all Judd would've needed to say. Everyone here knew the history.

"I've got best friends. Don't look at any of them like that."

Judd bristled. "You had something relevant to the investigation to show me?"

Charlie lifted his hands in truce. "Yeah. Come on and suit up. We'll look before we lose the light."

AUTUMN SHOULD'VE GONE STRAIGHT BACK to Judd's house. Just hauled her stuff upstairs and curled up with Boudreaux, while her cloud drive synced. She needed to get back to the book. Estimate a release date and start working on marketing plans. God knew, she needed the distraction of losing herself in a world where she had some control.

Instead, she found herself driving across town to Mary Alice's house. Which was foolish on so many levels. Judd was finally single, and, with the investigation ongoing, he'd hardly have time to jump into things with someone else. She could finally have that conversation with him. It was what she wanted. What she'd wanted when she'd tried to talk to him at the fountain.

But breaking up hadn't been his choice. He hadn't chosen her. He'd been dumped because of her. It wasn't the first time, and had it been anyone else, Autumn would've just let it go. But he loved Mary Alice enough to buy her a ring. As much as it gutted her to do it, she had to try and make things right for him. He'd given her so much of himself. The least she could do was try to give this back.

Mary Alice answered the door in yoga pants, a pair of reading glasses shoved up on top of her head. Her eyes widened at the sight of Autumn.

"Look, I know I'm the last person you expected or probably even wanted to see right now, but can I come in?"

"Sure." She opened the door further.

"I can't stay long. Boudreaux's in the car." Hearing his name, the dog woofed out the cracked window. "I'll be back in a minute, boy."

Autumn stepped inside and felt the awkwardness descend like a boom. Determined, she moved on into the little living room.

"I'm really sorry about your house."

Oh no. Autumn couldn't handle the well-intentioned politeness. She'd say this and then get out. "Thanks. But I'm not here to talk about that. Judd told me you broke up last night."

Mary Alice crossed her arms with a disapproving glare Autumn felt certain she'd leveled on her third graders. "Are you here to gloat?"

The whip of insult almost had her marching straight out the door. But she stayed because she understood, in a way Judd never could, exactly how his girlfriends saw her. "No. I'm here to ask you to give him another chance."

"Another chance?"

Autumn took advantage of the complete and utter shock to push through. "I know he's been busy and tied up lately, and a lot of that is, unfortunately, because of me. As long as the investigation is open, that's not going to change. But you're important to him. More important than any other girlfriend before you. And I know that if you take him back, give him another shot, he'll prove it."

Mary Alice frowned. "You're seriously standing there telling me I'm important to him. *You.*"

"Yes, me. Are you really going to stand there and tell me that your breaking up with him had nothing to do with me?"

"No. It had everything to do with you. I just don't understand why you'd be here asking me to take him back."

"Because it isn't what you think between us. I'm not a threat."

Mary Alice crossed the room to pick up a glass of wine from the coffee table. "Oh, but you are, Autumn."

"We aren't...we've never been anything more than friends." Never mind that she'd wanted to change that mere days ago. That she still wanted to change it.

"Oh, I'm not worried about that. I know he was faithful on that point, at least. But his life revolves around you, and that's just not something I can live with anymore."

Of course she couldn't. Autumn's whole relationship with Judd was absolutely toxic if they weren't actually together. She recognized that, even if he couldn't. "You won't have to. Not for long, anyway."

"You're still planning to leave?"

"It'll take me longer now, thanks to the fire. But yes. There's nothing between me and Judd." Her brain chose that inauspicious moment to remind her of those quiet minutes in his bed this morning, where that had been almost the literal truth. Swallowing hard, she shut the door on the memory. "The fact is, you matter to him. Trust me, I have insider information on this. If my father hadn't been released from prison, I think he would've already talked to you by now."

"Talked to me."

"About your relationship." *Come on, read between the lines. Don't make me say it and spoil this.*

One blonde brow arched. "You mean the kind of conversation that often takes place at the nicest restaurant in town? Where he apologizes for working too much and being distant and says he wants to make our relationship a priority? That kind of conversation?"

Oh God. Had she really called and interrupted his proposal? Autumn closed her eyes for a moment and cursed her crap timing. "How far did he get?"

"Far enough to pull out the box and make it clear we both thought we were having a very different conversation."

"What do you mean?"

"I thought he was proposing. He thought he was digging himself out of the doghouse."

That made no sense. "But…I thought he bought you an engagement ring."

"Oh no. That would've indicated we were on the same page." She crossed her arms. "He gave me the dozen yellow roses of bracelets."

"The what?"

Mary Alice held up a finger and disappeared down the hall. A few moments later, she came back with a long, slim jewelry case. Flipping open the top, she handed it over.

Autumn stared at the simple, unadorned twist of silver and gold. Every gift, every trinket he'd ever given her over the years had made her feel seen and cherished. But this…It wasn't ugly, exactly, but there was nothing personal about it. No detail that said, *I see you. You're special to me.*

She'd wound herself up for days thinking the door was closing for good, and she'd had it all wrong. This bracelet said clearer than any words that he didn't love Mary Alice. And she knew it.

"That's…wow. I knew he didn't do jewelry but, damn." Did the man know nothing?

"I'd thought maybe you helped him pick it out."

Autumn handed the box back. "If he'd solicited my opinion, I'd have steered him in a direction that wasn't going to piss you off."

Mary Alice studied Autumn as if she were a puzzle that made no sense. "You would have, wouldn't you?" She shook her head with a wry smile. "I really wanted to hate you. I wanted to put this all on your head. All his other girlfriends did. But you really do try just to be a friend to him."

"It would be shitty of me to be anything else."

"But you love him."

It didn't surprise Autumn that Mary Alice knew it. Probably everyone in town knew it except for Judd himself. "I wouldn't be here if I didn't. I want him to be happy." *Even if it's with someone who isn't me.*

She picked up the wine again, giving Autumn a long look over the rim of the glass. "You really want Judd to be happy? Go after him yourself."

Autumn stared at her, so taken aback she could only sputter, "Excuse me?"

"Oh, don't look at me like that. You're both selling yourselves short if either of you ever thinks you're going to be happy with anybody else. No one else could ever compete with the bond between you."

She'd thought so herself for years, but hearing it so plainly stated by someone she knew loved him left Autumn feeling off balance.

"I don't know what his reasons are for not crossing that line with you, but I think it's time you pushed him over it. If you don't, you'll regret it for the rest of your life."

"Why are you doing this?" Autumn asked.

Mary Alice polished off the wine. "Because I

love him, too, and I want him to be happy. You'll make him happy and whole in a way I never could."

It was as close to permission as she was ever going to get and the idea of it terrified her. Because that wasn't something she was prepared to discuss with Mary Alice, Autumn edged toward the door. "I should go."

"It's probably best if you don't mention this conversation to Judd."

"No arguments there." Autumn stepped back out into the cooling night. "For what it's worth, I really am sorry about the bracelet."

"Eh, I'll pawn it and put the money toward something fun. Maybe a weekend out of town with my girlfriends."

"I wish you all the best."

Mary Alice studied her. "I believe you mean that. So thanks. And I'll wish you good luck. Judd's a stubborn man. You're going to need it."

By the time Judd got home, Autumn was sound asleep, curled up in her own bed with Boudreaux. She'd had two incredibly rough days and the skin beneath her eyes looked bruised. So he pushed the questions he needed to ask off until morning. He slept poorly, one ear cocked for any signs of distress from her room. But no screams dragged him from sleep. When he woke in the gray light of dawn, he didn't know whether to be relieved or disappointed.

Her room was empty, the bed neatly made,

the suitcases stacked in a corner. Maybe she hadn't spent as easy a night as he'd thought. He found her downstairs, already dressed for work and pouring coffee into a travel mug. Boudreaux sprawled at her feet. Catching sight of him, the dog's tail made a steady thump against the cabinet.

Judd scratched him between the ears. "Hey. Been up long?"

"A while. I forgot how beautiful the sunrises are out here."

He stepped up beside her and followed her gaze out the kitchen window. A thin mist scudded along the surface of the water. That was the view that had sold him on this nineteen eighties monstrosity of a house. He could admit to himself now that a part of him had bought it for her, because he knew how much she loved the optimism of dawn. "Been a long time since you've seen one."

She hummed an acknowledgment. They stood side-by-side, watching the watercolor blush of color fade and the mist dissipate. But for the first time in a long time, the silence between them wasn't easy. Her expression was shuttered, and he didn't know where her head was. Was she thinking of her father? Was she still planning to leave? The idea of it cut him to the quick. A life without Autumn in it wasn't something he wanted to contemplate. She'd been his compass almost all his life. Without her he'd be…lost.

He thought of Nanna's assertion. *You have the power to make her stay. You always have.*

But what good was that power if he couldn't keep her safe?

Turning away from the window, Autumn scooped up her purse.

"What are you doing?"

"Going into work. I'm behind after the last couple of days, and I want a couple hours of quiet to myself before we open and all the Lookie Lous invade the library to ask about the fire."

"Not by yourself, you're not. Give me ten minutes. I'll follow you in."

He expected her to argue, but she just nodded and sat to wait with the dog.

He hated this withdrawn, muted version of her. It was too redolent of the way her father had drained all her life and vibrancy. The bastard didn't have the right to terrorize her back to silence. And after the evidence Charlie had found at the fire, hopefully he'd be well on his way to building a case that would get the son of a bitch put away for whatever remained of his time on earth.

They caravanned into town, with a brief stop by Leo's place to drop off Boudreaux. By the time they rolled into the library parking lot, Wishful was stirring, with parents toting kids to school or squeezing in a stop at Sweet Magnolias or The Daily Grind. His stomach growled at the scents of hash browns and bacon the breeze carried over from Dinner Belles.

Maybe he'd slip over and grab some breakfast to go and bring it back before Autumn got too far into her work.

She stopped on the sidewalk. "Judd. The door."

As he caught sight of what she had, his hand moved to the butt of his gun. "I see it."

The plate glass door had been broken. Even from here, he could see something red spilled across the worn tiles of the lobby. Tension whipped through him, but he didn't voice the question that immediately sprang to mind. When was Livia due to arrive?

"Wait here."

The lock was nothing special, and there was no security to speak of. The vandal had simply been able to reach through the hole in the glass to unlock it. Hell, a smaller person than him could've fit through the hole itself. Judd strained to listen as he pulled the door open, mindful of where there might be prints. He heard nothing but the crunch of broken glass beneath his boots as he stepped inside carefully avoiding the pools of what was very definitely paint. Paint, not blood. There was no broken body sprawled out of sight, and some of the strain eased. This was vandalism, not murder. More than likely, whoever had done it was long gone.

Graffiti was scrawled on the walls in the same red paint dumped on the industrial tile floor. *Faithless whore. I see you.* Over and over around the big bulletin board for local announcements. And smack in the center was a grainy, photocopied black and white picture of Autumn. Stepping closer, he identified it as the shot from the staff page on the library's website. But it wasn't her name scrawled beneath in bold, block letters. It was Harper Jackson.

"What the hell?"

Moving beyond the small lobby into the library proper, he circled the perimeter. No one bolted for one of the other exits, and there was no other obvious sign of vandalism. The damage seemed to be confined to the entryway. He'd do a more thorough search in a bit.

Autumn stood in the lobby, face pale and stricken as she stared at the bulletin board.

"I told you to wait outside."

"How could he possibly have found out? I was careful."

A sick feeling set up in his gut. "Careful about what?"

She closed her eyes, wincing. "I never wanted you to know about it."

Before the last couple of days, if anyone had asked, Judd would've staked his life on the fact that they told each other nearly everything. But she'd kept the secret of her mother for years. And apparently there was more. He couldn't stop the dual flashes of hurt and dread that spurted through him.

"Know about what, Autumn?" He knew he was pulling out his no-nonsense cop voice but couldn't seem to dial it back.

"You've been wondering how I've been supporting myself with my hours cut back so far at the library. You haven't asked, but you're not stupid. You know I haven't been making enough off the pools at Dinner Belles to truly balance it out."

Dear God, had she gotten into something illegal? "Have you been gambling?"

She snorted out a humorless laugh. "No. Nothing illegal. I've been writing."

"Writing what?"

"Novels. I started self publishing them nearly a year ago, and they're doing pretty well."

Whatever he'd expected, it wasn't that. His muscles loosened. "Why wouldn't you want me to know about that? I think it's great you're doing something you like and making a success of it."

"Because of *what* I'm writing."

"What, are you gonna tell me you're writing those drug store novels with the women ripping the men's shirts off?" One glance at the look on Autumn's face wiped the smirk right off of his. *Oh, crap.*

"Um…" he cleared his throat and tried to salvage. "So the half-naked men books. That's…" *Great? Interesting? Nice?* "And it's going well?"

She rolled her eyes. "There are no half-naked men on my covers, but yes, it is romance. Romantic suspense. So…like if we went to see an action movie, but the romance part of the plot—you know, the part that *I* like—was the main part of the story."

Huh. Chick-Action. Okay… "Help me out, Firefly, because you look like Jimmy Newman when I have to go haul his ass in after a three-day bender. There's nothing to be ashamed of. Hell, you're doing something you like, right? And you're doing well with it? So I'm happy for you."

"Thanks." She said it grudgingly, like maybe she didn't want his support in this.

What was that about?

"I'm just surprised this is the first I'm hearing about it. An author in town is something people like to talk about. I'd think Reed Campbell would have you signing books over at Inglenook and everyone making a fuss."

"It's not that glamorous. And also, no one knows because I write under a pen name."

"Oh."

"Because of the sex."

"Oh." There was no other safe thing to say.

"Because we live in the buckle of the Bible Belt and there are a lot of Puritanical people who feel like they have the right to dictate what other people read based on their own religious or moral beliefs. People who think it's okay to denigrate the most popular genre of fiction because it's written predominantly by women, for women, and it celebrates feminism and a woman's right to not only choose but also demand and expect satisfaction from her partner." Her eyes snapped to his and her finger got all up in his face. "If you ask whether that's like women's porn, I'm going to hit you. It's not."

Judd held up his hands in peace. "I didn't say anything." But he was thinking plenty.

Autumn wasn't repressed. She'd had adult relationships, same as he had. But it was one of the rare things they never discussed. Knowing she'd written books with *that* kind of explicit content made him wonder exactly what was in her head. Were those scenes purely made up for the story or were they fantasies of hers? What would it be like to see that side of her?

You need to stay the hell away from that side of her.

Pulling his mind out of the gutter, he circled back to the topic at hand. "What does that have to do with this?"

"Because Harper Jackson is my pen name. I don't know *how* my father could've found out about it, but the subject matter of these books is exactly the kind of thing he would've punished me for. He'd have used it as evidence that I am exactly the faithless whore he accused me of being. Case in point." She waved a hand at the walls. "If this isn't a threat that he wants to carry out the promise he made that day in the courtroom, I don't know what it is."

Judd clenched his fists until his knuckles went white. He'd seen the results of her father's form of punishment. The man had a gift for beatings that left no permanent scar. He would bring hell itself down on Jebediah's head before letting him lay a finger on her again. Breathing out the rage, Judd forced himself to focus on the immediate problem.

"He's not going to get near you." Reaching for his radio, he called in to dispatch and gave the order for Jebediah to be brought in for questioning.

Autumn stared at the vandalized wall. "You're going to have to tell the rest of the department, aren't you?"

"Probably. Unless I happen to find conclusive evidence that Jebediah was behind this directly."

She wrapped both arms around her middle. "I…Are people going to have to read them? The books? In the department, I mean." She obviously wasn't comfortable with that. And given her prediction about how the locals might take the news, he couldn't blame her.

"Listen, I can put a gag order on everybody. Keep the details under wraps for the sake of the investigation. We'll do everything we can to keep your pen name a secret."

"I think that cat's out of the bag. There's no way you'll get the scene processed fast enough that we can clean all this up before we open. Word's going to get out."

Judd hated the dejection in her eyes and how this whole thing had dimmed something for her that she clearly loved. He gripped her shoulders and turned her to face him. "I'll work fast. We'll go ahead and call Tyler at the hardware store to get some paint prepped. We don't need to leave the flyer up. I'll be bagging it for evidence. It will be okay."

"Mitzi may kill me herself."

"She won't. You can't be blamed for someone else's actions."

"My boss is absolutely one of those conservative pearl clutchers who thinks she can push her own agenda on everyone else. She's going to say that I've sullied the good name of this institution by association or some similar bullshit."

Judd had some creative suggestions as to what Mitzi could do with her attitude, but he kept them to himself. "It's going to be okay," he repeated. He just hoped it was a promise he could keep.

WHILE JUDD PROCESSED THE SCENE, Autumn searched the rest of the library, making certain nothing else was out of order. The computers were fine. Nothing else appeared broken or vandalized. He'd targeted the entrance, where she couldn't fail to see the threat. Given what Judd had said about her father's health, he probably couldn't manage more than that. But it was enough to destroy her peace of mind.

It infuriated her that he still had any power over her. For years she and her mother had been victim to his special brand of psychological warfare. She'd thought herself finally free of it. But that had only been true while he was caged. She'd worked so very hard to build a life she was proud of, a life on her terms—not his— and now within forty-eight hours, he'd managed to threaten all of it. Her home, her job, even her relationship with Judd.

Judd hadn't actually answered her question about whether they'd have to read the books as part of the investigation. Maybe she'd luck out and her father slipped up enough to leave a nice, clear fingerprint somewhere. Maybe it wouldn't come to them combing through her work. She couldn't think about what it would mean for Judd to read it. Not if she was going to get through today.

"Whoa." The sound of the stunned male voice drew her from the circulation desk.

Contractor Brody Jensen stood in the entryway, looking up at the bulletin board wall. Autumn's pulse jumped, but Judd had already taken down her picture. There was only the graffiti left.

"That's a helluva thing. Any idea who'd do this?"

"I've got some thoughts on the matter," Judd rumbled. "I'm done collecting evidence, so you're clear to take care of this."

"Take care of it?" Autumn echoed.

"Tyler told me what happened," Brody explained. "I've got some time this morning before I have to be on another job, so I figured I'd get things sorted for you. I'll get the primer on before I go back for supplies to patch the door. Not quite sure what we'll do about the floor."

Autumn wasn't at all sure that they had the right to do that without involving the library director, but she decided it was better to ask forgiveness than permission. "Thank you, Brody. I really appreciate it. And if you'll get me the bill, I'll—"

"What on earth? Oh my God!" Mitzi's horrified screech echoed in the tiny lobby as she stepped through the door that had been propped open.

Autumn fought the urge to cover her ears with both hands.

"Now Mrs. Farnham, calm down," Judd began.

"Calm down? Calm *down?* The library has been vandalized!"

"Yes, and I'm investigating."

"With all due respect Officer Hamilton—"

"Chief."

"Excuse me?"

"That would be Chief Hamilton. Chief Curry had a heart attack and has stepped down." That announcement shut Mitzi down long enough for Judd to finish. "I assure you, the department will be treating this with the utmost priority and sensitivity. Now, as I'm sure you don't want patrons to see this, we should all get out of Brody's way so he can get to painting."

"But the library's budget—"

"Think nothing of it," Brody assured her. "Consider it a joint donation from Edison Hardware and Jensen Construction."

"And your building insurance should cover the door and replacement of the floor," Judd added. "Go on inside now. Get some coffee going if you need it. I'll be along shortly to ask you some questions."

"Me?" Her voice shot up another half an octave in outrage.

"Yes. I'll be questioning all staff about anyone they've had trouble with lately."

Mitzi's shoulders dropped and Autumn could practically see her feathers smoothing out. "Fine. I'll be in my office."

As she walked on into the library proper, Autumn mouthed, *Thank you.*

Judd just double tapped his chest in their signal for *Got your back.* "Go get some work done, if you can."

There was work. There was always work. Books to reshelve, requests to process. She fumbled her way through it, distracted, as Judd went upstairs to Mitzi's office and Brody began to bring stuff in from his truck.

He worked fast. He'd already put down a drop cloth and managed to get the obscenities covered with primer before the library officially opened for the day at nine-thirty. It didn't stop the talking among the early birds. This kind of vandalism just didn't happen in Wishful, and that meant it was big news. But at least nobody would have the chance to post pictures on the town social media pages.

After questioning Mitzi, Judd stopped by the circulation desk. "I'm heading over to the station for that interview. I'll let you know as soon as I find anything out."

Autumn blew out a breath. "I'll be here." Assuming Mitzi didn't get a wild hair to fire her.

"Oh, one last question before I go. I was gonna ask earlier, but we got derailed by all of this. You didn't happen to have any bottles of Evan Williams bourbon in your apartment, did you?"

"What? No. You know I can't stand the smell of it. It's what my father always…" She trailed off as she realized what he was saying. "You found some in the rubble?"

"Yeah. Charlie's gotta run some more tests, but he reckons that was the accelerant used. It's not enough on its own to pin your father, but it's another piece."

And Judd would, she knew, keep searching

them out, stacking them up, until he had enough for a conviction. So she'd trust him to do the job he'd prepared for his entire life.

Eyes wide, Livia came around the desk, dumping her purse in a drawer. "Girl...what happened?"

Judd straightened. "I'm gonna let y'all get to it."

Reaching out, Autumn caught his hand and squeezed. "Don't let him get to you." As much as Jebediah knew how to manipulate her, he was also perfectly aware that she was Judd's soft spot. If he saw a way to use that, he probably would.

Judd squeezed back. "I've got this."

A constant stream of patrons meant Autumn didn't get a chance to tell Livia more than that they'd been vandalized before she got caught up in morning story time. People had heard she was back at work and the gossip hungry wanted to come by and get the scoop on what was going on. Many expressed their sincere condolences about the fire, which she appreciated, but more than a few just wanted an in on news of the investigation. That there was still evidence of library vandalism just added fuel to the gossip fires. Every new face wound her up tighter. She kept waiting for someone to ask about her father. So far, his release had been kept out of the media, but it was only a matter of time before someone saw him and word got out.

The reporters would come. How could they not? The original story had been so juicy, so sensational, and the day he was released, her house was burned to the ground? They'd spin the whole thing as a revenge plot—which wasn't outside the realm of possibility. And if her alter ego came out, the press would have a field day Romeo and Julieting Judd and her as they had fourteen years before. If they hadn't so heavily played that angle, would he have reconsidered wanting to be with her before now?

A familiar, lanky form stepped in from the lobby and Autumn tensed. She'd never again be able to see Mark Caulfield without thinking about the moment of confession he'd ruined. Over in the children's section, Livia was wrapping up story time, but it would take a bit for her to shake loose. There'd be no backup. But maybe he wouldn't linger. By the time he made his way around the stacks and over to the desk, she'd found a politely neutral expression.

"You forgot your inter-library loan books the other day."

"Yeah. I came back to pick them up." His gaze bounced around, not quite able to settle on her face. "I…um…read about the fire in the paper. I…it seems stupid to ask if you're okay, but I just…I wanted to check on you."

She softened a little. He meant well, in his weird, awkward way. "Thanks. That's really sweet of you. I wasn't at home when it happened, so I was lucky there. Everything else is just stuff, right?"

It wasn't just stuff. There'd been so many irreplaceable memories lost. But it seemed ungrateful to focus on that in the moment, and she didn't want to be an object of pity.

Mark shoved his glasses up his nose and seemed to finally get up the guts to look her in the eye. "If there's anything I can do to help, just name it."

Autumn grabbed his stack of books. "I appreciate it, Mark. If I think of anything, I'll let you know." She shoved the books across the counter.

He ran his fingers around the edges, straightening the stack. A slip of paper stuck out of one of the volumes. Mark tugged it out, opening it to skim the text written there. His face went scarlet, all the way up to the tips of his ears.

"Uh…is this some kind of a message?"

Frowning, Autumn held out her hand for the paper and read it herself.

Cooper's voice was low and rough. "What do you want, Lilah?"

"What I've always wanted." She took his cock in her hand, stroking a thumb over the silky steel of him until he groaned. "You. I want you."

Her head swam as the blood drained out

and came flooding back into her cheeks. This was part a love scene from *Forged In Blood*. And God, it had been spelled out. Both her names and the title, right there for anyone to see.

"I…this is…I didn't do this," she stammered.

Panicked, she looked toward the children's section. Story time was finished. Livia caught sight of her face and immediately began heading for the desk amid the stream of parents and kids with their stacks of checkouts.

"What's wrong?"

Wordlessly, Autumn just handed over the paper.

Livia's eyes widened, and somewhere on the other side of the desk, a child's voice asked, "Mommy, what's a cock?"

CHAPTER 10

Judd took his time getting back to the station, making a detour to talk with Tyler. The red paint hadn't come from Edison Hardware, which meant it had been purchased out of town or by someone else well prior to Jebediah's release from prison.

How much planning had gone into this? Her father would have needed to find out where she worked—not that difficult to guess when the library had been one of her safe spaces growing up. Books had always been her escape, so that in and of itself wasn't a stretch to imagine. But knowing her pen name? That was the part that made no sense. How would Jebediah have found that out in prison when Judd himself hadn't known as part of her everyday life?

In the back of his mind, he could admit to a little hurt over that. Why hadn't Autumn trusted him? How could she possibly believe he wouldn't support her in this? He'd been her biggest cheerleader all their lives. And, hell, it was a relief to know she had something else to fall back on if things at the library continued to worsen. But his hurt could take a backseat to the rest.

The fact was, outing her like this was exactly the kind of psychological warfare Jebediah had specialized in. It made him seem all knowing, all seeing, as if she had no escape. As if he knew all about her perceived "sins." So much of her child-hood had been spent in anticipation of what in-nocuous thing he'd punish her for next in the name of his twisted religion. She'd come so far since then, but Judd had seen her face at the sight of those words scrawled on the wall. Neither of them had forgotten the hatred he'd spewed as he'd been hauled out of the courtroom after his conviction. This would set her back. And the bastard doing it at the library had violated yet another safe space for her. She wouldn't be able to walk in there again without being aware that her father knew exactly where she was. She'd wonder, all day, every day, whether he'd show up and what he'd do when he did.

Judd's blood was at a steady boil by the time he shoved through the doors of Wishful PD. "Report."

Darius fell into step beside him. "Buchanan is in interrogation."

"What's his attitude?"

"Annoyed but cooperative."

"Let him stew a while longer." It was an unabashed power play, but it also gave Judd a chance to gather more information. "Is the rookie back?"

While Darius had hauled Jebediah in for

questioning, Corbett Raines had been tasked with reviewing security footage for the motel.

The kid emerged from the back. "Here, Chief."

The title still gave Judd a little hitch but he'd take the clout that went with it. "What did you find?"

"The suspect's car didn't move all night, and he didn't leave his room, except once to get ice."

"Was he in frame the whole time?"

"No. There was a four-minute window where he was off screen."

"Not long enough to get to the library and back, but maybe long enough to meet with somebody," Judd mused.

"Who?" Corbett asked.

"Maybe nobody. Maybe the same somebody who did the actual legwork to torch Autumn's apartment. The fact is, he didn't do this himself. Even if he didn't have physical limitations because of his illness, he's too smart to be this direct. He knows I've got my eye on him, just waiting for him to fuck up in any possible way that violates his parole. So he has to have help. The question is who?"

"Somebody he did time with?" Darius suggested.

"Maybe. Maybe somebody he knew from before. Corbett, dig back in our records and see what you can find about his former associates. Maybe he's looking to reconnect with some people. Darius, contact Parchman and get records of all visitors, phone calls, emails, and mail he had for his entire incarceration."

One dark brow winged up. "That's potentially a lot of records. I don't reckon they're gonna get back to us with that information fast."

"Probably not, but it's an angle. Do what you can. Also, compile a list of any former inmates in town who served time at Parchman while Buchanan was there."

"You got it."

The door opened again and Tyrell Weller strode in. "We already doing this again?"

"Looks like," Judd said equably.

"What is it this time?"

"Vandalism at the library. More harassment of his daughter."

"Surely, he wouldn't be that dumb."

"Oh, he's not. Not directly. I know he wasn't the one who physically did the deed, same as the fire. But somebody's had eyes on Autumn for him, reporting back. I don't for a minute believe he isn't behind all of it."

Tyrell looked skeptical. "You sure about that?"

"Tell me something. Why is he here? Why, when he got out of prison, didn't he go to Lawley or Jackson or the coast or anywhere in the state where people didn't know his name, didn't know what he did? He's gonna have a helluva time finding anybody willing to hire him here to do anything."

"He insisted he needed to come back to Wishful."

"Exactly. Because here he gets a front row seat to the destruction of his daughter's sense of safety. I think it's mighty damned coincidental that the day he gets out of prison, her house burns down. And the day after that, her place of work is vandalized in a way that directly points to the threat he made when he was hauled off to prison. He always used to get a power trip out of controlling and manipulating her. That hasn't changed. He's just having to go about it less directly. Give me enough time, and I'll find the evidence to back up my gut."

Tyrell lifted a hand in acquiescence. "All right."

"You want to sit in on the interrogation?"

"Sure."

Jebediah looked up from where he sat in one of the folding chairs, arms crossed, a scowl firmly in place. "Is this really how we're going to do this? You're going to keep coming up with excuses to bring me in and harass me?"

"Well now, that's gonna be up to you. If you stop finding ways to harass your daughter, we can work our way toward live and let live."

"I don't know what you're talking about."

"Maybe this will refresh your memory." Judd

pulled the evidence bag with Autumn's picture in it out of a folder and put it on the table between them. "Oh but you wouldn't have seen the full effect." He added a picture of the entire graffitied wall and watched Jebediah's face.

The older man's eyes narrowed, but there was no flicker of approval, no hint of a smile or recognition. "I didn't do this."

"Oh, I know. But see, all that shit painted on the wall sounds a helluva lot like you, don't you think? It was one of your favorite things to call her when we were growing up."

"Doesn't mean anything."

"See, I disagree. I think it means you've found somebody to do your dirty work for you. Just so you can remind Autumn you're out and could show up at any time."

"Why would I do that?"

"Because you want control over her. You always did. That got taken away from you fourteen years ago and you want it back."

"I was a sick man."

"Oh? Is that what you're telling yourself? It

was sickness that made you beat your wife and daughter? Sickness that had you going after her with a gun to keep her from leaving you, too?" Judd had meant to keep his tone bland and uninterested, but by the end he was growling.

Jebediah's eyes flared with something. Temper? Triumph? It was gone before Judd could read him.

"I've been rehabilitated. The state says so."

"No. The state says you're old and sick and less likely to cause problems than a lot of other offenders that need to be locked up more than you. But I know better, and I won't underestimate you."

"You're starting to sound like a broken record, *Chief.* Maybe if you made a recording of all your threats, I could listen to it on a daily basis and save us both some time."

"Oh, but why wouldn't I want to make sure you run out of yours?"

Jebediah looked to Tyrell. "Are you hearing this? For all we know, he's doing this stuff himself in the name of framing me."

Even as the insult whipped through him, Judd snorted. "Oh, you can be sure that if I were unethical enough to try to frame you for something, it wouldn't be with all this circumstantial bullshit. You'd be caught, ironclad, and we wouldn't be having these conversations."

The phone in Judd's pocket vibrated. He pulled it out to find a text from Autumn.

We were wrong. There's more. I need you. She followed it up with a GIF of a dumpster fire.

That sure as hell wasn't good. What had he missed on his search through the library this morning?

Shoving the phone back into his pocket, Judd rose, gathering the evidence. "You're free to go, for now. Be looking out for one of my officers to serve a restraining order in the next couple of days." It would take time to get the permanent one in place, but he'd get it done, if he had to corner Judge Carpenter himself.

Without a backward glance, he strode out of

the room and went to see what shape the next phase of this shit show of a day would take.

"WE'RE GOING to have to go through every book," Autumn hissed, frantically pulling children's books off the shelf in front of her and shaking each one to check for loose paper. They'd found half a dozen already.

"It'll be okay. We'll get it done. Riley will come help after work. As long as nobody tells—"

"Autumn!" Mitzi's shriek cut through the hushed atmosphere like a serrated blade.

Autumn squeezed her eyes shut. "Too late." Praying for some fortitude and a miracle, she replaced the book in her hand and pivoted to face the library director. "Yes, ma'am?"

Mitzi held a sheet of paper in her hand. The pinched expression and vaguely puce shade of her face was confirmation enough of what it was. "What is the meaning of this?"

What the hell could Autumn even say? *I can explain.* She couldn't. Not really. The idea of spilling out her personal business, trying to tell her boss how her father was determined to ruin her life, made her vaguely ill.

"I don't know. Someone is playing a very not funny prank."

"Someone? It's your name on these."

"I—"

"Excuse me." Liza Keeney smiled, a sheet of paper in her own hand. "I just wondered if y'all had this book available for checkout?"

Under other circumstances, Autumn might have laughed at the choked noise coming from her boss. But there was nothing at all funny about the current situation. "No. I'm afraid not."

"Where can I find it?"

Did people not understand how to privately google titles or search on Amazon? Autumn swallowed. "Any online ebook retailer."

Liza grinned. "Can't wait. I can't believe I

know an author." She gave a happy bounce as she strode away.

Mitzi waved the paper. "These don't just have your name on them. You wrote them." She said it as if writing romance was akin to sowing seeds of the worst kind of sedition. To someone like Mitzi, it probably was.

Sick of the moralistic judgment, Autumn squared her shoulders. "They are excerpts from books I wrote, yes. But I did not do this."

Mitzi's gaze fell to the small stack at Autumn's feet and went back to the books. Her voice dropped dangerously low. "These are in the *children's section?*"

"Apparently. Livia and I are taking care of it."

Her nostrils flared. "In my office. Now!"

"With all due respect, we need to finish going through—"

"Now!"

Wonderful. I've lost my home, and now I'm probably going to lose my job.

She trailed her boss up the stairs to the office.

"Explain yourself," Mitzi demanded.

"What exactly do you want me to explain? Am I writing? Yes. I had to do something to make ends meet when my hours got cut. But I did it under a pen name, and I told no one here about it. I've done absolutely nothing wrong."

"You're telling me this," she slapped the paper on her desk, "isn't some kind of a publicity stunt?"

The accusation sent Autumn's temper soaring. It took three long breaths to reel it in enough she could speak. "I did not do this," she repeated. "Why would I? I'm well aware of how you feel about romance as a genre. Why would I do anything to imperil my position here? That makes absolutely no sense."

"I found this on the copy machine. Someone made these copies right here. If you didn't do it, then who did?"

"I don't know. Probably the same person who broke in here to vandalize the place last night. The one who posted a picture of me and outed me about my pen name on the bulletin board where everyone could see. This was an attack on me. Just like the arson on my house. Or are you going to accuse me of doing that, too, as some kind of a cry for attention?"

"Everything okay here?" The sound of Judd's voice caused a few knots to loosen before Autumn remembered why he was here.

Striving for calm, she turned toward him. "It seems last night's vandal also decided to make use of the copier. A number of…explicit passages…were printed and randomly inserted into books throughout the library."

Something flickered in his eyes at "explicit," but he remained professional. "It's likely our perp wore gloves doing that, too, but I'll check for prints. I'll need copies of the pages."

Of course he would. "I'll get them for you. If you're finished with me?" She looked back at Mitzi, who looked at least a little abashed.

"Yes, for now. We've got a couple of our volunteers coming in this afternoon. Let them man the desk while you and Livia search the stacks."

"Yes, ma'am."

Judd caught her eye as she strode toward the door, and she recognized the question there. *Are you okay?*

Not even a little bit.

He frowned as she scurried past. The door shut behind her and she heard the rumble of his voice as she hit the stairs. She told herself she didn't care what he was saying to Mitzi. That it didn't matter what he was sharing to try to protect her. But it was a lie. Her personal business was spreading through town. It was only a matter of time before this went beyond gossip and into the actual media, and every hope of privacy she had would be lost.

"What happened?" Livia whispered. "Did she fire you?"

"Not yet. But if this keeps up, I wouldn't put it past her. How far did you get?"

She pointed to a shelf, and Autumn automatically moved to continue.

"I've got to give the stack to Judd."

"Seriously?"

"They're evidence." Not that she was under any delusion that they'd lead him to who'd done this. It was just another way to undermine her and destroy the life she'd made for herself.

They'd found three more by the time Judd joined them in the children's section.

"Well, that's a wrinkle. Sorry about all this."

"Not your fault." Autumn reached for the next book, shook it, put it back.

"Firefly." He gripped her hand, tried to turn her to face him.

"Please don't," she whispered. Tears of frustration and sheer mortification were threatening to choke her, and if he held her, did anything to comfort her, she was going to break. There was too much work to do for that.

"Do you want us to save all the ones we find?" Livia asked.

"If we don't find prints on these, we probably won't find them on the rest. But hang on to them for a bit just in case."

Autumn just nodded and reached for the pile. She couldn't look him in the eye as she handed it over. All her heroes were Judd in some form, but these scenes in particular were from her first book, the one that was most obviously him. Now he was going to read them—out of context—which was somehow worse. And it was going to force the conversation she wasn't yet ready to have because she hadn't figured out how to approach the whole thing. She didn't know how that conversation would go, didn't know how he would react. Either way, time was running out.

Judd took the papers. "I won't bring anyone else in unless I have to."

"Okay."

He waited, but what else was she going to say?

"What time do you get off today?"

"It doesn't matter. I'll be here well after hours going through every book in the building, looking for more."

"Not alone?"

"I'll be here," Livia promised. "And Riley's coming to help when she can."

"All right. I'll be by when I'm finished for the day, and we'll head home."

She nodded, still looking at his shoes.

Judd chucked her under the chin, tipping her face up toward his. "It's going to be okay."

"How will it?"

"I don't know. It's a mystery." Even his crooked grin and a quote of one of her favorite lines from *Shakespeare In Love* couldn't drag a smile out of her.

"You've got work to do, Chief. And so do I."

He dropped his hand and stepped back. "I'll see you in a few hours."

Livia waited until he'd walked out. "Do you want to talk about it?"

"I really don't. Let's just get this done."

Judd hadn't planned to read the book, not when Autumn was so clearly shut down about sharing anything about it. But in the course of trying to suss out how Jebediah could have found out about her work, he'd looked her up online, read the book descriptions. *Forged In Blood* was all about the daughter of a cult leader. Jebediah hadn't been that, but certainly the twisted religion he'd espoused would've lent itself to that kind of narrative, and Judd had been curious how much personal experience she'd drawn from.

"Daddy, no! Nothing happened."

"I got eyes in my head to see otherwise, girl."

"It was just a kiss." But it wasn't just a kiss. It was everything. He was everything.

Jesus Christ. She'd put it all in here. Almost every fucking detail. Except Cooper had gotten the kiss Judd never had. He'd been there that day. He'd thought he'd known what she'd gone through. But reading it like this… It was like his own memories had been covered by a haze of smoke and with her words, she'd stripped that away, leaving the stark, unvarnished truth.

This was *their* story. Or something very close to it.

No wonder she hadn't wanted him to read it.

Hell, anybody in town who'd been here when the whole thing went down would recognize it in the thinly veiled backstory. After he and Autumn had worked so hard to curb the rumors, she'd gone and written this?

And dear God, the love scenes. It had been obvious they were erotic when he'd skimmed the passages that had been hidden in the stacks. But reading them in context, knowing he *was* Cooper... He'd spent so many years actively avoiding thinking about her like that. How the hell was he ever going to unsee those mental images? He'd spent most of the afternoon hard as a rock. It was as if she'd reached into his brain and unearthed every dark fantasy he'd never allowed himself to have and spilled it onto the page. Along with quite a few he couldn't have imagined but now desperately wanted to lose himself in. With her.

This was a nightmare. He needed brain bleach. A mind wipe. Something to help him get back the status quo.

What he had, as he pulled his cruiser into the library parking lot at the end of the day, was a whole lot of pissed off.

This wasn't the time or place for a confrontation. He'd just hold it together until he could get her home, and they'd talk about this like civilized people.

Nothing Cooper and Lilah did was civilized.

Shut the fuck up, he told himself as he stepped inside and followed the sound of voices. He could carry on a basic conversation. He could be normal.

But the moment he spotted Autumn by a library cart full of books, wearing one of those prim little librarian dresses that only made him wonder what she had on underneath, his mouth ran away without his brain. "You could've warned me."

He could tell by the look on her face that she knew he knew. With obvious resignation, she slid another volume onto the shelf. "What would I have said? How would that conversation go?"

"Oh, I don't know. Maybe, 'By the way, Judd, I poured every detail of our own private hell into a book that who knows how many people have read.'"

He'd expected some kind of contrition or

embarrassment, but what he saw in her eyes was a spark of temper. When she spoke, her voice was deadly quiet. "I had to put it somewhere."

"Put what somewhere?"

"The truth," she snapped.

Autumn rarely lost her temper. Growing up in a house of violence, she considered it the ultimate loss of control. But Judd could see the simmer and bubble of it in her eyes.

Fine. If she wanted a fight, he'd give her one.

"What you put in there wasn't the truth. Cooper walked away. I stayed." And damn, that chapped his ass.

"No, you didn't walk away. What you did was almost worse." She turned away from him, head dropping, shoulders slumping, as if he'd hurt her somehow.

Insult added fuel to an already raging fire. "What the hell are you talking about? Everything I've done has been to protect you!"

Autumn rounded on him, hands fisted, eyes blazing. "I am not a fucking job! I don't need you to protect me! I need you to love me!"

The shot hit him straight in the heart. It took everything he had to recover, to try and salvage something of what was because he knew everything they were was collapsing around him.

He aimed for reasonable. "Of course, I love you. You're my best friend."

"No." She stalked toward him, the expression on her face dialed to a level of fury he'd never seen in her before. "You don't get to hide behind that excuse. I'm done being quiet. My father spent seventeen years trying to make me and nothing ever worked. Not his hand, not the switch, not the flogging with his thick leather belt. Seeing you take the bullet meant for me is the only thing he's ever done that scared me into silence. Not because he meant to end me—because I resigned myself to the fact that he hated me a long time before that—but because you were the only thing I ever cared about, and I saw how easily he could rip you away from me. So I've stayed quiet, swallowing down everything I feel because you seemed to want it that way. *You* decided—without ever giving me a say, giving me a voice. But I'm done. I'm done with censorship, with judgment. I wouldn't be quiet for him, and I'm done being quiet for you. I won't let you ignore what's between us anymore."

Before Judd could process any of her accusations, her hands fisted in his shirt, hauling him against her. Her mouth crushed his in a savage kiss, and he stopped thinking at all as every drop of his blood drained south. Shock held him immobile as she assaulted his senses.

She tasted of devastated fury and desperation and heat—so much unrestrained heat, he wondered she didn't incinerate them both. With his head full of every erotic image she'd written, his traitorous hands curled around her hips and dragged her closer. He couldn't keep up, couldn't stop himself from responding to the demanding thrust of her tongue against his.

He growled, every possessive instinct he had roused beyond belief.

But just as he slid his hand into her hair, she shoved with both hands, propelling him back a full step. "I'm moving out," she snarled. "Good luck putting me back into your goddamned box."

Move out? Autumn couldn't move out. They had to discuss this. Because she sure as hell had obliterated the goddamned box, whatever that meant.

But as he stepped toward her, hands outstretched, his radio crackled. "Chief, we've got a situation here."

It took him a full five seconds to scrape together enough brain cells to answer the call. "This is really not a good time, Inez."

"But Chief, the rookie ran his squad car up a tree."

"What?"

"I don't quite know the details of what happened, but Officer Raines ran off the road and hit a tree. There was something about a cow."

Judd pinched the bridge of his nose, responsibility to the job warring with the need to finish this. "Is Raines injured?"

"His status is unclear. He's not responsive. The home owner called it in. Medical's been dispatched."

"Just go." Autumn's words, an echo of Mary Alice's just days ago, reverberated through him.

This was bad. So very bad. But they'd find their way back. They had to.

On a rough exhale he radioed back. "Send me the address. I'm on my way."

"Incoming."

"This isn't finished."

Autumn's face was ravaged, tears magnifying those big, green eyes. "Yes, it is. I can't live like this anymore."

The declaration slid into his gut like a knife and panic spilled out like so much blood. He'd done everything right. He hadn't rocked the boat, hadn't taken any risks, hadn't given in to everything he'd wanted for years. He couldn't lose her. He couldn't.

"Autumn—"

"No. You have a job to do. And so do I. Go, Judd."

Greasy terror held him to his position. "Promise me you won't run off. Promise you'll wait and talk to me when I get loose from this shit."

She just stared at him, indecision written all over her face.

"If the last twenty-five years have meant anything to you, then you'll promise me." It was a low blow, and he knew it, but he was desperate.

At last, she nodded, and his feet unfroze from the floor. Duty alone had him moving toward the door, knowing somehow he'd just made the worst mistake of his life.

THE SNICK of the closing door echoed like a gunshot through the library. Autumn trembled where she stood, her blood pounding with a mix of fury, arousal, and fear.

She'd been prepared for his anger. She *had* written in explicit detail about an experience that had been intensely personal and horrifying for them both. After all the efforts they'd made toward privacy in the wake of the shooting and the trial, she understood he'd feel that was a betrayal on some level. But for him to continue to willfully behave as if he didn't understand what the rest of it meant, when she'd poured out her heart and soul on those pages, laying out everything she felt for him? That had been the last straw.

She'd wanted to scream and rage. She'd wanted to punch him. Instead, she'd kissed him, holding nothing back as she'd ravaged the mouth she'd dreamed about for years, irrevocably shattering his carefully constructed status quo.

"Oh God, what have I done?"

Riley's arm slid around her waist, holding her up. "What you had to, I think."

"In spectacular style, I might add. Awards

for best impassioned speech and best on-screen kiss, for sure." Livia fanned herself.

"He kissed me back." Autumn lifted a hand to the lips that still tingled from his. The erosion of his iron control had been glorious.

"Yeah he did!" Livia started to lift her hand for a high five, then dropped it with a wince. "I feel like it's too soon for that."

"Maybe a little. The whole damned thing might backfire on me. I could have stopped with kissing him. It made my point. But I know him. I knew if I didn't keep pushing, didn't do something to unequivocally show him that I won't go back to what we've been, he'd just backpedal and start herding me like a damned border collie back to what we've always been. The fact is, I broke us. I did it knowing that we can't ever go back. I'm trusting in him, in what I know we can be together. At the end of this, we'll either be more or we'll be nothing."

The idea of nothing had the bottom dropping out of her stomach. "I feel sick."

Riley squeezed her shoulders. "I saw the

look on his face, honey. He doesn't want to lose you. And with Mary Alice finally out of the picture, there's nothing stopping him from meeting you exactly where you are."

"Except whatever's been stopping him for fourteen years." Autumn had never known what that was and hadn't ever been brave enough to broach the subject.

"Listen." Livia cupped Autumn's shoulders. "I don't know what lies he's been telling himself all this time, but it's obvious to everyone with eyes that he loves you, and I know exactly where I'd lay my money on this. In fact, you should lay your own money on it."

"What?"

"March yourself down to Dinner Belles, right now, and put money on yourself in the pool. It's good karma. A sign of your faith that everything's going to work out."

"What about finishing up in the stacks?"

"Riley and I can finish up this section. Then we're down to the areas people almost never browse in. You and I can get to that tomorrow.

You've been here since before opening this morning, and it's been a stressful day. Go, place your bet, then go home and do something to destress before your conversation with Judd."

It was crazy, probably foolish. But what the hell did she have left to lose?

Dinner Belles was in the midst of the dinner rush as she shoved through the door. From the surprised glances that came her way, Autumn had the sense she must look a little like a wild woman. Well, she felt it.

With purpose, she strode to the counter. "I need to see Omar."

Mama Pearl just arched a brow before calling back to her son in the kitchen.

A few minutes later, the former Ole Miss running back emerged, a broad smile on his dark face. "Hey there, Lady Luck. What can I do for you?"

"I want to put five hundred in the pool for this week." The low hum of the diner's patrons fell silent as she slapped the bills down on the counter. It was the last of the cash she'd pulled out for her essentials shopping.

Both brows shot up. "Which one?"

Autumn straightened her spine. "Mine."

Surprise turned into a delighted grin. "About damned time."

"Hey now," someone called, "is that even legal to bet on yourself?"

"Hush up, Tony," Mama Pearl called. "Long as this pool's been runnin', she can do anything she likes. Go get him, sugar."

Autumn sucked in a breath. "That's the plan."

The applause started as she turned. By the time she'd reached the door, the smattering of claps had turned into a crash of cheers. Nice to know the rest of town was in support of this lunacy because now that she'd made this very public declaration, she was starting to wonder if she'd lost her mind.

Blindly, she reached for the door, stumbling when it opened. "Oh excuse—" The words died in her throat as she took in the man blocking her path.

Her first, inane thought was that he was so much smaller than she remembered. In her mind, he'd been a giant of a man—objectively nowhere near as big as Judd, but somehow filling their house with his hatred and twisted religion. The gatekeeper to her freedom and happiness.

Prison and illness had winnowed him down. The flesh hung on his gaunt frame like an ill-fitting thrift-store suit. The eyes so like hers looked dimmer, somehow less substantial, as if they were a battery meter showing how much life he had left. He'd aged almost three decades in the years since she'd last seen him.

"Autumn."

That voice. No matter the physical packaging, that voice hadn't changed. At the sound of it, Autumn felt the whip of the belt across her skin, and with the phantom of remembered pain came the deep-rooted fear. The sick slither of panic wormed through her belly and sweat broke out down the middle of her back. Every instinct shouted for her to run.

She didn't move. Couldn't.

Judd, you swore you'd be here. The thought came unbidden, and she hated herself for that weakness. Hated that she needed him, even now. Hated that she couldn't control the fear rising up like bile in her throat.

"Nothing to say?" Jebediah asked.

Autumn's mouth went to cotton, her jaw refusing to move. Her pulse beat fast in her ears, drowning out everything but that hated voice.

"Finally lose all that sass?" His thin lips curved in something that might've been a smile, as if he enjoyed the idea that he'd finally succeeded in shutting her up.

Where was her fight? The sharp tongue that'd earned her so many beatings in her teen years, when she'd started fighting back and challenging his delusions? Why could she only *stand here*? She should be stronger than this. But shoulds didn't stop the paralyzing fear, didn't stop the shallow breaths or the trembling that wracked her limbs.

"She doesn't have to talk to you."

What?

Someone came to stand at her shoulder. Autumn couldn't tell who because that would require being able to move.

"You're lucky she doesn't haul off and punch you," someone else said.

"My daughter isn't violent." Jebediah sounded almost proud of that.

No. No she never had been until he'd threatened Judd. Her hand shook with remembered impact as she'd struck him.

Blood. So much blood slicking across the checkerboard floor. Autumn felt hers draining out of her head, saw the gray at the edge of her vision and squeezed her eyes shut. *Not here. Not now.*

"Can't say as I can make the same claim." Omar closed a big hand around her shoulder, and Autumn wanted to weep with relief.

"Reckon you can move along, find somewhere else to eat. Permanently," Mama Pearl added.

Autumn was dimly aware of chairs all over the diner scraping back as customers stood, crowding behind her. It gave her the power to open her eyes. The vision of blood was gone. But her father still stood in the open doorway.

Jebediah's gaze scanned over the assembled crowd before coming back to rest on her. "There are things I need to say to you."

"I don't care," she rasped. With the strength of numbers at her back, she took a deeper breath. "There's nothing you can say that I want to hear. The time when I have to submit to listen to your ravings and hatred is long past. So stay away from me. And you sure as hell stay away from Judd or I *will* finish what you started in that kitchen all those years ago."

She expected him to start ranting, raging about respecting the Holy Spirit and how she was bound for hell for breaking a commandment. But Jebediah lifted his hands in concession, backing away and letting the glass door swing shut.

Autumn was shaking so hard, her teeth nearly rattled. A warm, comforting arm slid around her waist.

"Come on back to the kitchen for a little while," Mama Pearl urged. "You're white as a sheet."

She wanted to say no, wanted to escape all the eyes that were now turned on her. But she didn't have the strength to resist as the older woman led her behind the counter and through the door into the back. The familiar scents of grease and burgers made her stomach roil. Mama Pearl didn't stop, just steered her on into an office and nudged her into a chair.

"Head between your knees. Omar, get some ginger ale."

Autumn simply did as she was told. Bent over in the chair, the gray started to recede and her breath began to level out. She'd made it through. Barely, but she hadn't lost her shit out there. And she'd done it without Judd.

She'd had panic attacks away from him before. Certainly the night terrors in college had been brutal without being able to reach over and touch him. She'd learned to get through those. And up until finding out Jebediah was getting out of prison, it had been years since anything had triggered a full on attack. But she'd faced down the source of her nightmares. She'd faced him down and survived. If she could stand up to her father, she could stick to her guns when it came to Judd himself. She was so much stronger than he gave her credit for.

"Here, sugar."

Autumn slowly straightened, taking the glass of ginger ale from Omar's big hand. "Thank you." She sipped, the fizzy sweet liquid quenching her parched throat. "I'm sorry about that."

"Honey, don't you be apologizin'," Mama Pearl chided. "Gotta be a shock. When did he get out?"

"A few days ago. Patty asked Myles to keep it

out of the paper." She worked up a rueful smile. "Guess that's done now."

"You already did away with your low profile when you marched in here and made that bet," Omar pointed out.

"Yeah, well. It seemed like a good idea at the time."

"Don't you be backin' down now," Mama Pearl said. "Not when the way's finally clear."

Autumn's mouth dropped open. "How did you…?"

"Where *else* you think she got her breakup pie?"

"Point taken." She drained her glass. "Thank you. I should go."

"You go on out the back. Omar will walk you to your car."

"Oh, it's back at the library, I walked. You don't have to—" She swallowed back the rest of her protest under Mama Pearl's gimlet stare. "Yes ma'am."

CHAPTER 12

The city boy rookie was an idiot. Scared shitless by one of Mel Bailey's cows loose in the road, he'd swerved and managed to drive halfway up a tree. Got a broken shoulder for his trouble and likely totaled the squad car. Judd was still waiting on the estimate from the garage. The City Council was gonna love that.

As if that hadn't been enough, he'd been called in to deal with a bar fight at the Mudcat Tavern. Harley Forbes was drunk off his ass and had gotten in a sucker punch while Judd was trying to talk him down. That was almost a relief because it gave Judd somewhere to funnel his filthy mood. Not that dropping the asshole with one punch had exactly been standard police protocol, but Jesus Christ. The world was conspiring to keep him from getting back home to talk to Autumn. What was she thinking? What was she *doing?* Packing, probably, despite her promise. He only hoped he could get back to the house before she'd finished.

His cheek ached like a sore tooth as he dumped Harley in one of the two empty cells to sleep it off. Slamming the door shut, he snarled at Cleveland Timmons, the night dispatcher. "Unless the town is outright under attack, nobody better bother me for the rest of the damned night. Do I make myself clear?"

"Yes, but—"

"I don't wanna hear any 'buts', Cleveland."

"It's about Miss Buchanan, sir."

Judd stopped in his tracks. "What about her?"

"There was an incident earlier at the diner. With her father."

Judd worked his jaw, trying to keep his voice controlled. "Why am I just hearing about this now?"

"You were tied up with bigger stuff. Nothing really happened. He came in to pick up food as she was leaving. She was understandably taken by surprise. A bunch of folks at the diner more or less ran him off. Mama Pearl told him he wasn't welcome back. I had three different people call to tell me about it."

Autumn had faced off with her dad, and he hadn't been there? He'd promised her. He'd sworn she'd never have to do that alone. And yet she'd survived it. No panic attack, no cardiac incident. She hadn't needed him. Could this day get any worse?

No, dumbass. Don't ever say that. It's tempting fate.

"Is there anything else?"

"No, Chief."

"Then radio silence for the rest of the night. Get me?"

"Yes, sir."

He just hoped it was enough time and that he wasn't too late.

Her car was still in the drive when he pulled up. *Thank Christ.* After her encounter with Jebediah, maybe she'd changed her mind about moving out.

The sky had clouded up over the last couple of hours and thunder began to rumble as he sprinted for the house. They were in for a gullywasher of a storm. He took off his duty belt on his way through the door, setting it on the table behind the couch as he passed. His service weapon went into the lock box, then he was pounding up the stairs.

"Autumn?" He found her in her room, one suitcase open and mostly full on the bed. No sign of the other one, which meant it was probably already in her car. He dragged his gaze from the bag to her, searching her face. "Are you all right? I heard about Jebediah."

"I'm fine, Judd." That excruciatingly calm, polite voice was not his Autumn.

"I'm sorry I couldn't come straight back. I got dragged in on a couple of calls and only just now managed to shake loose."

"Full moon. The crazies are out." She folded another shirt and laid it on top of the pile, as if he was just giving his excuse for missing the weekly trivia night at Los Pantalones. "Leo dropped Boudreaux home earlier. You owe him a six-pack for dogsitting."

Now that he was here, Judd had no idea where to begin. She'd blown the foundation out of his world, and she was obviously serious about leaving if he didn't get this right. He didn't want to fuck it up.

"You said earlier you had to put the truth somewhere. The truth about what?"

A ripple of temper disturbed that too calm exterior. "Really? You're going to make me spell it out? Fine. I haven't maxed out my humiliation capacity for the week yet." She hurled two more pairs of jeans into the bag and closed it.

The zipper sounded too loud. "Because I'm in love with you. I think I have been my entire life."

He'd known. Of course, he'd known. But hearing it out loud gave twin shocks to his system—elation and grief.

"In my defense, you haven't exactly made it easy on me to be anything else. You've been fulfilling my rescue fantasies since I was six years old. Time after time, you've put yourself on the line to protect me. You took a *bullet* for me. Why is that?"

"You're my best friend." But the truth he'd been telling for years felt hollow now. She was his compass. He'd do anything for her.

Pain flickered over her lovely face. "There was a time when you wanted to be more." She shook her head and looked away. "You were almost my first kiss, and you don't even remember."

Judd couldn't bear the grief in her eyes. His own throat felt tight. "You changed that part in the book. You were wearing that yellow dress with the daisies that day. The one that made you look like summer sunshine. It was always my favorite."

Slowly, she turned back toward him. The betrayal on her face slid straight between his ribs and into his heart. "All these years, you said you didn't remember."

"Autumn, I couldn't risk it. After he tried to kill you, I couldn't risk changing things between us and it not working out. I couldn't risk losing you and leaving you unprotected."

She stared at him. Whatever was brewing in her eyes was so much worse than the temper he'd seen flash earlier. "So all these years, you let me think that I was in this alone. That you felt nothing." Devastation trembled in her voice.

"No, I—it wasn't like that. I never wanted to hurt you. I just had to keep you safe."

"He was in *prison*."

How could he make her understand? "I knew one day he wouldn't be. I couldn't leave you without protection."

"Is that all I am to you? Some convenient damsel in imagined distress to feed this perpetual hero complex?"

"What? No, I just—"

"I'm not fragile." Even as she said it, he thought she looked like she could break at any moment, and he could too easily see her lying pale and still as death in that hospital bed.

"Your heart fucking stopped!"

"So did yours!" she shouted.

An enormous boom of thunder shook the house. Rain began to lash at the windows as the storm finally struck.

"Do you think there's a day that goes by when I don't have a moment where I see your blood on my hands? Where I don't worry that somebody, somewhere is going to finish what my father started? But I've never tried to run your life because of it. I've never made decisions for you because I thought I knew best."

He was handling this all wrong. He'd been handling everything wrong for fourteen years. "I should've talked to you about it."

"Yeah, you should've done a lot of things." Tears gleamed in her eyes, but she didn't let them fall. "You should have been my first kiss, Judd. You should've been my first lover. My first everything. My only everything. It's what I wanted. And instead you chose to be less out of some misguided sense of duty...because you didn't trust me enough."

"It had nothing to do with trust." He trusted her with everything he had.

"Of course it did. You didn't trust that we would work, that we were right. That we've been right since the day you saved me on that playground. You were so goddamned terrified that I'd push you away, and the irony is that's exactly what you're getting."

The first true spurts of panic flickered through him like lightning from the storm outside. "What are you saying?"

"Exactly what I told you earlier. That I'm done, Judd. I'm done with this half-life. I'm done hanging around begging for the crumbs of your affections. You either love me or you don't. You're either with me, completely, or you're not. I won't take anything less than all. Not anymore. I deserve better."

JUDD STARED at her as if she'd tased him, so much pain on his face Autumn half expected him to hit his knees. But he said nothing. In all her imagined versions of this scenario, he'd never said *nothing*. With frustrated disbelief, she grabbed her last bag and moved past him, anticipating with every step that she'd hear him behind her. That her actions would shock him into doing *something.*

It wasn't until she stepped off the porch, into the lashing rain, that the grief set in. Her chest seized up and her lungs stopped working, because she was dying. She'd been near enough before that she remembered the feeling. She'd just laid it all on the line, and he'd done *nothing*. Everything she'd thought, everything she'd believed about them, was wrong. He didn't love her. Not enough. And now she had to put her money where her mouth was and leave for real. There was no way she could stay in Wishful after this. No way she could see him day after day and know he'd never be hers.

At the next clap of thunder, a hand grasped her arm. For an instant, terror overrode everything else. She dropped the bag, already leading with her fist as she was spun around. Judd caught her hand. Another flash of lightning illuminated him. There was nothing calm or rational about him now. He looked almost crazed with the rain dripping down his face as he speared both hands into her hair.

"I love you, damn it. I've always loved you."

Stunned, she could only stare. His mouth crashed down on hers. It was like being hit with a defibrillator and shocked back to life. Joy and relief shot through her as she wrapped around him, holding tight, tight as she met the fevered assault of his kiss with equal fervor. He hadn't let her go. She hadn't lost him.

There was none of the careful reserve he'd

shown the first time he'd tried to kiss her. She had, at last, stripped away his restraint, leaving behind only a deep, desperate need. Her body went to flame, and she wondered the rain didn't steam right off them both.

Judd's hands slid down her back, under her ass to boost her up. She wrapped her legs around his waist without hesitation, nipping his bottom lip with approval as he headed toward the house. They barely made it inside before he was spinning, using her body to shut the door. Then he was devouring her mouth again, trapping her between the hard plane of the door and the hardness of his body.

There were too many wet layers between them, too much distance. Her fingers fumbled with the buttons of Judd's uniform shirt as his mouth left hers to trail down the column of her throat. She moaned, dropping her head back against the door to give him better access. She wanted to feel him everywhere. Desperate for skin, she gave up on the buttons, taking a good grip on either side of the shirt and yanking hard. Buttons flew, pinging off the wall. Together, they stripped off the kevlar vest and undershirt, and at last her hands found flesh. Greedy, she ran her fingers over the defined ridges of his abs, wanting to feel them flex and release as he moved over her, in her. He groaned, pressing his hips harder against her, and she realized she must've spoken aloud.

"I want you to do so many things to me."

"Anything. Everything," he promised.

She shuddered as he slid the straps of her dress down her shoulders, tugging until her breasts were bared. He sucked one puckered nipple into his mouth, swirling his tongue as if committing the taste of her to memory. Autumn gripped his hair, holding him in place as he sucked and licked and drove her out of her mind, until she squirmed against the erection she could feel through his pants. So close and yet so far away. With the other hand, she reached between them, trying to work at his belt.

Judd lifted his head, his eyes glazed with

passion as they stared into hers. "Autumn." A wealth of questions lay that single, rasped word. *Slow down. Think about this. Are you sure?*

"Please." She wasn't above begging. Not now. Not when everything she'd ever wanted was a touch, a kiss away.

Seeing whatever he needed to see, he kissed her again, cupping both her breasts in his big, strong hands. She needed so much more. Dropping her legs to the floor, she went to work on the belt in earnest, tugging it open. The button took only a moment, then the zipper. And then she had him in her hand, hard and hot and pulsing.

He cursed and slapped a hand against the door to brace himself as she palmed him, rubbing her hand down his length, then back up again, spreading the bead of moisture at the tip around the crown. How many times had she imagined this? Touching him? Tasting him? Before she could indulge herself, he shrugged out of the shirt and reached for the zipper of her dress. His eyes were midnight dark as he shoved it to the floor, along with her panties.

Autumn slid both her hands inside his boxers and over his glorious ass, until he was bare. She pulled him against her, digging her fingers into the strong muscles of his back, rising on her toes to take his mouth again. Her breasts flattened against the hard planes of his chest and the contrast made her dizzy. God, the feel of all that slick skin against hers was heaven.

"Need you," she gasped. "God, please, I need you inside me."

He kissed her deep as he lifted her again, pressing her back against the door, the heat of him poised at her center. Autumn dug her heels into his ass. That was all it took. He pressed into her, inch by slow inch, until he was buried, and all she could think was that she'd been made for this, for him. Emotion tightened her throat. At last. At long last, she was his and he was hers. No more excuses, no more lies, just this connection as it had always been meant.

Then he began to move and she was caught again in the riptide of sensation. His tongue thrust against hers as he pumped into her. Pinned against the door, she could do little more than hang on for the ride. And what a ride it was. Her hands slipped along his sweat-slicked skin. Dropping her head forward, she nipped at the tendon in his neck, urging him faster, harder. With a growl that made her inner muscles clench, he lost whatever control he had left. He drove into her, rocketing them both toward a brutal peak. She shot over the edge, screaming his name. He plunged into her once, twice more, pressing his face into her throat before finally shuddering over the edge behind her.

BREATH HEAVING, Judd stayed where he was, face tucked against Autumn's neck, his body buried deep in hers. Every cell vibrated with a primal call of *Mine.* She slumped against him, the fingers of one hand stroking lazily through the hair at his nape. At this point, it was more physics than actual intent keeping them both upright. He felt hollowed out, emptied of all that pure, unadulterated need. Years of wanting finally unleashed.

He was appalled at his behavior. He hadn't even made it to the damned sofa.

Autumn stirred in his arms, shifting to drop her legs. He eased back so she could slide down, but didn't let her go. He had to find a way to apologize.

"Autumn."

She lifted her hands in the air and stretched with a sound that couldn't be described as anything but a purr. "That was—"

Too rough. Too crass. Too out of control.

"—the best sex of my life."

Judd straightened to stare at her, taking in the smug, feline smile curving her lips.

"Not surprising, I suppose. Fourteen years is a helluva lead up," she said.

"I just took you against *the door.*"

She grinned in obvious delight. "I know. First time in our lives you didn't treat me like I was fragile. It was amazing." Stepping away from him, she headed toward the bathroom. "I think we embarrassed Boudreaux."

The dog lay behind the sofa, nose just barely peeking out.

Judd scooped up his boxers. How could she not be upset? Everything they were to each other and he'd turned into an animal. No care. No finesse. No condom…

Oh shit. The boxers fell from his hand.

She emerged from the hall bathroom, still gloriously naked, stopping short when she saw him. Her smile faded, expression turning stricken. "Please tell me you don't regret what we just did."

He crossed to her in two strides, taking her into his arms. "No." Whatever consequences there were, he couldn't regret being with her.

"Then why do you look like you've just been mule kicked?"

He led her over to the sofa and sat, pulling her across his lap.

Despite her look of concern, she snuggled in. "That's your Very Serious Discussion face."

"My what?"

"Whenever you have something to tell me that you think is going to upset me, you get this look on your face. And you always touch me. Albeit never quite like this. I've always thought it was for my benefit, but now I'm wondering if it goes both ways."

The arm she slid around his shoulders had her breast pressing against his chest and almost distracted him from what he needed to say.

"Started out for you. But after the hospital, yeah, just as much for me, I guess." He rubbed a hand down her back. "Firefly, I didn't stop to think about protection."

"Oh." Her face smoothed out. "It's fine. I've been on birth control since college."

Okay that was one concern down. "I'm clean," he assured her.

"I know. You've been a serial monogamist

your whole life. I wasn't worried." She pressed a sweet kiss to the underside of his jaw. "Besides, I really, *really* enjoyed seeing you lose control."

It was hard to argue with the evidence of her pleasure. But that wasn't entirely the point. Judd stroked the wet hair back from her face. "You deserved more than that. You've always deserved more than I've given you." Guilt at the knowledge that he'd hurt her weighed heavy on his heart.

Autumn pressed closer. "You gave me everything you could. You had your reasons for not doing this before. They were damned stupid reasons, but you thought you were doing the right thing."

He thought back to her shouted accusations. "I'm sorry. I never ever meant to make you feel like I was trying to silence you. I'd never in a thousand years want to make you feel like he did."

"It was a cheap shot. I was angry." On a sigh, she tucked her head against the hollow of his throat. "I've loved you all my life, and after we both got out of the hospital, when you didn't remember—*said* you didn't remember—and never pursued anything more with me, I thought my father had made it so you couldn't love me. That I wasn't worth it."

Horrified, Judd tightened his arms around her. "No. God, no. Staying away from you all these years, not doing exactly this, took everything I had." Along with a string of relationships that he'd known, in his heart, would never go anywhere. Judd didn't care to analyze how much of a dick that made him.

He felt her lips curve against his throat. "If I'd known that, I'd have given in way earlier to all those fantasies I had about jumping you." When she lifted her head, her amusement had faded. "The truth is, you've always treated me as the most important person in your life on every level but this one, and I just couldn't do it anymore."

"What changed?"

"I thought you were going to marry Mary Alice."

"You…what?" The pieces of a puzzle clicked into place. "You mean that day outside Sanderson's, when you bolted? *That's* why you thought we were there?"

"It was a logical conclusion. You don't buy jewelry."

"So all this talk of leaving Wishful, leaving me, was because of her? Because you thought I was serious about her? Why didn't you just ask?"

"And have to test my acting skills to the max when you told me to my face you were going to marry someone else? No, thank you. I'm not that good. Not with you."

"I knew you were lying. But I thought you were upset about the flowers. What were you really going to tell me that day?"

"The truth. That I love you and I wanted to be with you. I had a plan and a speech that didn't involve losing my temper and kissing you brainless in front of my two closest girlfriends. I was going to ask you to choose. But then Mark came and blew the timing, then the jewelry store happened, and I just couldn't face you right then. So I ran. And I was going to keep running, as far as I had to. If someone else was truly going to make you happy, I could've given you up. But I couldn't stick around and watch it. I'm only human."

He'd come so close to losing her to something that would never have happened. God, he'd been a fucking idiot.

"There was never a choice. I love you. It's always been you." Overwhelmed with the desire to soothe whatever hurts he'd caused, he brushed a soft kiss over her lips. "Let me show you."

She melted into him without hesitation. That instant surrender sparked his blood, made him want to roll her under him. But he'd taken her hard and fast already. Now he wanted her slow. To take the time to explore the body he'd fantasized so long about, learn her taste and texture. Scooping her up, he headed for the stairs.

"That was a perfectly good couch," Autumn murmured against his mouth.

"Not enough room. And we have time." He hoped like hell it was true. He'd left his radio and phone downstairs. But surely fate couldn't be so cruel as to drag him away when they'd finally come together. He prayed everyone in town would have the sense to stay home in this foul weather.

Pushing the thought from his mind, he laid her out on his bed and looked his fill. She was long and slim and beautiful, her wet hair spread out over the pillow.

"Do you know how often I imagined you here, like this?"

"I very seriously doubt it was anywhere near as much as I thought about you."

Judd chuckled as he lifted her leg to press a kiss to her ankle. "Probably not. I spent a *lot* of effort trying not to think about this. But I failed more often than not."

"That should've been a sign."

He paused, stroking light fingers over the

tender flesh behind her knee. "I suppose my sentence will be a nice long stretch with regular reminders of how long I've been an idiot?"

"It does seem fair. But it's possible I could be induced to reduce the sentence if you proceed with efforts to make up for lost time."

"I have every intention of making you lose time. Hours, days, years. Isn't that how you put it with Cooper?"

She smiled with wicked pleasure. "Somebody paid attention."

"Always."

He slid his hands beneath her hips, dragging her to the edge of the bed so he could drape her legs over his shoulders. Those jade green eyes held not an ounce of self consciousness as she splayed out for him. Goddamn that was sexy.

Judd rubbed his cheek against the sensitive skin of her inner thigh, loving her low moan. Eyes on hers, he pressed his mouth against her, drawing his tongue through her wet folds. Autumn cried out, hips bucking beneath him. Downstairs, Boudreaux began to bay.

The taste of her barely on his tongue, Judd lifted his head. "What the hell?"

Even from up here, Judd could hear the dog hurling himself at the door.

"Stay here." He untangled himself from Autumn and sprinted for the stairs, not bothering with pants. Boudreaux's howls turned to frantic barking. He pawed at the door, glancing back at Judd as if to say *Hurry the hell up!*

Grabbing up his service weapon, Judd strode toward the door, giving the order for the dog to shush. He hauled Boudreaux back and saw the arc of wet on the floor. The door had been opened since he and Autumn came inside, shoving their clothes to one side. The deadbolt was unlocked. Wary now, he grabbed up his pants and slipped them on. He pointed for the stairs. "To Autumn. Guard."

Growling low in his throat, Boudreaux did as commanded. The way he was behaving, likely whoever had opened the door wasn't inside, but to be certain, Judd did a quick sweep, clearing the lower floor and killing lights as he went. He listened hard but heard nothing out of the ordinary over the drum of rain outside. Satisfied no one was in the house, he slipped out the front door, keeping to deep shadow.

Autumn's suitcase still lay where she'd dropped it in the driveway, the contents soaked. Hopefully not all ruined. He saw no signs of a vehicle or any movement as he slowly circled the house. Not that he could see far in this monsoon they were having. Whoever had tried to come in was likely long gone, using the rain for cover.

Returning to the door, he saw a small square glinting from the porch. Something protruded from the middle. Had this been here when he stepped out? Or had the intruder circled back around?

Judd went back inside to grab a flashlight and some gloves.

"What is it?"

He whipped toward the stairway. Autumn stood in one of his shirts, one hand on

Boudreaux, the other holding the 9mm Ruger from his nightstand by her side.

"I told you to stay upstairs."

"What's going on?"

"Someone left us a present."

Autumn started to come down. "No. Stay there." She was safer out of sight.

Judd went back outside and turned on the flashlight to see what had been left. It was a picture frame, one he well recognized, as it had graced one of the bookcases in Autumn's apartment for years. The picture inside had them both mugging for the camera on a camping trip sometime during college. The glass in the frame was cracked around the knife driven through the image all the way through the cardboard backing of the frame. It was a pocket knife. A Swiss Army number with a faded insignia. But he could still make out the initials he'd had engraved before he gave it to her when they were thirteen.

AEB.

Shit.

CHAPTER 13

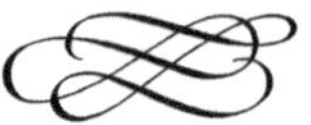

Stabbed through the heart. Her picture. Her knife. Both precious memories she'd thought lost in the fire. Twisted now into something ugly.

Long after Judd's officers had left, long after the scene had been processed and she'd gone through her encounter with her father at Dinner Belles, Autumn lay awake thinking about the message he'd left her. It hadn't been him, of course. A sentry had been posted to watch him after Judd heard about the diner, and he hadn't left the motel. But they'd been operating under the assumption he had someone else being his eyes, ears, and legs. The idea of it terrified her. Jebediah himself might have been limited in what he could do, but whoever was acting for him wasn't.

How far was that person willing to go to carry out her father's vendetta?

In the four days since he'd gotten out of prison, her house had burned down, her place of work had been violated, and her pen name outed. She'd confronted her father, issuing her own threat, and in a matter of hours, he'd made one in return.

I nearly took him from you once. I could do it again.

She didn't dare close her eyes for fear of going back there. The memory was too close, even with the warmth of Judd's big body wrapped around her, his chest rising and falling in a reassuring rhythm. For the first time in her life, she'd gotten everything she'd always wanted. The man she'd always loved loved her back. The foolish wall he'd thrown up between them was gone. And, in a way, it was her father's actions that had led them here.

But what would be the cost? Because if life had taught her anything, it was that there was always, always a price. Consequences for those wants. Those desires. A pound of flesh, literal or figurative. She'd paid for their friendship gladly, enduring the beatings and the lectures and even the occasional imprisonment because the light Judd brought to her life was brighter than any of her father's darkness.

Jebediah had nearly snuffed out that light once, and Autumn couldn't shake the terror that he'd try again. That this time, he'd succeed.

In the deep hours of the night, as fear took her by the throat, she turned to Judd, taking comfort in his body. They made desperate love as the night waned, and she shattered with the first rays of dawn. But the light wasn't enough to banish the shadows.

She couldn't lose him. Not now.

As they readied for the day, she struggled to tamp down her anxiety. It would only make him worry, and she didn't want to do anything to dull his edge. But as he dressed, her eyes went, unerring, to the scar just to the right of his heart.

"I don't know how to do this," she whispered.

Judd froze, his undershirt half on. Expression serious, he tugged the shirt down and crossed to her. "Do what, Firefly?"

"Let you go out there." She slipped her arms around him. "I've always worried about you. It's the nature of the job. But it feels different now. After last night, part of me wants to just lock us both inside and hide. Part wants to take you and run far, far away where he can't find us. I know we can't. And I'd never ask you to walk away from the job you've worked so hard for. But I just…I'm so afraid of losing you."

He stroked her hair back from her face, his big hand lingering on her cheek. "It's what he wants. To make you afraid."

"I know. And I hate that it's worked. I hate

that we can't just bask in finally being together without his pall hanging over everything."

"It won't last. The hits are coming one after another. There's no patience to what's being done. Sooner or later—probably sooner—he's going to slip up. He'll get arrogant. Or his help will. And when that happens, I'm going to nail him. He's not going to be free to terrorize you for much longer. I promise."

Autumn didn't doubt that Judd would find whatever there was to find. He excelled at the job. But her fear of Jebediah was old and deeply ingrained, and she didn't think she'd sleep easy until her father was put back in a box—whether that was a cell or a coffin.

Judd pressed a kiss to her brow. "How about, when all this is over, we do a little of that running away and take a vacation? We could head up to Tennessee to the mountains. Rent a cabin and spent a week just the two of us. Clothing optional, so I can keep working off my stupid debt."

Her lips twitched into a smile, as he wanted.

"I can't say as I have any objections to being the creditor to whom that orgasmic debt is owed. But before we go running off together…maybe we should tell the family. Do they even know you and Mary Alice split?"

"I haven't told them. All my focus has been on you since the fire."

"Well, that'll make the twins' birthday party tonight interesting."

"Ah, shit. I lost track of time with everything going on. And I volunteered to host the thing."

"It'll be fine. I sorted the details with your mom on Sunday. And I'm glad to have something else to focus on for a little while. I just…" She trailed off, not sure how to articulate what she was feeling.

"You're not worried about how the family will react, are you? They adore you. I mean, it might be a surprise—"

Autumn couldn't stop the burst of laughter. As he fixed her with a bland stare, she framed his face in her hands. "Oh, my love, literally the only surprise will be that you finally pulled your head out of your ass. Everyone in town has been expecting this for years."

His brows drew together. "I can't decide whether I should be insulted by that or not."

She grinned at him, unable to resist a little teasing. "There might be a parade."

His lips twisted in a decided pout. "Definitely insulted."

Amused and feeling somewhat lighter, she drew him down for a kiss. "I love you."

His fingers began to knead at her hips. "If I stay insulted, will you keep saying it?"

"I'll say it as often as you want for the rest of my life." As soon as the words were out, she wished she could pull them back.

She'd loved him all her life, and she knew he loved her. But they'd had one night. That didn't automatically equate to a lifetime commitment, no matter how much being with him felt like a foregone conclusion.

Eyes gone softer than she'd ever seen them, Judd pulled her closer, brushing his mouth over hers. "I love you. I should have been saying it all these years. And I'll tell you every day for as long as you'll let me. You're the best thing in my life, and I'm sorry my bullheadedness wasted so many years."

Heart settling, she wound her arms around his shoulders. "You're making it very hard to be a responsible adult who goes to work."

"Same. If there weren't so damned many eyes on me as Chief, I'd take you right back to bed and keep you there. But the sooner I go in, the sooner I get to the bottom of all this and get us both some peace."

With one last kiss, she pulled back. "Then we'll go in." She quirked a smile. "But come closing time, you're mine."

"From your mouth to God's ear."

They drove in together, and he walked her inside the library, where Livia was already getting started on the backlog of work from yesterday. She looked up from some paperwork spread across the circulation desk, her gaze skimming over their joined hands.

"So you two finally—"

"Yeah," Judd said.

Autumn supposed it didn't actually matter how Livia had planned to finish that sentence. They'd finally—a lot of things.

Livia's grin was megawatt. "That's awesome."

"It is." He turned his attention back to Autumn, lifting her chin. "I need to get to work. What time are you supposed to be done today?"

"Three. Then I really need to pick up some last minute gifts for the twins. We never did manage that shopping trip."

"If I can get loose, I will. If not, I'm sending someone as escort."

She still didn't love the idea of a bodyguard, but she wasn't about to argue with him. "Okay. See you later."

He kissed her again, easily, as if he'd been doing it for years, then headed for the front door.

"Judd." When he turned, she called, "Be careful."

He gave a smart salute, then blew her a kiss and walked out.

As soon as the door shut behind him, Livia stomped her feet and squealed. "Oh my God, tell me *everything!* You have beard burn on your throat."

She had beard burn in quite a few places this morning.

Not knowing where to start, she went straight to the most important point. "He loves me."

"Well there is the world's biggest non-newsflash."

"Okay, fine. He admitted and acted on it."

"That's more like it. Details, girl."

As the door opened and their first patrons of the day trickled in, the story had to wait. But over the course of their shift, Autumn managed to fill Livia in on all the pertinent details. She was an incredibly satisfying audience, squeeing and gasping in all the right places. It made it easier to focus on the bubbles of happy instead of the worry underscoring everything.

"So Judd seems to be pretty over the top protective today, even for him. Did something happen?" Livia asked.

Autumn had left out that part of the story. The details of the night were being kept under wraps as the investigation continued. "Someone tried to break into the house last night."

Livia's eyes went wide. "Oh my God."

"Boudreaux scared him off, but Judd's not taking any chances."

"Yoohoo! Autumn, dear!"

Autumn turned toward the older, sing-song voice to find Betty Monroe hot-footing it across the library in her orthopedic sneakers and baby blue velour track suit. "Hey, Miss Betty. How are you today?"

"Fit as a fiddle. I just wanted to come by to see how you were doing after all that ugliness."

"All that ugliness" could cover a whole host of things, but she didn't much want to get into any of it with one of the biggest gossips in town. She offered a smile to the older woman.

"I'm doing okay. It's an adjustment, for sure. But I was lucky not to be there when it happened, so I wasn't hurt."

"Such a shame. If there's anything I or the girls can do, you just let us know."

"I sure will. Thank you."

"Are we still on for book club Thursday? We'll totally understand if you need to cancel."

"I'm sure I can still make it."

Miss Betty clapped her hands. "Wonderful! We're very excited. And don't you worry about those ninnies making a fuss on the sidewalk. They don't know what they're talking about."

Autumn's smile froze. "What ninnies on the sidewalk?"

"The protesters, dear." She leaned across the counter. "You ask me, they're only making a fuss because nobody's taking care of *them* in the romance department, and God forbid anybody else have a satisfying love life."

Gut curdling, Autumn circled around the desk. "Excuse me for a minute." She strode across to the front of the building and peeked out the tall windows.

A half dozen people with picket signs were marching in a circle where anyone driving past could see. She saw flashes of her name on the signs.

Autumn Buchanan contributes to moral decay!
Autumn Buchanan, Sin Seller
Autumn Buchanan threatens family values.
"Oh my God."
Her day was about to get a whole lot worse.

"GOT a minute to talk about this requisition you submitted?"

Judd looked longingly at the door leading out of City Hall and onto the street. So close and yet so far away. Resigned, he turned toward Councilman Cam Crawford. "I'll make one."

"Do you *really* want to try to push this through right now?" Cam asked. "I mean, with the totaled cruiser, that's far and away above the department's budget."

Judd felt a headache set up behind his eyes. "The cruiser was an unfortunate accident and replacing it is a necessity. So is this training seminar in Jackson."

"Are you sure it's a good time?"

The timing was crap with the ongoing investigation, but he had hope that things would be wrapped up by the time the seminar rolled around on Friday. "I submitted the requisition before the car." Hell, he'd done it his first full day on the job because Robert hadn't gotten around to the paperwork of doing it himself. "The fact is, the course isn't being offered again for six months."

"But you're proposing sending nearly everyone in the department. What about covering the shifts for that day?"

"Sheriff Riggs has already agreed to lend a few of his reserve officers to help bridge the gap in coverage for both days. Look, Cam, I know it's shit timing, but the bottom line is, my people need this training."

The city councilman, who'd been a couple years behind him in school, sighed. "All right. I'll push it through."

Judd made the requisite noises of appreciation and escaped. The moment he stepped out of City Hall, he released a sigh of relief. Rather than following up on the investigation into Autumn's harassment, he'd spent most of the morning answering to the city council and mayor for the rookie's squad car disaster and injury. There were endless discussions of departmental budgets he hadn't even had a moment to look at, let alone get a grasp on. Sitting through it, remaining polite and professional instead of announcing how he really felt—that the whole meeting was a waste of time that could have been an email—took every shred of patience he had. And after last night, he didn't have much.

Fuck all of it. He just wanted to get through this case, put Jebediah away, and make Autumn's world okay again. He couldn't stand seeing fear in her eyes.

For efficiency's sake, he opted to pick up lunch and take it back to the station. Dinner Belles was hopping, as it usually was during the weekday lunch rush. He nodded to several familiar faces and broke several cardinal rules of southern etiquette by not stopping to speak. But he didn't have time for those sorts of social games today. Working his way to the counter, he slid onto the last available stool.

Mama Pearl finished her conversation with one of the old timers at the other end, slapped a new ticket on the wheel leading back to the kitchen, and ambled in Judd's direction. "Afternoon, Judd."

"Mama Pearl. I'm in something of a hurry. What have you got that'll get me out of here fast with a to go order?"

"That'll be the blue plate. We got barbeque chicken or the fried pork chop."

"Let's go with the chicken. Thanks."

Instead of moving to put in his order, she

studied him with her fathomless dark eyes.

Judd resisted the urge to reiterate he was in a hurry. There was breaking social etiquette, and there was pissing off the purveyor of the finest pie in a three hundred mile radius. He had his priorities.

At last, she nodded to herself. "'Bout damned time."

Before he could ask what she was talking about, she strode over to an old fashioned dinner bell hanging in the corner and began to clang it.

"Attention. Attention, please! The Judd Hamilton/Autumn Buchanan pool is officially closed. Winner will be announced later this week."

Judd's jaw dropped. "But I didn't say—"

"You didn't have to. It's written all over yo' face. Looks good on you. I'll get that order in."

His ears burned. Did he have some kind of neon sign tattooed on his forehead? *Slept with my best friend, the love of my life.*

He didn't regret it, and he wasn't ashamed of

how he felt about Autumn. But news hadn't yet gotten around about his breakup with Mary Alice, and he didn't want the situation to reflect badly on any of them.

Casting a cautious glance around, he noted lots of smiles and nods of approval. But exactly as Autumn had predicted, nobody seemed surprised. He saw money changing hands at several tables, including between two of his best friends.

Mitch held out a hand to Riley's fiancé, Liam. "Give it up. I take partial credit for this."

Judd moved over to join them. "And exactly how is that?"

"The bracelet, man. It did exactly what it was supposed to do."

"It most definitely did not. It dug me deeper into the hole I was already in."

"Exactly. It nudged that relationship over onto the rocks, where it needed to be."

He stared at Mitch. "Are you telling me you deliberately torpedoed my relationship with Mary Alice?"

"I did that woman a kindness and gave her the motivation to cut you loose. She deserves a chance to be happy, and it wasn't ever gonna be with you."

"You sneaky son of a—"

Liam held up a hand. "When we tried to talk to you about this last year, you kinda lost your shit, so you didn't leave us a lot of choice."

"As I recall, we were talking about you seeing a future with Riley, not about me and Mary Alice."

"Yeah. And I'm betting if I asked you the same question now about Autumn—about whether you see her in your life in five years, in ten—you'd have an answer."

Judd opened his mouth to reply, then shut it again. Of course he had an answer. Because the future he'd never allowed himself to dwell on had always been built around Autumn. He'd been such a fool. For years, he'd lied to himself that he could love someone else. He'd given it his best effort. But his best effort with only part of his heart. Nothing he'd ever experienced with anyone else had ever come close to what he'd felt with Autumn last night. He loved her. He'd always loved her. And he wished he'd trusted in them the way she had.

Mama Pearl materialized with his order. "On the house. With a slice of pie. You look like you need it."

"Thanks." He glanced to his friends and acknowledged, at least to himself, that he probably wouldn't have gotten here without their interference. "Thanks. I gotta get back to work."

Relieved to walk away from the uncomfortable attention, Judd headed back to the station. But his relief was short-lived as he pulled up to see Nash helping a very irate-looking Robert Curry up the few steps to the door.

"I'm not a damned invalid!"

"You're damned well not well, either. Rowan's going to have both our hides if you do something stupid and have another episode that requires her coming back from Texas."

"Robert, what the hell are you doing here? You had a heart attack barely a week ago. And in case that addled your brain, you don't actually work here anymore, remember? You're retired."

"Retired doesn't mean useless. And I didn't get the chance to smoothly hand over the reins. I heard about your trouble and wanted to see how you were getting on."

Resigned to the fact that he wasn't going to get any peace to work for a while yet, he led them inside to the office that he hadn't actually personalized. As they stepped inside, he moved the box of Robert's personal effects out of one of the visitor's chairs. "Inez packed these up for you. Haven't had a chance to run them out to you."

Robert grunted and sat. "It'll keep. Tell me about the case."

So Judd laid it out, from the fire all the way to the picture and knife left on his porch last night, leaving out exactly what he and Autumn had been doing at the time.

"We're in the process of chasing down Jebediah's former associates and anybody in the area who might've served time with him. And we're waiting on some additional records of his time at Parchman."

Robert frowned. "You're being blinded by your personal connection."

"Excuse me?"

"You're making assumptions that it has to be Jebediah because you want it to be. But the fact is, his release is a matter of public record. Somebody else could be using that to cast suspicion in his direction. If that's the case, obviously it's working. Have you even looked at anybody else?"

Judd worked his jaw, hating that he was being called out. "There hasn't been anybody else to look at."

"So go back to the beginning. Go over everything that's happened, without Autumn's father in the equation. Figure out who has a motive here."

"He's the common factor," Judd insisted.

"Seems to me Autumn is the common factor. Her house, her work, her books. With a pseudonym, it seems beyond unlikely that her daddy somehow found out about them while he was in prison and has just been sitting in there planning all this for the past year."

That detail had been bugging Judd, too, but he hadn't had the opportunity to work through it.

Hands curling around the arms of the chair, Robert shoved up. "Now I've said what needed saying, I'm going home for a nap. You need to bounce ideas off somebody else, call me."

With a minimum of additional fuss from Nash, he was gone, and Judd was left staring at the empty whiteboard on the far wall.

Robert wasn't wrong. He'd let his personal involvement cloud his judgment, looking for confirmation of his assumptions rather than allowing the facts to speak for themselves. So what had he missed?

Grabbing a dry erase marker, he went back to the beginning to trace everything all over again.

CHAPTER 14

"I can't believe you didn't call me."

Autumn piled grocery bags on the kitchen counter and prepared to soothe Judd's ruffled feathers. "What was the point? I knew you had that meeting with the city council this morning. You had more important things to do than come rescue me from peaceful protesters exercising their right to freedom of speech. Even if they're basically supporting censorship." She'd had sufficient time to lock away her own hurt and offense over the whole thing. Licking that wound would have to wait until they weren't about to be inundated by family for the twins' birthday.

Judd scowled. "I guarantee I could have come up with something to make them disperse."

Turning into him, she lifted her hands to frame his face. "You can't keep using your position as chief to shield me, as if you're my own personal private security. It'll come back to bite you in the ass, and you can't afford that if you really want to keep this job."

"It was a personal attack on you. How can you expect me to just stand by and let it happen?"

"Because measured against arson and vandalism, a picket line by a bunch of holier-than-thou pearl clutchers is nothing. Hurting my feelings is not a crime."

"It is in my book."

Rising to her toes, she kissed him. "You're sweet. And if we have a prayer of being ready when everybody gets here, we've got to divide and conquer. Go get the picnic table and seating sorted and prep the grill, while I get started on the food. I'll bring out all the stuff to set the table once I've got the potatoes on to boil for the potato salad. What did you do with the outdoor table cloth and containers I bought you?"

"Closet under the stairs."

"'K. Take Boudreaux, otherwise he'll be laid out right where I need to be standing in hopes I drop something."

Ever hopeful, the dog leaned against her legs, rubbing his head against her in adoration. Laughing, she kissed his ears and shooed them both out of the kitchen.

As soon as the pair of them were out of sight, Autumn let the easy mask drop. She was more rattled about the protesters than she'd let on. Mitzi was furious. Shocker. There was only so much the library director was going to take before Autumn was just flat on the budgetary chopping block. Beyond that, there'd been a steady stream of people coming into the library to ask what it was all about. They were making her the center of attention again, somewhere she absolutely hated to be. Too many eyes looking, judging. Too many people whispering behind her back. Except, instead of being the daughter of the town zealot, now she was being judged for her own alleged misdeeds. It wasn't everybody. It wasn't even a majority. But it was enough when they were actively hitting on her biggest fear as an author. This was exactly why she'd chosen to write under a pen name. But a pseudonym was apparently the equivalent of paper armor and whatever false sense of security it had provided had been ripped away.

No help for it now. What's done is done. The truth is out.

Probably she needed to do something to spin that truth so that it was her version that got bandied about, but that would take more thought and consideration. For now, she had food for the small army of Hamiltons about to descend. That brought its own worry as she scrubbed and chunked potatoes.

She didn't know what to expect out of this

family dinner. Had the family heard about them yet? She and Judd had decided it was news best delivered in person, but he'd told her about Mama Pearl's announcement. *Someone* had likely spilled the beans by now.

Autumn didn't know how they'd feel about it. The Hamiltons loved her. And certainly they all knew how she felt about Judd. Patty would be beside herself with excitement. But it was one thing to know that she and Judd were to-gether. It was entirely another for the family to know they'd been…*together.* Autumn was pretty sure that there was a blinking neon sign hanging above both their heads. Their body language toward each other had changed. She wasn't a prude, wasn't embarrassed or ashamed, but the whole situation was a little awkward.

Looking out the kitchen window, she spotted Judd down by the water hurling a stick for Boudreaux. The dog lumbered after it, galumphing into the water like a self-contained herd of elephants. The sight made her smile, and she decided that it didn't matter. Finally having Judd as hers was worth absolutely any price.

On the stove, the potatoes had come to a boil. Reducing the heat, she put a top on the pot and went in search of the rest of the picnic supplies. Judd had rolled his eyes in affectionate forbearance when she'd showed up with a table cloth and assorted decorative caddies as a gift when he'd bought this monstrosity of a house. Matching buckets for utensils and drinks were not manly and certainly didn't get hauled out for poker night. But he'd kept it all, as he'd kept everything she'd given him over the years, even if he did keep it well out of sight when it wasn't being used.

Opening the door, she flipped the light switch inside. Nothing. Apparently the bulb had blown. Retrieving a new one from the laundry room, she ducked into the closet, reaching up to the angled ceiling for the bulb.

The door slammed behind her.

The bulb tumbled from her fingers, crashing

to the hardwood floor as she whirled, heart in her throat, to reach for the knob.

It wouldn't turn.

"No. No no." She jiggled the knob. Still, nothing.

Desperate to stay calm, she looked down at the thin ribbon of light below the door and saw the twin shadows of legs.

The relief came hard and fast. "Judd! Something's wrong with the door. I'm locked in."

When he didn't reply, her blood ran cold. Judd would never leave her in here. He'd be working to reassure her and to take the door off its hinges if he had to. He'd never just stand there, cold and silent. That purview was her father's.

He was here. In the house. In their *home.*

In the dark, the walls began to close in and childhood nightmares woke and stretched to life. Hours locked away in the tiny, dark closet, where the air had been close and humid. Jebediah's version of solitary confinement, when he felt she needed time to reflect on the nature of her sins. No food. No water. No contact.

Panic crawled up her throat and she pounded at the door. "Let me out! Let me out right now!"

She didn't care if she was giving him what he wanted. She couldn't see, couldn't breathe. She had to get out. Had to get to light. Sobbing, she threw herself against the door, over and over. It shuddered with every strike but didn't budge.

"Let me out! Let me out!" The words came out in a wheeze as her lungs seized up.

She was going to pass out, going to—

The door was yanked open.

Autumn careened out, almost hitting her knees before strong, familiar arms wrapped around her.

"Autumn! What the…?"

"He was here." Pressing her face into Judd's throat, she shook and tried to find enough air to speak. "He locked me in."

Judd pulled back, eyes fierce. "Did you see him?"

"No. No. Just the shadow of someone standing outside the closet." More scalding tears spilled over. "He was in the house. You were right outside, and he was *in the house.*"

The back door opened. Judd spun, putting himself between her and whatever was coming. But it was his brothers and parents spilling into the kitchen across the hall. The laughter seemed entirely surreal, when panic still flickered in her blood.

"Mom, take Autumn. The rest of you, come with me."

The good humored ribbing stopped as if he'd flipped a switch with his serious cop voice. They all piled into the hall.

"What on earth? Oh, honey." Patty drew Autumn into her embrace.

"What's going on?" Owen demanded.

Judd's expression was grim. "We're going on a manhunt."

"I DON'T THINK we're gonna find anything, son."

Judd clenched his jaw, hating to agree with his father on this, but there'd been no sign of anyone. He was still batting a big, fat goose egg on this entire investigation. Meanwhile, this son of a bitch was rapidly eroding whatever sense of safety Autumn had.

He dragged a hand over his head, down the back of his neck. "How can I even face her?"

Leo shook his head. "She's not going to blame you for this."

"I promised I'd keep her safe. I swore no one would get to her. And this bastard just waltzed right into our damned house while I was fifty yards away. He locked her in the fucking closet, Dad. Jesus, the look on her face when I opened the door." Ashen, terrified. He shook his head, as if that would wipe away the image seared into his brain. "I never saw her right after one of Jebediah's confinements. She told me about it some. I thought I understood how bad it was.

But I didn't have a clue. Not really. And this was just a few minutes."

Eli clapped him on the shoulder. "You're doing the best you can, man."

"Yeah, well, my best isn't good enough." And Judd didn't know what the hell to do with that.

He hadn't figured it out by the time they made it back to the house. As they trooped inside, Autumn turned from the sink and the potatoes she'd just dumped into a colander. She'd washed her face, the only sign of her recent tears a faint puffiness around her eyes. If he hadn't seen it himself, he wouldn't have known she'd been hysterical twenty minutes ago. How the hell could she pack it away like this?

Anticipating her unasked question, Judd jumped straight in. "We didn't find anything."

Her hands twisted the kitchen towel she held, and there were the remnants of the anxiety and fear. Those hands trembled, the knuckles white with their grip.

Bracing himself for what came next, he

stepped forward, catching her hands in his. "I understand if you don't feel safe here anymore."

"I'm all right, Judd."

But he felt the tremor that made it a lie. Unable to stop himself, he cupped her cheek. "He locked you in."

"And you got me out."

That wasn't the point. No one should have been able to get to her here in the first place. He'd been careless. Foolish. That stopped now. "Tell me where you still feel safe. I'll figure out a way to make it so."

"With you. Always with you." She reached up, mirroring his touch. "I can handle this—all of this—because I know you'll do whatever it takes to get me out. You always have. So I'm not going anywhere."

Relief that she didn't want to move out hit hard and fast. On its heels came guilt that she was the one comforting him when she'd just been freshly traumatized. He didn't feel worthy of her faith in him, but selfishly, he'd take it.

Brushing a kiss over her lips, he pulled her closer. "I don't deserve you."

Her smile was sweet. "We can agree to disagree. But you have me either way."

A watery "Oh!" came from somewhere near the table, and Judd abruptly remembered his entire family was in the room.

"So, uh, I'm guessing you and Mary Alice broke up?" Eli asked.

Leo nudged him in the ribs with an elbow. "I told you I heard something about it earlier."

"The rumors have been wrong before."

"Not this time." Might as well set that straight himself. "I finally got my head out of my ass."

His mom shot her hands into the air. "Hallelujah! *Finally.*"

Insulted, Judd gave her a flat stare. "Gee, thanks."

"I'm sorry, son, but you're the slowest mover in the history of slow movers. This has been sitting in front of you your whole life."

Autumn tipped up to kiss his cheek and whispered, "Told you."

As soon as she stepped back, Patty grabbed her hands, leading her into a brief little dance. "When do I get to hit number seven on my speed dial?"

Autumn threw back her head and laughed, an impossibly light, happy sound considering the grave situation they'd just been discussing. Judd was struck again by how damned beautiful she was, inside and out. Maybe that was partly how the Universe was balancing things out.

"Don't get ahead of yourself. Judd's still catching up."

"Who is number seven on your speed dial and what am I catching up on?"

Autumn just grinned. "Don't worry about it."

Oh, like that didn't make his curiosity ten times greater?

His brothers simultaneously ambushed him with thumps on either shoulder.

"What was that for?"

"Took you long enough," Leo said.

"Moron," Eli muttered.

Judd rolled his eyes and grabbed them both in a headlock, one under each arm. "Happy birthday, dweebs."

He grunted as they punched him in the ribs, struggling to escape, but he was still bigger and better trained.

"Boys," his father's warning tone rang out, and they all straightened.

Eli angled his head. "Dude, is that a bite mark on your neck?"

Autumn's head whipped around, her eyes wide, cheeks going pink. "I did not—"

His brother laughed. "Made you look."

She goosed him in the ribs. "You are an ass, little brother."

"You love me."

"I do. And because it's your birthday, I won't even steal your cake for that remark."

"Speaking of, we should probably relocate inside for the festivities, under the circumstances." He could put off dealing with additional security until after dinner, at least.

"No, we're going to eat out by the lake like we originally planned," Autumn insisted.

"I'm not sure that's such a good idea."

"No, I've been thinking about it. Whoever's doing this wants to scare me. And yeah, okay he got some screams out of me. But I'm not going to let him win by hiding inside and cowering. I need some normal. So I want to put all this away, at least for a little while, and have a lakeside picnic just like we planned. It's an act of defiance, even if he's probably long gone and not still watching."

Judd didn't like it. But he understood her need to assert herself and take back control. "Okay."

Because they all wanted to give her what she asked, they slid into the easy rhythm of family, razzing each other as the potato salad was finished and burger patties were made. With some juggling and a great deal more ribbing, they trooped outside carting dishes and food.

Bringing up the rear with a bucket of utensils, Judd caught sight of his mother's phone on the kitchen table. With a glance after his family, he snatched it up and pulled up her contacts. Swiping over to favorites, he scanned down to the seventh number.

Reverend Paul Prescott.

His mother had the preacher on speed dial?

Judd let the implications of that sink in. Then he texted himself the contact. They'd see who needed to catch up.

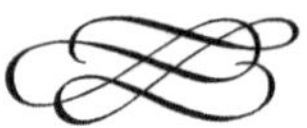

CHAPTER 15

Autumn eyed Nash Brewer's full police uniform. "Are you *sure* you don't want to change first?"

As one of Wishful PD's reserve officers, he'd been her shadow during business hours the last couple of days. But he'd done so in plainclothes, under the auspices of working on some genealogy research. Today he'd shown up in full cop mode, duty belt and all. Hadn't she reminded him that today was the Thursday afternoon book club at the senior center? She was a little concerned he'd get mobbed by a bunch of enthusiastic blue hairs.

Nash's easy smile widened. "Nah. I'm perfectly comfortable."

"That totally wasn't why I asked. Never let it be said that I didn't *try* to save you from having your ass pinched."

His brow shot up in question. "Beg your pardon?"

"You're an attractive guy in a cop uniform. Chances are we'll have to work hard to convince them you're not a stripper. These ladies can be mercenary."

Some of Nash's amusement faded. "I mean, I've heard about the Casserole Patrol. You can't live here more than a couple of months and not hear rumblings, but I've never had any real interaction with them."

"Then you, sir, are in for an education." Resigned to his fate, she started the two block walk.

"Are you sure you don't want to drive?"

"I could use the fresh air." She'd gotten little enough of it since the cookout. Judd had beefed up his security system, and they'd begun keeping all the doors locked and the alarm set even when they were home. It made for a bit of a production when the dog needed to go out, but it was the best they could do under the circumstances.

All had been quiet since the invasion. Autumn didn't trust it. It was the longest stretch they'd gone without escalation, which didn't make sense. Where was the harassment? The steady stream of actions designed to leave her off balance? Then again, wasn't she off balance simply by the waiting?

"Thanks for helping out as my bodyguard this week. I know it's not exactly a dream posting."

"Beats traffic duty. And babysitting crotchety retired police chiefs."

"How is Chief Curry?"

"Grumpy, and sadder than he's willing to admit that Rowan had to head back to Houston.

He really wanted to talk her into coming onto the force here."

Something in his tone had Autumn's interest piquing. "Oh yeah? *He* does?"

Nash just gave her the side eye. "Yes *he* does, Miss Matchmaker."

"But you wouldn't mind if she did either."

"Rowan and I are friends. We enjoy hanging out on the occasions she comes to visit her uncle. That's it."

Autumn hummed a noncommittal noise. She knew interest when she heard it. But she'd let it go for now. No reason to torture the poor man before the Casserole Patrol got ahold of him.

As soon as they stepped inside the senior center, a cheer went up.

"There's our girl!" Maudie Bell Ramsey crossed the room, as fast as her orthopedic shoes could carry her, and wrapped Autumn in a hug scented with Chantilly and peppermint.

"Oh, and look! She brought us a surprise!"

Miss Betty looked Nash up and down with approval.

"Not that kind of surprise, Miss Betty. Nash is just…" What was he "just"?

"I'm just here to check out the book club. My grandma is coming in for a long visit, and I thought it might be something she'd enjoy."

Nice cover.

Looks of disappointment swept through the assembled group. "Well, he's still nice to look at," Miss Betty declared.

Nash's cheeks colored under the sandy scruff of his stubble. "Uh, thank you, ma'am."

Miss Maudie Bell looped an arm through Autumn's. "We're so glad you're back. Book discussion went totally off the rails without you."

Autumn didn't doubt it. Keeping this group in line was like herding a bunch of drunk cats. "I'll do my best to get everything back on track. Where's Miss Delia?"

"Flirting. The boys are playing with their toy soldiers again."

Toy soldiers. Which meant Mark was here.

Damn it. Twice a month, he hung out with the senior men, reviewing major military campaigns of history, complete with enormous maps and complements of little plastic soldiers. He hadn't been back to the library since the day all those love scenes had been found.

Miss Betty nudged her toward the door. "Why don't you go get her, dearie? Your legs are a little more spry than ours."

"Yes ma'am." Inwardly, Autumn cringed, but she headed into the back room of the center, where a fairly epic battle was laid out on the ping pong table.

A cluster of elderly men were hunched over the table. At the side, Mark gestured in broad strokes, his face alight with passion for his subject.

"You can see here, if the other Confederate generals had listened to Stonewall Jackson and marched on Washington when he suggested it, it would have cut off—" He broke off as he caught sight of Autumn, his cheeks coloring.

She gave a little wave and wished they could

still look each other in the eye. "I was just coming to retrieve Miss Delia for Book Club."

The older woman stepped out from behind the knot of men, preening in her purple velour track suit. "You should come join our book club, Cecil. You might learn something." Miss Delia punctuated the statement with an unmistakable eyebrow waggle as she leaned in.

The elderly man jolted.

Oh my God. She totally pinched his butt.

Message delivered, Miss Delia sailed by Autumn into the meeting room—insofar as one could sail in sensible sneakers.

"Not going to ask," Autumn muttered.

She shot one last look at Mark, who studiously avoided her gaze and seemed determined to find the Battle of—whatever he was teaching—the most interesting thing ever. It was official. She would never recover from having explicit descriptions of a cock handed to a library patron. Maybe he'd start going to the library in Lawley instead and spare them both the embarrassment.

More senior ladies were congregated in the meeting room than was usual for a book club meeting, and as soon as she stepped through the door, Autumn understood why. A banner stretched across one wall. *Welcome Harper Jackson!*

Oh God, they know.

She wrestled with instant and profound regret for not having asked what the book was today because she knew—she just *knew*—it would be one of hers. And that would have been better to control.

Well, you're in it now, Buchanan, so suck it up, Cupcake.

Nash had positioned himself in a corner—ass to the wall, she noted—and looked like he wanted to bolt, but there was a quartet of grannies flanking him on all sides. Time to give the poor guy a rescue.

Autumn clapped her hands for attention. "Okay y'all, let's get started. I see several new faces since our last meeting. Welcome. Y'all probably already know each other, but let's do a quick round of introductions for me."

They went through the round robin intros and Autumn picked up the thread of conversation again. "Okay, so I understand y'all already had your discussion on Dinah McClure's *Catch My Breath?*"

"Yes, we picked a new book last meeting," Miss Betty said.

"Okay then. Since I wasn't part of that, perhaps one of you would like to lead the discussion?"

"Actually, we'd love if you've do a reading for us," Miss Maudie Bell said. "You do such lovely readings, and we're so excited to read your work!"

Maybe I can still salvage this. "I appreciate the enthusiasm, but I didn't come prepared—"

"Oh, that's all right, honey, you can borrow mine. I have the passage marked already." Delia handed over her ereader, a terrifying gleam in her eye.

With some trepidation, Autumn swiped the

screen awake and began to skim. The blood drained from her cheeks. *Forged In Blood*. Worse, it was one of the love scenes.

Struggling to control her reaction, she arched her brows. "I'm not entirely sure this is appropriate."

"Oh come now, we're all adults," Miss Betty argued.

"Yes, but we might scar poor Officer Brewer for life." Autumn prayed they'd take pity on him.

"Strapping young man like that could stand to be educated," Miss Delia insisted.

"Or he could plug his ears!" Miss Maudie Bell suggested. "Please read for us."

Autumn swallowed. She was far from prudish, but reading her work aloud in front of a crowd—especially one of the scenes she'd now experienced in a very intimate way… She could refuse, but what other excuse did she have? So she did the only thing she could. She read.

"Lilah trembled. She didn't know how much

was from being soaked to the skin and how much was the shock starting to set in.

"Cooper came back with a towel, wrapping it around her shoulders. 'You're freezing.' He rubbed his big hands up and down her arms, and she had to resist the urge to lean into him.

"'It's my fault she's dead.' Lilah's teeth chattered as she said it. 'It's always my fault for asking the questions, breaking the rules. Someone else always pays the price. Just like you did.'

"Eyes fierce, Cooper shook her—not hard, just enough to make a point. 'No. Nothing about this is your fault. Nothing about what happened with your father was your fault.'

"This was the first glimmer she'd seen of *her* Cooper—of the boy she'd so desperately loved. The sight of it broke her heart all over again. 'I don't blame you for leaving. Why would anybody stay after that hell? I'm sure being shot pretty thoroughly destroyed any delusions of love.'

"'My leaving had nothing to do with not

loving you. I don't blame you for what happened. And I've thought of you every day since I walked away.' He tucked a chunk of her wet hair behind her ear, his fingers grazing her cheek, and she turned into the touch, needing the elusive warmth, the connection."

Autumn closed her eyes for a moment, remembering not tenderness, but unleashed passion as Judd's hands speared into her wet hair and he claimed her.

Her voice shook a little as she resumed. "'I've thought about what would have happened if your father hadn't come home that day.'

"So had Lilah.

"'I wanted you.' Cooper skimmed his thumb across her lower lip. 'I've always wanted you.'

"The touch lit little fires in her belly, along her skin, burning through the lingering cold of wet and shock. And looking up at him, into the deep blue pools of his eyes, she knew she didn't want to walk away from this, didn't want to walk away from him, even if they had no future. So she leaned forward, sliding a hand around his nape to pull him close enough that his lips were a whisper away from hers. 'Then take me.'

"His breath shuddered out, the warmth of it fanning across her mouth, and Lilah closed the distance.

"Cooper didn't move. His body, pressed so close to hers, hummed with leashed tension.

"'Please, Cooper. I need you to touch me.' She needed this. Needed him. But that was something neither of them was ready to hear.

"*Please don't make me beg.*

"His hands came up, tunneled into her hair as he pulled back to look into her eyes. 'Lilah.' That was all he said. Part question. Part apology. Part something else. And then his mouth was on hers, and she stopped asking the questions, stopped thinking entirely because she could only feel."

They were a rapt and attentive audience, something Autumn usually enjoyed. Not even the faint, omnipresent click clacking of knitting needles interrupted her reading. She did her utmost to divorce herself from the fact that these were her words, immersing herself in the story. There was no stopping the blush that crept up her neck and cheeks, and Autumn cursed her red-head's complexion. But her voice wavered only a little, even when her body flushed with remembered heat as she reached Lilah and Cooper's climax.

"His fingers laced with hers, an anchor as that magnificent body stroked into hers with endless, exquisite patience. He drove her up, a long, slow climb that destroyed her sense of anything but the glorious pleasure building between them. Desperation grew as he kept them there, on that narrow edge, for what felt like hours, maybe days. Lilah shut her eyes, wrapping her legs tighter around his hips, trying to pull him deeper.

"'Stay with me,' Cooper rasped.

"But she was too lost to sensation, reaching too hard for that final peak to respond.

"'Lilah, I need you with me.' There was a vulnerability beneath the strain in his voice, and that pulled her back. 'With me,' he ordered. 'Come with me.'

"Opening her eyes, she stared into his. And it was Cooper—her Cooper—looking back at last. The only man she'd ever fully trusted. So she let go, crying out as waves of rippling pleasure pulled him over with her."

Around the room, women were fanning themselves with their ereaders or paperbacks.

"Lord have mercy! Now *that* is a love scene," Miss Delia declared.

Echoes of agreement peppered the room.

"So much more meaning in the context of the story," Miss Maudie Bell said. "But still just lovely on its own."

So far so good. Maybe nobody had cottoned to the fact that she'd written about her and Judd. As the senior ladies took over discussion, debating whether Cooper should have stayed or gone, Autumn struggled to get her own reaction under control. The room was two shades under a hundred degrees on the best of days, and today she felt like it was a bikram book club. She didn't dare chance a look at Nash, not wanting to see either his embarrassment or smirk if he'd gleaned what she'd actually been reading.

"Cooper obviously did what needed doing for the purposes of the story," Miss Betty insisted. "But what I really want to know, Autumn dear, is whether Judd's as good in bed as he is on paper."

IT WAS OFFICIAL. Judd hated being Chief of Police.

He'd wanted the power and control that went with it, believing he'd be able to leverage that, when and if Jebediah got out of prison, to better protect Autumn. But his being Chief hadn't stopped anything, and all the other responsibilities of the job were keeping him from being front and center on the investigation himself. He was having to delegate the search, as well as her protection, so he could play nice with the powers that be. And, oh goody, he had a meeting with those powers that be tomorrow for a performance review. After two weeks on the job. That didn't bode well.

He knew he was a good cop, but he was coming to understand he was a shit politician, and he'd absolutely underestimated how much of the job was exactly that. Robert had made it look easy. After that many years in the position, that wasn't surprising. Judd knew he was under additional scrutiny because of his interim status. But Jesus, couldn't they just let him alone to do his damned job?

Armed with a big ass bag of takeout from the Lucky Palace and a six pack of beer, he tucked the folder full of research from his officers under one arm. He'd comb through all of it after dinner and maybe something would spark for a new direction to try. But first he wanted to kiss his woman and pop open one of those beers. In that order.

His first sight of her, leaning one elbow on the kitchen island, fiery hair spilling down her back as she lifted a glass of wine to her lips, hit him in the gut and the heart. Knowing she was here, that she wasn't leaving at the end of the night, that she'd be going to sleep in his bed, in his arms, made the big, rambling monstrosity of a house the home he'd been missing. Because she was his home. He'd wasted way too many damned years denying it.

"—sure you don't want a glass of wine or a beer?"

"Not while on duty," Nash said. "Besides, I'm pretty sure you need it more than I do after that ambush."

Judd snapped out of his momentary reverie and felt the headache behind his eyes ratchet up a few notches. "What ambush? What happened?"

Autumn shifted to face him and offered wan smile. "The Casserole Patrol happened. Well, the entire seniors book club, really, but they were the ring leaders. Don't let Nash be all modest. He bravely waded in to rescue me from a mob of nosy blue hairs."

"My ass will recover." He winced. "Eventually."

No bodily harm. No malicious harassment. At least not the kind Judd had been prepared for. He relaxed a fraction, noting the bottle at her elbow was already half down. "Can somebody please start making sense?"

She took another hefty sip of wine. "I'll tell you all about it. But we should let Nash get on out of here. He's maxed out his mortification quotient for the day. God knows, I have."

"Sure. Thanks for all this."

"Anytime. See you later, Autumn."

As Nash let himself out the door, Judd closed in on Autumn, caging her in on her barstool. "Am I going to need alcohol for this story?"

"Undoubtedly."

Nodding, he carefully plucked the glass from her fingers and set it aside. "Noted. I just need this first."

She flowed into him, her hands snaking up around his shoulders, her mouth opening beneath his. He tasted the boldness of the wine and the indefinable something else that was just her. Everything in him that had been wound tight eased loose. She was okay, she was still here, she still wanted him. Everything else came second to that.

He could have chased the lust that curled through them both, boosting her up and carrying her up to bed, where they could both work off the frustrations of the day. But that was just a delay tactic. Better to get that beer and get the details out there. There'd be time to lose themselves later.

On a sigh, he pulled back, pressing his brow to hers. "Missed you today."

"Mmm, missed you, too."

"Does it make me a Neanderthal if I say I really liked coming home to you?"

"Only if you suddenly expect me to turn into a 1950s housewife."

"I came bearing Chinese takeout."

"Oh excellent. Humiliation goes so well with fried rice and wantons."

Brows up, Judd studied her face, deciding some of that flush was from the wine instead of him. "You're already feeling that wine, aren't you?"

"Better the wine than the embarrassment. Which was entirely the point."

"That bad?"

"Worse." She shuddered and picked up her glass.

At this point, he was almost afraid to hear the full story. The Casserole Patrol was legendary for its nosiness, and given it was book club day and she'd recently been outed as an author, he could imagine the direction this tale would take.

"Then let's see about getting some food in you before you suck down much more of that wine. You don't want to go to work with a hangover tomorrow."

He made a sweep of the house under the auspices of changing clothes and stowing his firearm. Once the doors were locked and the alarm reset, he went about fixing them both plates of food.

"Before I deep dive into tales of octogenarian terror, how was your day?"

"Meh. Less time spent on the investigation than I wanted. I brought home some stuff my officers put together, but I don't actually expect it to be more than dead ends. I want this to be your dad so I have an excuse to put him away again. But I can't make all the pieces fit. Some of them do, but some don't. And if this is all meant to be some revenge is best served cold shit, then what's the end game? And why would somebody be willing to do his dirty work for all this? He didn't have money going into prison, and he hasn't managed to find a job since he got out. Beyond all that…I cannot come up with any logical way he could have found out about your alter ego. I wish I had some ideas about who else stands to benefit from all this, but right now, I just don't."

As he slid onto the stool beside her, she

tipped her head to his shoulder. "You'll figure it out."

"That's it? You're not freaked out by the fact that there's a strong possibility that somebody other than your dad is out there doing this stuff?" He sure as hell was because that meant there was a threat he hadn't seen coming, and what did that say about him?

"I've had sufficient wine that whatever level of freak out is very, very muted. But either way, I trust you. I believe in your abilities as an investigator. And if it's not my dad, then you probably need to be interrogating me about other stuff." She straightened on the stool, swayed a little. "But maybe when I'm a bit more sober."

"Noted. So what happened at book club?"

She stuffed a wanton in her mouth and washed it down with more wine. "As you might surmise, they knew about Harper."

"Did they hassle you about it?" He wasn't sure exactly what he'd do to a bunch of old women, but he'd come up with something.

"Not the way you're thinking. They were extremely supportive and enthusiastic fans. They had me do a reading from *Forged In Blood.* That first love scene. So, of course, I'm already fire engine red, but I get through it. And they're discussing the plot and character arc and a lot of the same kinds of stuff we discuss no matter what book we're reading."

That didn't sound *so* bad to him. "Clearly, this isn't the end of the story."

"No, it is not." She shoveled in some pork fried rice and drained the last of the glass for fortification. "And *then* they asked if real life you was as good in bed as you were on paper."

Judd choked on his egg roll.

"Oh yeah. Yeah, they went there. Because it's every bit as obvious as I feared to anybody who was around back in the day that Lilah and Cooper are us."

"You didn't actually *answer* them, did you?"

"Of course not! I'm pretty sure I just sat there looking like a gasping fish, while they continued the discussion without my contributing a word. At least until Nash waded in to rescue me. God love him."

Shoving her plate aside, she pressed her face to the bar. "I never wanted this to get out. Which is stupid to even say when I wrote it. But when I put it out there, I honestly never thought anyone from Wishful would ever stumble onto them. And it never occurred to me that my pen name would get publicly out-ed." She heaved a sigh. "My fault. I made as-sumptions and trusted too much in the flimsy protection of a pseudonym. In truth, I brought this on myself."

A part of him agreed, not that he was foolish enough to admit it out loud. He didn't have a problem with the romance or the graphic sex. But he didn't understand why she'd risked putting so much of the truth out there, when they'd both spent so much time and effort trying to put it behind them.

"Why did you write it? I mean, I know you said you needed to put the truth somewhere, to try to get me out of your system. But why the rest of it? Why did you write about what happened to us? Why not just take who we are and plunk us down into some other story?"

She looked at him over a forkful of Mongolian beef. "Do you really think we'd be who we are without going through that hell?"

He considered the question. Without that defining horror, what would their lives have looked like?

"If Jebediah hadn't shown up that day, you'd have kissed me. Everything would've changed between us. And I would've followed you anywhere, the moment we turned eighteen. My heart condition would've gone undiagnosed for some unknown amount of time. You probably wouldn't be a cop. We'd have been together, probably blissfully happy, but it wouldn't have made for a good story."

"It sounds pretty great to me." It was an alternate version of events he'd never allowed himself to consider.

"To live, maybe. I won't lie and say there's a part of me that doesn't regret all the years we lost. But in terms of the book, it was a no go. Story is all about conflict." She speared more beef and onions.

"But why *that* conflict? It had to be brutal on you to write. God knows, reading it took me back." And it'd been worse, re-experiencing everything from her perspective. He thought he'd known what it'd been like for her. They'd talked about it often enough in the dark hours of the night. But she'd minimized all of it.

"I wrote it out a long time before there was ever a book. My therapist in college suggested it. The night terrors were really bad. I wasn't sleeping for longer than a couple of hours at a time. She had the theory that if I could write it all down, really capture the detail, that I could exorcise it."

He hated thinking about her going through that alone. "Did it work?"

"Not really. Mostly I just had to get used to sleeping without you. It was a rough year." She shrugged, as if that was no big deal. "As to the book...I was trying to work through stuff about you. The day you were shot was the root of all of it." A shadow passed over her face, and she set her fork aside. "I know you're angry, and you have a right to be. It's your story, too, and I put it out there for public consumption."

"I'm not angry."

She just looked at him with her *Really?* face.

"Okay, I'm a little angry," Judd admitted. "It's just that…well, like you said, there's just enough reality that people who were here and re-member will recognize it. But they don't know which parts are true and which are fiction. So there will be people who take the whole thing as largely fact."

Judd paused, beer halfway to his mouth as he ran back through what he'd just said. *They don't know which parts are true and which are fic-tion. So there will be people who take the whole thing largely as fact.*

"The bourbon. You made a thing about the bourbon in *Forged in Blood.* Did you put any-thing else personal in your other books? Any-thing about the knife I'd given you or the fear of small spaces because you'd been locked in as a child?"

"I—yes. The knife got mentioned in my second book. It was a gift from the hero to the heroine who helped him escape a terrorist compound. One of those home-grown, anti-government militia groups. And my heroine in the first *Redemption Ridge* book is claustrophobic because she'd been locked in a box by human traffickers as part of the backstory."

Judd stared at her.

"What? I've got some dark stuff in my head."

"Clearly." He started working his way back though the pieces. "The graffiti at the library said '*I see you.*' We thought it was supposed to be some kind of a threat from your dad but what if it wasn't? What if it literally was an announcement that they see *you*, Autumn, as Harper. They figured out the secret of your identity."

She considered. "I don't know how they would have."

"I mean, the books are popular. That part could have just been chance, a random reader, who was here back when, who remembered what happened to us and recognized it in the first book and put two and two together."

"Okay, so say that's true. Someone read it, figured out who I was. That's well within the realm of possibility given the Casserole Patrol was so quick to jump on it. But why expose me?"

He thought about the protesters. "Maybe someone who disapproved of the subject matter? One of those moralizing pearl clutchers you've talked about?"

Her burst of laugher was a surprise. "I'm sorry, I'm having a hard time imagining any of those women taking this kind of action or going to this kind of extreme."

"You assume it's a woman. It's not so far fetched that a guy could also disapprove. Your father would. We know that."

"Except it seems highly unlikely that a guy just *happened* to stumble across the book—a romance—and read it, if it's something he disapproves of. Why be looking in the first place?"

"I don't know, but chase the thread for a minute. They figured out who you are, enough to believe everything you wrote in that first book as truth and make some major assumptions that they know *you* as a person. There was enough detail in that first book alone that someone could reasonably have plenty of fodder for the same kind of tactics your dad would have used to harass you. If they knew he was getting out of prison, it would be a very convenient misdirect. One I fell for hook, line, and sinker."

"That's a lot of supposition without a motive. Who would want to harass me like that?"

Judd met her eyes. "That is the million dollar question."

CHAPTER 16

"The protestors are back." Livia brought the news, along with a pizza from Speakeasy for their lunch.

Autumn dropped her head in her hands. "Of course they are."

Livia set the pie aside and rubbed her shoulders. "At least Mitzi probably hasn't seen them yet."

"I don't know that it matters. There's only so much of this she's going to take."

"It's not your fault."

"Except it's my name on those signs." She

exhaled a slow breath. "I'm going to pull a Scarlett O'Hara and think about it tomorrow. I've got enough on my mind today." Like who, besides her father, would want to torment her and why.

Livia frowned. "You look like you're thinking deep thoughts."

"I don't know about deep, but certainly disturbing."

"Care to share?"

Autumn glanced around. It was the early afternoon lull before school got out. "Can you think of anybody who really dislikes me?"

"You mean other than Mitzi?"

Autumn tried to imagine the older woman vandalizing the library in the name of making her look bad and couldn't make it play. "Yeah." Checking again for anyone nearby, she lowered her voice and explained Judd's latest theory. "I just…can't quite wrap my brain around a motive that works."

Livia tapped her fingers, gnawing on her lip as she considered. "Okay, here's another theory.

It's kinda out there, but roll with it. Someone figures out your secret identity. The how doesn't necessarily matter, but they figure it out. It was a serious *secret,* one you didn't tell anyone. And it is, arguably, part of the real you, not the you that's your public persona, as it were."

"Okay, I'm with you so far."

"You and I have had conversations before about how a lot of women struggle with being seen as who they actually are, rather than whatever shallow, socialized roles dictate and that, because of that, arguably the best romance heroes truly *see* the heroine for who she is and that's what makes him Mr. Right For Her. It's that huge moment of romantic fulfillment for readers, when the hero sees the real her and realizes that she is his perfect match. What if this is…some kind of subversion of that?"

"How do you mean?"

"Like…someone read your book, figured out who you are, and fixated on who they believe you to be and decided you're Miss Right for them? Like...crazy stalker fan."

"That is...an incredible leap and beyond disturbing." Before all this had started, she'd been researching stalkers for a future book idea. The idea that one of those psychos had latched onto her because of her work left her cold. "But maybe it makes a sick kind of sense. There was the vandalism. The totally inappropriate grand gesture of 'I see you.' If all this stuff was meant to get my attention, it didn't work. At least, not the way it was intended. All of it just pushed me closer to Judd. It finally pushed us over the line from friends to something more. The thing with the picture happened right after that. The knife was stabbed through Judd. What if it wasn't a reference to the shooting like we thought? What if it's symbolic of the idea that this person finds him to be a threat because they view him as a rival?"

Livia's eyes widened. "And then the whole locking you in a closet at Judd's house. Maybe that was meant to make him look bad. Like, hey see, I got to you here. He's not worthy."

Autumn eased back onto a stool, her knees going to jelly. "Oh, I don't like this. I don't like it all. It's creepy as hell. Maybe we're over-reaching with this. Maybe it's a Your Brain On Fiction cautionary infomercial."

"I don't know. But it seems worth mentioning to Judd."

"Yeah. Yeah, I'll tell him tonight."

A throat cleared behind her. "Autumn, can I see you in my office, please?"

She turned to find Mitzi looking expectantly over her bifocals.

Called into the boss's office. Nothing good can come of this. Stomach twisting into knots, she pasted on a confident smile for the library director. "Of course."

Miming wide eyes at Livia, who widened hers back and shrugged, Autumn followed the older woman, noting that her tight, iron gray curls didn't even vibrate as they went up the stairs. She shut the door behind them, and the sound of the latch struck Autumn with the finality of a cage door closing.

Don't make assumptions. Just breathe.

"I'll get straight to the point. Word has gotten around about your…extra-curricular employment."

No sense in denying the obvious. Better to meet the problem head on. "I know. And I apologize for that. I never intended for my pen name to be known. If it's caused you any awkward questions from patrons, I'm really sorry, but I'm sure everything will die down pretty quickly." *I hope.*

"I'm not so sure it will. You've seen today's protesters?"

Autumn held in a wince. "It's just gossip. Pretty soon, someone will do something else scandalous, and it'll be old news."

Mitzi heaved a put-upon sigh, folding her hands on the desk blotter in a power play that reminded Autumn of a Catholic school headmistress. "This library is a venerable institution of Wishful. Its employees are expected to comport themselves with a certain level of dignity, class, and morality."

Autumn's gut twisted again. "I've been nothing but professional since the moment I walked through this door to work here. What goes on outside work hours or in my personal life has no bearing on the job."

"I'm afraid quite a few people feel that it does."

"Excuse me?"

Mitzi reached for a sheaf of papers. "This is a petition calling for your removal as head librarian on the grounds of being an immoral influence."

Autumn stared at her. "You can't be serious. What have I done in the context of this job that's immoral?"

"You wrote what's tantamount to pornography."

Insult mixed with the first traces of panic, and Autumn struggled to remain objective. "Oh please. It's romance, and it's tame compared to a lot of what's popular since *Fifty*

Shades came out. Tamer even than a lot of what's on our shelves. And yes, I wrote it, but under a pen name, which I told no one. I have not pushed the books. I haven't added them to our catalog. I haven't promoted them in any way locally. This has nothing to do with my job here."

"Except there was that dreadful incident with those...excerpts."

"Which I told you I didn't do."

Mitzi ignored that. "The public is concerned about your access to children."

"Oh bullshit. I've never made age inappropriate recommendations about books in my life." Her gaze dropped to the top signature. Clarice Hopper Morris. Of *course* she'd be behind this. She'd been making Autumn's life a living hell since elementary school. "Mitzi have you even read my books? Do you even know what they're objecting to?"

The library director's lips pinched in disapproval. "I don't need to read them. They're inappropriate. The entire genre is inappropriate.

There's nothing about it that's noble or pure or praiseworthy."

Because, of course, she was one of the sainted pearl clutchers who wanted to pretend sex didn't exist. "That's censorship, and as a librarian, you ought to be ashamed of yourself for even suggesting it."

Autumn wished she could take the words back the moment they fell from her lips.

Before she could apologize, Mitzi's eyes narrowed. "Miss Buchanan, this library has been under dire financial strain for some time. You've been a good employee for many years, and I've done what I can to keep you on as long as possible. But the fact remains that I cannot, in good conscience, ignore the wishes of the public. I'm sorry to have to do this in light of your difficult circumstances, but I have to let you go."

The knife of betrayal slid in so fast, she didn't even have a chance to feel the pain. "You're ignoring my years of service to this library, from the time I was seventeen, up to now, and firing me for something that has no direct bearing on my job?"

"I'm doing what I have to do."

Autumn rose, hands curled into fists. "You're being weak and caving to the opinions of those who have nothing better to do than try to ruin other people's lives over something they don't know or understand. I've just lost everything I own and now you're taking away my primary source of income. So thanks for that. And good luck sleeping at night."

She stalked out, slamming the door behind her. Startled patrons looked up as she made her way down the stairs.

Livia waited at the bottom. "What happened?"

"I'm fired."

"*What?*"

"There was a petition. I am apparently an immoral influence, who cannot be trusted around children."

"That's ludicrous! She can't do that!"

"Unfortunately, Mississippi is a no cause

firing state. She can do anything she wants." She shoved both hands through her hair, feeling the first traces of panic begin to leak through the fury. She needed to be far, far away before the full implications sank in. "I'm getting out of here."

"But what about the no bodyguard thing?"

Most of the department was in Jackson for a training today. It wasn't ideal, but it wasn't as if she could just stay here. "I'll go straight to the police station. It's only a few blocks. I'll be fine."

She held it together long enough to pack her small box of stuff. A decade of giving her all to this job and her things fit into a carton not even half the size of a banker's box. How sad was that? She promised Livia she'd call later and made her escape. As she backed out the swinging front door—still waiting to have the glass replaced—she juggled the box to one side and dug one-handed for her phone to text Judd and let him know she was coming.

"Miss Buchanan, do you have any comment on your father's release?"

"Miss Buchanan, is it true you based Cooper Danes on the now current Chief of Police?"

"How do you feel about having your pen name exposed?"

Autumn froze as questions peppered her from all sides. Microphones and cameras were shoved in her face as the throngs descended on her. The air in her lungs seemed to harden, along with the muscles in her legs. She couldn't make herself go back into the library and couldn't seem to force herself to push forward through the mass of reporters. Flashbacks to the trial flickered through her mind. She started to shake.

"Autumn, are you and the Chief now an item?"

"Miss Buchanan, have you and your father reconciled?"

An arm wrapped around her and a taller body urged hers forward. "Let's go," a low, gravely voice murmured.

Autumn froze. Slowly, she turned her head to look over her shoulder in disbelief. It was

Jebediah with an arm around her. Jebediah trying to lead her.

"Mr. Buchanan, do you believe your time served is sufficient recompense for nearly killing your daughter's lover?"

She stumbled back. "What are you doing?"

"Trying to get you through this mob."

She didn't know what to think about that, didn't know what to feel about the fact that he was *here,* at her place of employment—former—in direct violation of the restraining order. What did he want?

Dimly, she was aware of the sudden silence as cameras and recorders rolled. "I'm not going anywhere with you."

Irritation flickered over his gaunt face. Irritation, but not the rage she'd learned to expect as a child. "Must you always defy me?"

He sounded tired and looked bone weary, likely from whatever cancer was eating away at him. For a fleeting instant, she thought about what he'd said to Judd, that he'd come back to make amends with her. And then she couldn't think because the mob of reporters pressed closer, sucking up all the oxygen.

"You aren't supposed to be anywhere near me." She said it as much to the media as her father.

"Be reasonable, girl." Jebediah reached out, trying to take her arm.

Autumn flinched back from the touch, her mind's eye seeing a fist where there was none.

"Stay away from her!" Another, taller man in a hooded jacket was suddenly between her and her father, hands curled to fists.

Jebediah stepped back, lifting his palms in surrender.

Her rescuer turned, one hand shoving glasses back up the bridge of his nose. "Are you okay?"

"I..." She didn't know what she was. The crush of people was suffocating and the confrontation with her father had her vibrating with tension. She couldn't think, could barely breathe.

Beneath the shaded bill of a baseball cap,

Mark's eyes softened a fraction in sympathy as he looked at her, then hardened again as he shouted at the gaggle of reporters. "Back off, all of you." His voice rang with an authority she'd never heard from him before. It made him seem somehow bigger, more powerful than she'd always seen him. Autumn wondered if this was his lecture voice. In the face of it, the crowd did, indeed, back up a few paces.

Jebediah held his ground, watching with an inscrutable expression. But he said nothing more, made no move to approach her again.

Gently, Mark cupped a hand beneath her elbow. "Are you coming or going?"

"Going. Definitely going."

"Okay then. Let's get out of here."

He led her toward the parking lot. None of the assembled reporters seemed willing to intervene. Thank God, for small favors.

"Where's your car?"

"I don't have it with me. Judd dropped me off at work this morning."

"I'll drive you. Where do you need to go?"

"Police station." She needed to get to Judd.

"Okay." Mark unlocked his older model Explorer and immediately started tossing piles of papers from the front seat to the back. "Excuse the mess. I don't often have passengers." He grabbed the camera bag and tossed it into the backseat.

"It's no problem. I appreciate the rescue." The words came out on autopilot. She looked back toward the building to see if Jebediah was there or if the reporters had followed. If they'd press her again, but so far, they'd held back. Hand on the door, she braced herself for the moment the seat was empty, then vaulted inside.

"You've got your hands full. I'll just get the seatbelt."

"I—oh, thanks." As he leaned over her, she tried to work up some semblance of a smile. "I really appreciate the rescue."

"No problem. We were both in the right place at the right time."

At the sharp stab of pain in her arm, Autumn yelped. She looked down to see a hypodermic needle sticking through her sleeve. As the seatbelt clicked, her gaze snapped back up to Mark's. "What the…?"

"Sorry about this, but you just weren't cooperating."

JUDD ROLLED HIS SHOULDERS, trying to release some tension before he walked into the conference room. This wasn't the sort of performance review he was used to. Likely they wouldn't be going over his cases, his close rate. He hadn't even been in the job long enough for there to be a follow through conviction rate based on his investigations. Because investigations were no longer a primary focus of his job. Not directly.

Mayor Sandra Crawford sat at the head of the table, flanked on either side by the five City Council members and her personal assistant, Avery. They'd been in much the same configuration when he'd been brought in two weeks ago to take the job. His shoulders tightened up again because they looked every bit as grave now. This didn't look good.

Understanding his role in all of this, Judd sat in the remaining chair at the opposite end of the table from Sandra, facing both her and the Council.

"Chief Hamilton, thank you for joining us," Sandra began.

The radio at his shoulder crackled. With one ear, he listened to the call from dispatch about the fender bender on Lawson Street, heard Nash take it.

"Could you turn that off, please?" Sandra asked.

That was tantamount to being blind to what was going on in his town. Judd didn't like it. But conscious of the need to play nice here, he hit the call button on the handset at his shoulder and hailed his dispatcher. "Inez, I'm going radio silent. If anybody needs me, I'm at City Hall for a meeting."

"Got it, Chief."

Judd switched the radio off and immediately felt the weight of silence descend on the room.

"Thank you. Let's get started."

They began with the budget. Again.

"It's been an expensive few weeks," Hank van Buren observed. "Totaled cruiser, training courses, the cost of bringing on reserve officers while most of the department was attending the training. And I see here another equipment request?"

"First, what you have in your hands is an inventory of the department's equipment, outlining the condition of our resources and making recommendations about the extent and order of replacement as the budget allows in the future." It had been a project he'd assigned to the rookie since Raines was riding the desk with his injuries. "It's for information purposes. Second, the training for my officers was long overdue. We are, thankfully, generally a sleepy town, but that's no excuse for ignorance of current investigative techniques. We hope they aren't called into practice, but in the event that they are, we ought to be prepared to do the job to the best of our abilities. And third, I had no way of knowing Officer Raines would panic when faced with a cow in the road. The loss of the cruiser is unfortunate, as are his injuries, since it leaves us short-staffed on patrol duties, but it is what it is."

"When you were appointed to this position, you were informed that the position was probationary, pending review of your performance." Connie Lockwood folded her hands. "How do you feel that performance has been?"

For fuck's sake, really?

"I have never given this department anything but my all, as I believe my record indicates."

"What about the execution of your duties as pertains to Jebediah Buchanan?" Ed Falk asked.

Judd fought to keep his hands from clenching on the table. "My duty pertaining to Jebediah Buchanan, or any convicted felon released back into our community, is to make certain they cause no harm or disruption to the community, most especially the victims impacted by that release."

"A noble intention, but surely you're somewhat biased in this particular case," Hank suggested.

"Bias has nothing to do with the facts."

"Doesn't it? Does it really justify round-the-clock guard of one person, when the department is, as you've already indicated, short-staffed?"

"Mr. Van Buren, if someone tried to murder your wife and was then released from prison, coincidentally the same day your house burned to the ground, I assure you, I'd be arranging a round-the-clock guard for her as well."

"But you haven't managed to tie Jebediah Buchanan to the fire," Grace Handeford said.

"The investigation is ongoing and not a matter of public record. There's been a documented string of harassment aimed at Autumn since Jebediah's release. And in case you missed it, the fire also burned the home of another Wishful resident. There's no way of knowing how escalation could affect others in town, so my use of departmental resources is not just for Autumn."

"How many officers are assigned to Miss Buchanan today?" Hank asked.

"None."

"Not even with all the reporters roaming town?"

Reporters? How the hell had he not known the press was here? Not wanting to be caught unaware of what was going on in his town he skated the edge of a lie. "Against my better judgment, no. While the press is a definite nuisance, they generally do not justify protective custody."

Hank scribbled something on his legal pad.

In Judd's pocket, his phone vibrated. Autumn letting him know about the reporters? Were they bothering her at the library? He itched to check but knew better than to pull the phone out in the middle of all this.

"What about the reason they're in town to begin with?" Connie asked. "These books she wrote." Her tone dripped with contempt.

Judd was willing to bet she was one of the offended pearl clutchers Autumn talked about. "That has no bearing on today's proceedings."

"No?" She feigned surprise. "The public is making some interesting assumptions about you based on what she wrote."

Oh, for the love of... Judd knew his tone had chilled to arctic. "Fiction has no bearing on my ability to do my job."

"I'm afraid I disagree. It impacts how the public perceives you, and this position is one that demands respect."

Judd ground his teeth. "With all due respect, *ma'am,* that's ludicrous. My record with this department stands. My actions, both as an officer and as Chief of Police, have been exemplary." He'd stand by that statement with his hand on a stack of Bibles.

Sandra held up a hand. "Okay, I think we're veering a little off topic here."

"Respectfully, madam Mayor, what is the

topic? Why am I here? Are you actually dissatisfied with the performance of my duties?"

"We simply have concerns," she said easily. "Chief Curry had reservations about our putting you in this position. We're merely exploring those. We have continued with the nationwide search and have two other candidates for the permanent position. The first was interviewed last week and the second should be arriving any minute now."

That was news to Judd. But he'd been far too occupied with the actual execution of the job to concern himself much with the politics.

"We're just gathering information in order to make a final decision in short order," Ed added.

So his tenure as Chief might be drawing to a close? Judd couldn't deny the sense of relief he felt at that. He didn't want the job anymore, not beyond closing out this case, seeing Autumn safe. But he couldn't have his authority ripped away just yet.

Cam, the youngest Councilman and Sandra's son, finally spoke. "You've got to admit, things have been rather personal the last few weeks."

"We live in a town of five thousand people. There's no such thing as doing the job here without getting personal. Getting personal is half of what allows me to do the job well. It's what allows you to do your jobs. People and their connection to each other are a huge part of what makes Wishful what it is. That's exactly what your wife-to-be is always preaching."

"We're just concerned that being so personally involved limits your objectivity," Grace said.

"Have there been complaints about my performance?" Judd demanded. "Documentation that I have somehow shirked my duties?" He knew his tone had slid past respect and well into belligerence, but he couldn't seem to stop it. He had zero tolerance for anyone questioning his integrity.

"We're just trying to—"

The door flew open, effectively cutting

Sandra off. Judd automatically surged to his feet as Nash burst into the room.

"Couldn't get you on the phone."

"What's going on?"

"Someone took Autumn."

Judd's blood turned to ice, the sharp shards of it stabbing through his whole body. "Talk and talk fast."

"I went by the library after my last call, just to check on her. I saw the protesters and the press. Livia said she left over an hour ago, planning to go straight to the station. But she never got there. I talked to the reporters. They said she had a confrontation with her father, then left with another man."

Hanging on to the last bit of his control, Judd managed, "Who?"

"We don't know yet. There's video footage of the confrontation, but he was careful. Hood up. Nobody caught his face."

There was something else. Judd could see it in the tense line of his jaw. "What else?"

"We have a witness who claims the guy injected her with something before he drove off."

The strength went out of Judd's legs, almost dropping him to his knees.

I shouldn't have let her go to work on her own. I shouldn't have taken her protective detail off. A dozen other recriminations rang in his head. But they didn't matter. Only action mattered. Because the son of a bitch had taken her.

Rage burned through the paralyzing ice.

Turning back to the City Council he said, "The personal's interfering with my objectivity, huh?"

A few of them had the grace to look abashed.

"I'm done here. You do whatever the fuck you need to do about the job. I don't care anymore. Because I will go to hell itself to bring her back, with or without the badge."

He stalked out with barely a glance at the cool-eyed stranger in the hall. Autumn was in danger and the clock was ticking on finding her alive.

"Where's the witness now?"

"At the station." Nash hurried to keep up as Judd all but bolted down the stairs. "There's one more thing you should know."

"What?"

"The witness is Jebediah Buchanan."

CHAPTER 17

Autumn woke slow and queasy, a situation not at all helped by the full rumble in her head or the general rocking of the bed. She tried to moan at Boudreaux to settle down already, that it wasn't time to play, especially not with this hangover she'd been utterly unprepared for, but all she managed was a faint wheeze of sound. Her limbs felt heavy and stiff, like she'd fallen asleep in some awkward position. What the hell had happened?

There'd been that awful reading at the senior center and all the invasive questions about her love life. That had merited all the wine. But…no, she'd eaten. She'd had fluids. That was…yesterday?

Something splashed on her face and began to cool in the breeze.

Breeze?

Fighting through the cotton of her brain, Autumn forced her eyes open to slits. At first they refused to focus, too glued together by the remnants of the night to open all the way. It was daylight, and she was…where the hell was she? Outside. A brilliant blue sky stretched out above, and she could feel the heat of the sun beating down on her fair skin. The rocking wasn't Boudreaux turning infinite circles to get comfy on the bed. It was a boat. She was in a boat.

What the hell?

She struggled to sit up but found she couldn't move properly, so she applied all her concentration to getting her eyes the rest of the way open.

She was slumped on the floor of an aluminum boat, toward the bow. A man perched on the seat at the stern, steering the outboard motor. Not Judd. A cap covered his head and sunglasses obscured part of his face. He wore a dark hoodie. Why was he wearing a hoodie when it was still hot out?

Gradually memory filtered in. The library. Getting fired. The protesters. The crush of reporters. Her father.

She must've made some noise because the driver looked toward her.

"Oh good, you're awake. I was getting a little worried. I estimated what you weigh, so I had to guess at the dosage. I think I went over a little."

Dosage? Her throat was dry as the Sahara as she rasped, "Mark?"

"We're well away from the reporters and your father, in case you were worried. I'm just sorry I didn't get to you sooner. I never intended that Jebediah should have the chance to lay a hand on you." His mouth pressed into a grim line.

What kind of alternate reality had she fallen into? Had she hit her head? Was she dreaming?

The pinch and prickle in her hands and feet as she attempted to wiggle them proved she was very much awake. So what the hell was she doing here with Mark Caulfield?

"What...? I don't...understand."

"That, sadly, has been abundantly clear. I tried to be subtle. Really, I did. Everything I've done was to show you that I know you, Autumn. I see who you really are. But none of the subtlety worked to properly get your attention, so I'm taking you to the compound. Or what's left of it."

"What are you talking about?"

"Oh, you don't have to play coy with me. I figured it out, you see. I figured all of it out. It was fate, really. I don't normally research anything so recent as what happened to you, but I stumbled across a news article from back then and I saw your picture. You were so lovely. Fresh faced with those haunted eyes. And that was no comparison to what you've grown into."

The look of profound adoration made her skin crawl.

Somewhere beneath the smothering sensation of whatever drug he'd shot her up with, panic was trying to work its way to the surface. She used that energy to continue flexing and rolling her limbs. He hadn't bound her.

"So I dug deeper, did more research. I pulled everything I could find on your case, the trial. And I decided to come to Wishful to meet you. But I didn't want to seem like some creeper. You needed the chance to get to know me first. And I tell you, Autumn, the more I saw you, the more I fell. You are…simply amazing."

Two years. He'd been trying to get to know her for two years. Had been researching her for *two years*. Like she was some kind of…what? Dissertation topic?

The boat beneath her continued to bounce as he cut across low waves. They had to be on Hope Springs. There was no other body of water close by. But where the hell was he taking her? And what were his plans when they got there? It was an enormous lake. What were the chances they were anywhere near Judd's place?

Judd.

Did he know she'd been taken? Was he looking for her yet?

"But the real kicker was the day I stumbled on your laptop."

"My…laptop?"

"It was a pretty slow day at the library, and I guess you'd brought it with you to write during downtime. You'd gone to help somebody in the stacks and left your screen up. I couldn't help looking. I was curious. And I found your book. It pulled me in from the first word, that personal account of what you'd been through. I don't blame you for putting it out under a pen name or taking a few liberties here or there. It was a powerful story, one I felt privileged to share, to have gotten an inside track on. And I knew the fact that it was right there waiting for me was a sign."

So their theory about a crazy stalker had been half right. But he hadn't just randomly stumbled across the book to read. He'd invaded her privacy to do it.

Bracing her hands on the side of the boat, she pushed herself into a seated position. "A sign of what?"

"Easy there. You'll be woozy for a bit yet."

She put a hand to her head. He wasn't wrong, but the mental fog was lifting.

"Anyway, it was a sign that I was the lucky one, the special one who could see behind the curtain. You've had to put up so many walls since the trial, and I'm the guy who saw beyond them. Because I see *you*, Autumn. The real you. And I've been trying to show you. I brought you the flowers because I knew how important they were to your past. That was just the beginning, but then you had to go and ruin everything by planning to move. I couldn't have that. I worked too hard and too long to get here."

"So you burned down my house?" she croaked.

"I was going to help you with everything after. So you could see how good we could be together. But you turned to the cop. I mean, he had a girlfriend. What were you thinking?"

There was no good answer to that question. Apparently he took her silence as contrition because he continued. "All I wanted to do was prove myself worthy, and you just kept missing all the signs. So it's time for a more direct approach."

"I don't understand. What do you think is going to happen here?"

His gaze slid over her with something like fondness. "You're going to realize that we're perfect for each other."

She opened her mouth to protest, but he just kept going.

"You're not meant to be with that idiot cop who couldn't even keep you safe in his own house."

The trip-hammer beat of her heart was starting to break through the lingering lethargy from the drugs, adrenaline spiking.

Escape. Escape. Escape.

But where could she escape to? How? She

needed more time for the drugs to wear off and maybe, maybe she could leap out and swim to shore. Maybe she could capsize the boat.

Keep him talking.

"That was you?"

"Yes. I'm sorry about that. I know you were scared. I knew you wouldn't be in there very long, and I had to make my point."

Autumn didn't want to ask what his point had been. He'd ticked enough boxes on the crazy stalker list for her already.

"You said we were going to the compound."

"Yep. Took me a while to figure out what you'd based it on, but I know I'm right. You'll see."

Looking around, Autumn tried to judge where they were on the lake. She could only assume he was talking about the cult's compound from *Forged In Blood*. But the place had been purely a product of her dark imagination. It wasn't based on anywhere real around here. So where could he possibly have found?

She didn't recognize anything, but they'd

gradually veered closer to shore. Her body trembled with the need to *move,* but she waited, looking for signs of habitation. Certain parts of the lake were more remote and difficult to access from town. Maybe that was why he'd brought them by boat. Or maybe it was because if the alarm had been raised about her disappearance by now, no one would expect them to be casually cruising on the lake.

Maybe she could reason with him. "Mark, I can understand your frustration that I didn't understand."

"It's okay, love. There'll be plenty of time for you to make it up to me."

Her stomach twisted, and she lunged for the side, afraid she'd be sick. The boat rocked, more spray hitting her face.

"Careful there. I told you you'd be woozy."

Curling her hands around the edge of the boat, she looked back at him. "I'm sorry, Mark, but none of this is ever going to happen. If you truly read my books, you'd know that. I'm in love with Judd. I've always been in love with Judd, and him with me."

Something dark rippled over his face. "He's wrong for you. He walked away from you."

"No. Cooper walked away. That was fiction. Judd has been there for me, always."

"He's not here now," Mark snarled.

"But he will be." She lurched to her feet, doing her best to rock and capsize the boat as she launched herself out of it.

She hit the water with a painful crash. It closed over her head, stealing half the breath from her lungs as she fought her way back to the surface. Breaking through, she sucked in a lungful of air and struggled to make her wooden limbs work. But her clothes and shoes were waterlogged, dragging her under with every attempted stroke toward shore.

It was so far. She'd miscalculated how well she could manage. The burst of energy from fear and adrenaline was already draining out. Was she really going to drown getting away from this lunatic?

Suddenly her head was yanked up and back. She cried out as Mark dragged her closer by her hair. The pain of it bowed her backward, seeking any kind of relief from the screaming of her scalp. She willed herself to fight as he hauled her back, but her limbs were too heavy with water and fatigue, and she couldn't make them work. The metal edge of the boat bit into her chest and belly as he dragged her over the side, and desperate panic threatened to choke her every bit as much as the lake water.

Mark's face was a thundercloud as he stared down at her where she lay, coughing, in a heap at his feet. "I tried, Autumn. I tried to give you the dream, but you don't want a dream. You want a nightmare. So fine. I'll give you a nightmare."

"I've already got a BOLO out on the dark blue SUV, with a description of the guy based on video from the reporters."

As Nash filled him in, Judd dialed Autumn's cell. Straight to voicemail. Checking the friend finder app, she didn't show up at all. Either location services was disabled or the phone itself was off.

"We're gonna find her," Nash insisted.

Yeah, Judd was going to find her, and when he got his hands on the son of a bitch who'd taken her, it was probably better he didn't have a badge. On the short, fast drive to the station, he kept an iron grip on his fear and the rage that threatened to boil over. He had to keep a level head to do the job. Had to divorce himself from the personal so he didn't make a mistake. But the moment he walked in and saw Jebediah waiting in interrogation, his control slipped.

He stalked into the room, slamming the door behind him and looming over the other man's chair, not laying a hand on him, but using his bulk to intimidate. "Start talking. And so help me, if you lie to me right now, you'll wish you'd never been born. What did you see?"

Jebediah didn't cower. He barely so much as

blinked. "I ran into her as she was coming out of the library."

"That was a violation of the restraining order."

"There's been no hearing about the permanent one yet. And are you really going to get on that high horse right now?"

Judd growled. "Don't test me."

"I just wanted to talk to her, but all those reporters were in her face. I tried to get her away from them. Once she realized it was me, she wouldn't go." His pale face twisted into a disapproving scowl. "The girl was always willful."

Judd snarled. "Get to the point."

"Someone else intervened with the reporters. I didn't know him but she seemed to. She went with him willingly enough and got into an SUV. Dark blue Explorer. As I already told the other officer, I didn't get the tag."

"What makes you think she was taken if she got in willingly?"

"He injected her with something."

"All those reporters and cameras around, and none of them caught that?"

"I was at an angle where I could see past the shield of the passenger door. He leaned in to buckle the seatbelt and jabbed her with something."

The tiny, lingering hope that Jebediah was making all this shit up to screw with him died a swift death. He could see the conviction and the worry—unfamiliar as it was—in the other man's eyes.

"And you just stood there and let it happen?"

"He was moving fast and there was a mob of reporters in the damned way. In case you've forgotten, I'm dying."

"Oh, I haven't forgotten. I've been counting the days." Judd straightened, needing some space to keep from taking his frustration out on Jebediah. That wasn't the way. "This was, what? An hour ago or more? Why the hell did you wait to report it? To give your accomplice a chance to get safely away?"

Jebediah pointed one bony finger at him.

"That. That's why. Because you've been bound and determined that I've been behind all of this, assuming I'm working with someone else. I didn't think you'd believe me."

Judd wasn't sure if he did. Except what motive did Jebediah have for admitting he'd violated the restraining order if he didn't see something? Chances were, Judd could use it to get him sent back inside for whatever days or weeks he had left.

"Hate me all you want," Jebediah rasped, "but if you love her like you claim to, you won't waste more time on me."

With no other leads, Judd couldn't risk not believing him. "What did this other guy look like?"

"He was wearing a hooded jacket and a hat. I didn't get a good look at his face."

"Height? Weight?"

"A few inches shorter than you. Thinner, too, but not small."

None of this gave them more than they already had video of.

"Anything else distinguishing?"

Jebediah considered. "Glasses. He was wearing glasses."

Something niggled the back of Judd's brain, but before he could follow the thought, Inez stuck her head through the door. "Livia's here."

He'd likely gotten as much as he was going to out of Jebediah.

Livia stood outside his office, hands knotted, face twisted with concern. "I shouldn't have let her go alone. I should have insisted she wait until we could get someone to go with her."

"Come on into my office. Sit down." It was easier to keep himself leashed with her. "What can you tell me? Why was Autumn even leaving the library?"

"She got fired."

He absorbed that. "Of course she did. Because the last two weeks haven't been shitty enough for her. What else?"

"Before that we were talking about your theory from last night, about who could be doing all this stuff." He listened as she quickly laid it out for him, filling in the possible motive. On a deep breath, she lifted her eyes to his. "I think it might be Mark Caulfield."

"The history professor?"

"Yeah. I know he's had a crush on Autumn forever. I mean, I always thought it was harmless. I'm even the one who told him where to find her that day he wanted to bring her flowers. But they were yellow tulips. She wrote about those in her book."

Caulfield was tall and slim. He wore glasses. He fit the physical description.

Judd yanked open the door. "Somebody get me an address on Mark Caulfield. Contact HR at Wachoxee County Community College, if you have to. He's a professor there."

He pulled out his phone, already searching the college's website for a faculty photo as he marched back into interrogation. As soon as the image loaded, he thrust the phone at Jebediah. "Could this be the guy?"

He stared at the picture something flickering in his eyes. "Maybe. I can't say for sure."

It wasn't the certainty Judd wanted, but it was the best he had to go on. If he was wrong, he'd apologize and buy the guy a beer.

He was already walking back out again when Jebediah called out. "Am I under arrest?"

Judd hesitated, looking back. Jebediah had violated the temporary protection order. But he hadn't hurt Autumn and had put his own ass on the line to report her abduction, even if it had taken him too long to do it. He was still a grumpy, bitter old bastard. But maybe he really had straightened up some in prison and found some remorse. Maybe being on death's door had made him reevaluate his life. If this was his attempt at some kind of atonement, arresting him would be a dick move.

"Not at this time."

Surprise widened those familiar green eyes.

"Don't make me regret it."

In the bullpen, Inez waved a slip of paper. "Got the address, Chief. He lives in the county, out near Chapel Creek, about halfway between

Wishful and Lawley. And he does have a blue Explorer registered to him."

There it was. The piece he'd needed. "Somebody find Judge Carpenter. We need a warrant. Inez, update the BOLO and expand to Tennessee and Arkansas. He hasn't been gone quite long enough to leave the state, but I'm not risking nobody looking if he's actually on the move with her. And call in Reuben. He wasn't on duty until tonight, but we need every ablebody to help. Put in a call to Sheriff Riggs, too. With the damned training day, we've got too few officers to help with a manhunt."

"I can help with that."

Judd turned to see the stranger he'd passed in City Hall. The competition, he realized. He noted the outline of a shoulder holster beneath the suit coat as well as the cowboy boots

"Ethan Greer. U.S. Marshal Service." He flashed his credentials.

"What the hell is a federal marshal doing down here?" Nash asked.

Why *was* a federal marshal applying for a

position as a small town chief of police? "He had business in town."

Something like approval flashed in those steel gray eyes. "I heard about the trouble and wanted to offer whatever assistance I could."

A tall man, if not quite as broad as Judd, Greer exuded a quiet confidence. A man who could handle himself and didn't feel the need to throw around his rank or his weight to prove it.

"I'm not here to step on any toes, Chief Hamilton. I just want to help."

Judd extended a hand. "At this point, Marshal, I'd take help from the devil himself. Welcome aboard." He made introductions to Nash, Inez, and the rookie who was still manning a desk.

"Catch me up."

Judd gave him the overview, outlining the particulars Greer would need to know in order to tap his federal resources and expedite the coordination of agencies, should it become necessary.

"And the victim, Autumn Buchanan, she's your wife? Girlfriend?"

Judd met the marshal's steady gaze. "She's my everything."

Sympathy flashed before Greer nodded. "Then we'll find her. I'll make some calls, get the ball rolling on the regional coordination."

"Got Sheriff Riggs on the phone," Raines announced.

Taking the receiver, Judd locked down his emotions and began to work the case.

CHAPTER 18

He'd drugged her again. It was the only thought Autumn could hold on to as she struggled toward consciousness. Her body ached, and her shoulders were rolled back into an awkward position.

"Wakey, wakey." Something cool and hard brushed her temple at the words.

Inhaling a slow breath, Autumn gathered what energy she could muster and opened her eyes.

Mark—or a very blurry version of him—crouched in front of her. His lips curved, and as his face resolved into a clearer image, she registered the cold fury behind the smile. How had she missed the signs of this in him all this time? She, who prided herself on being so attuned to others' behavior, hadn't seen. Maybe she hadn't wanted to see.

She licked her lips and tried to swallow, but her mouth felt full of cotton.

"Thirsty?" He produced a bottle of water and held it to her lips.

Autumn tried to turn her head away. What if he'd put something in it? She needed to come out of this stupor if she had a chance in hell of getting out of this.

"There's nothing wrong with the water. See?" He tipped it back himself and drank a quarter of the bottle.

When he offered it again, she drank. The lukewarm water tasted flat in that way of something left in the car in the heat of the day. But it helped quench her parched throat and made it a little easier to breathe.

"Now, what do we say?"

As much as she wanted to tell him exactly where to shove it, she knew the right response, knew she couldn't afford to piss him off any further. "Thank you." The rasp of her voice was barely above a whisper.

"There. Was that so hard?" He reached out to push her hair back and there was that cold, hard thing against her temple again.

Cutting her gaze to the side, she saw the gun in his hand and hissed in a breath. "Wh…what is that for?"

"Consider it insurance. As is the rest of this, since you've proved yourself a flight risk." He waved the gun as if to encompass the chair he'd bound her to.

It was only as she looked past him that she realized where they were.

Her blood ran cold.

He'd promised her a nightmare, and he'd delivered. He'd brought her back to where it all began. Or ended.

She'd never come back to her childhood home after the day Judd was shot. Someone else had been the one to retrieve her things. Someone else had dealt with the aftermath of violence. Her gaze skittered over old cabinets and worn vinyl floor, half expecting to still see the bright crimson pool of blood that had marked her memory.

The kitchen wasn't clean. Too many years of dust and decay saw to that. But the evidence of the shooting had been scrubbed away. Objectively, she'd known the bank had repossessed the house. They'd done the clean up, putting just enough effort into repainting the walls in this room, at least. But no one had wanted it. Why would they? The miasma of her father's drunken delusions and hatred had seeped into the very walls. She could feel it, pulsing in the room like some living thing. Or maybe that was her own fear of this place coming out of hibernation.

"I wondered what it would be like for you, coming back here to the scene of the crime, as it were. You painted it so vividly in your book. Do you still see it? Can you smell the blood?"

As if summoned by his words, red washed across the floor in a hideous flashback. Bodies blinked in and out of her vision. Judd. Her father. Her palms went slick with sweat and her chest began to tighten.

Mark strode to a window. Overgrown bushes blocked any view of the sun. There was just enough light that she could tell it hadn't gone down yet, but she had no idea how much time had passed.

"The kitchen table would have been here, right? And your dad would've come in the backdoor there." He gestured with the gun and continued to move, pacing with restless steps to the cased opening leading into the living room. "You and your precious Judd would have been in there on that old, broken down sofa. It's gone now. I guess they got rid of about everything. But whatever. You two would've been holding hands and making goo goo eyes at each other. I could see it so clearly. How, even then, he wasn't man enough for you. But you couldn't see anything else. Still can't."

Turning back to face her, Mark shook his head. "I did my best to show you the way, but you're exactly the faithless whore Jebediah accused you of being."

The words were a familiar lash, one she'd never thought to hear from another soul, and Autumn couldn't stop the instinct to curl in on herself. But with her hands lashed to the back of the chair, the motion was hampered.

"Does he even know what a gift he has in you? How can he, when he's wasted it all these years. He should have worshiped you all this time. It's what you deserve. It's what I wanted for you. For us. But you wouldn't even look my way. You threw the gift of my affection back in my face, tried to run away!" His voice rose to a thunderous pitch, his face mottled with temper as he closed the space between them, the gun in his hand lifted, as if to strike her.

Autumn tensed, barely holding in a whimper as she braced for the blow. In the sudden silence, she dared to look at Mark again. His shoulders heaved, the cruel twist of his mouth somewhere between fury and pain.

"We can't help who we love," she whispered.

He sniffed, nodding as he looked around the room. "Yeah. Yeah you're right. So, I tell you what. Since you love Judd so damned much, I'm gonna give you what you want. I'm gonna bring him here so you two can be together."

Confused, Autumn stared up at him. "What?"

"It seems only fair you should be together for the end. And make no mistake, there will be an end. I'm going to finish what your father started."

"No! Stay away from him!" She exploded into motion, struggling to pull her hands free.

"Silence, bitch!" He pistol whipped her across the face.

The explosion of pain in her temple stole her breath, even before the chair tipped and crashed, cracking her shoulder against the floor. Her vision went white, waves of agony rippling out from her face and shoulder. Of all the abuses she'd endured at her father's hands, she'd never once been struck in the face. Jebediah hadn't believed in leaving marks visible to anyone outside the family. The shock of it stunned her. The little girl she'd been wanted to cry out, but there was no air for screams.

Mark yanked her back up. The movement jostled her shoulder and the stab of a thousand knives all but blinded her. Dislocated. The joint was dislocated. Her thoughts splintered as she realized he was dragging her, chair and all, through the house.

She had to fight. Had to get free. He was going after Judd. But just breathing through the pain felt like more than she could manage.

Then he pulled her through the door to her old room, and she found something worse than the pain. Because something here had changed since she was a child. A brand new hasp and lock had been drilled into the wood of her closet door. The closet of her nightmares.

"No. No, please! Don't!" Sobs boiled up from her throat. She jerked at the ropes, feeling them bite into the flesh of her wrists, even as fresh waves of nausea threatened to take her under. But nothing stopped him from shoving her, still bound, into the closet.

"Don't worry, pretty lady. I'll be back with your lover soon, and then this will all be over."

He slammed the door, and Autumn began to scream.

JUDD POUNDED on Mark Caulfield's door. "Police! Open up!"

No one answered. Nothing moved.

"Fan out," he ordered.

The group of men he'd brought with him broke apart to search the property. Set well back from the road, the house was small but neat, an older ranch style common in Wachoxee County. The landscaping was a bit overgrown but not truly unkempt. Blinds were drawn on all the windows, but Judd could just see through the gap into a living room with a wide screen TV mounted to one wall and the expected bachelor sofa. The community college reported he'd taken some time off today—sick leave. He'd made arrangements for his class load to be covered for several more days. But if he was sick, he wasn't cruising the couch here. All in all, the place was as unprepossessing as its owner, with no real indicators where Mark had gone.

Autumn wasn't here. He felt it in his gut. But he needed inside to search the place. Maybe there'd be a clue where to look next. But that required the damned warrant and nobody had been able to pin down Judge Carpenter. Sheriff Riggs had his people working on obtaining one through a judge in Lawley. Judd needed to keep moving. Stopping meant too much time to think, to imagine all the things the son of a bitch could be doing to her, to review all the ways he'd failed her.

A radio crackled.

"Got a warrant!" Sheriff Riggs shouted.

Judd didn't wait for more. He kicked in the

door, moving inside, gun drawn, aware of Ethan Greer quickly bringing up the rear. They cleared the entryway and living room, moving efficiently through the rest of the three-bedroom home as more deputies followed. As he'd expected, no one was there.

"Holy shit."

Following Ethan's exclamation, Judd poked his head into one of the bedrooms. His own mouth fell open. "Holy shit."

Photographs covered most of one wall. Every single one of Autumn. Autumn at work. Autumn walking around town. Autumn at the diner with friends. Autumn through her living room window, sitting at the desk where Judd assumed she used to write. All moments where she was clearly unaware of being observed.

"I think we just found our smoking gun," Ethan observed.

Judd moved into the room, taking a closer look at the images. "These go back for months."

There were even several pictures of her with him. His image had been methodically destroyed in every one. Some scribbled out with Sharpie. Some sliced up with a knife. Some he'd been cut out of entirely.

Ethan followed his gaze. "That whole theory that you're the competition is starting to look pretty damned promising."

"Jesus. I met the guy, and I didn't suspect a damned thing." Hell, he'd seen the camera bag himself. He'd known Caulfield had a crush on Autumn and he'd even baited the guy. His gut roiled as that sank in. Guilt and a fresh terror. What was he planning to do to her?

A hand settled on his shoulder. "Don't go there, son," Bill said. "Keep your head in the case."

He kept scanning the images. "Wait, he didn't take all of these." Judd reached forward and pulled one from the wall. "My mom took this. And this." He grabbed another. "These were from Autumn's photo albums. We thought they were destroyed when her apartment burned."

"Guess he felt the need to keep some trophies himself. Looks like the photo gallery isn't everything." Ethan nodded toward a box beneath the desk. It was full of more framed photos and mementos from her apartment. Even journals. Not everything, but a damned lot of it. Things she'd be grateful to get back.

Pulling open the desk drawers, he found files. There were newspaper clippings of trial coverage from the local and county papers, as well as the *Clarion Ledger* out of Jackson. Another folder held the full transcript of the trial, with pieces of Autumn's testimony highlighted.

"What the hell is all this?" Ethan asked.

"It's research. On us. On the trial that put Autumn's father away."

But why? The pictures made sense for a stalker. She was the object of his obsession. Maybe he was some kind of true crime fanatic? Or was there something else? Did he think sifting through all this material was going to help him know and understand her better? As if a bunch of strangers' documentation of events could get inside her head?

Ethan lifted a printed stack of double-spaced pages bristling with post-its. "Looks like he dug pretty deep. Even did some interviews."

Something inside Judd went still at the words. "With who?"

Without a word, the marshal passed over the papers. They were transcripts, dated nearly two years before, of an interview at Parchman Prison. With Jebediah.

"The son of a bitch played me." Judd's hand crushed the pages. "I knew better. I knew he couldn't change. But I bought into that whole song and dance about wanting to redeem himself and let him walk. I showed him Caulfield's picture, and he said he couldn't be sure that was the guy. All this time they fucking knew each other." He slammed a fist down on the desk, making the contents jump.

If he'd been thinking clearly, he'd have put a man on Jebediah, to follow him when he left the police station. But with most of his officers in Jackson, he hadn't felt like he could justify it. Not when all signs pointed to Mark Caulfield.

He'd needed as many trained bodies as he could get.

"Slow it down," Ethan urged. "All it proves is Caulfield went to see him. Doesn't establish why. Buchanan may be in the wind, but we know with reasonable certainty that it's Caulfield that has Autumn. So work it through. Where might he have taken her? What's his end game?"

Judd scrubbed both hands over his head. "I don't know. To beat me? To possess her." He didn't want to think about what that could mean. "He couldn't have known she'd be coming out of the library when she did. He couldn't have known she'd be fired today. That makes the abduction a crime of opportunity."

"Okay, so he probably didn't have somewhere ready and waiting for her. It seems a reasonable assumption that he'd know the authorities would get after him in short order, so it makes more sense that he'd go to ground somewhere close. The question is where? Does he own any other property in the area?"

"Without doing a search of county records, I have no idea."

"I'll get someone on it," Sheriff Riggs promised, and moved away to put in the call.

Judd turned back to the wall of photographs, continuing to scan the layered collection, as if the answer would simply jump out at him if he stared long enough.

And in a way, it did.

It was a fairly recent shot, which he knew only because the vegetation had grown so much it almost obscured the house. But he recognized the lines of it. Knew that dingy siding and the sagging eaves.

"I think I know where he took her."

CHAPTER 19

Fear destroyed Autumn's sense of time. She had no idea whether Mark had been gone minutes or hours. Time passed in pulses of pain and ragged breaths as she struggled with the ropes. Her palms were slick—with sweat or blood, she didn't know. But no matter how much she fought, there was no give in her bonds.

Exhausted, she slumped in the chair. All her remaining energy went toward trying to level her breathing and get her blood pressure down.

Panic wouldn't help her. Panic wouldn't help Judd.

She focused on the feel of the chair beneath her. Hard and unforgiving. An anchor as much as a restraint. Letting it ground her, she focused on what she could hear. Nothing but the wheeze of her own breath and the pulse pounding in her ears. But gradually, the frantic gallop of it began to slow. The still, damp air in the closet weighed on her like a wet blanket. She opened her eyes. The enveloping blackness made her chest seize, but she fought her way through it, focused on the faint rim of light edging the door. It wasn't full dark. Not yet. She stared at that sliver until her eyes ached.

Judd was a highly trained cop. There was no way Mark could incapacitate and bring him here. No way he could carry out his threat.

But what if he decides it's not worth bringing him here? What if he just decides to eliminate the competition.

Kevlar didn't protect against a head shot.

No. No, don't go there.

The fact was, Judd wouldn't be alone. He'd be looking for her by now, commanding whatever army he'd managed to drum up in order to knock on every door, overturn every stone. He would find her. Somehow. And he'd stop Mark. They weren't going to have their chance at happiness stolen by someone again.

At first, she thought she'd imagined the shadow passing through the frame of light. Then she heard the scrape of the padlock being moved.

The heart she'd finally managed to slow leapt into a frenetic rhythm. Oh God. He was back. If he was back, did that mean he'd captured Judd?

Though she was terrified of the answer, she called out. "Hello?" Her voice rasped only just above a whisper, throat raw from all the screaming.

She expected Mark to speak. To brag about what he'd done, what he planned to do. She expected the lock to be removed and the door opened wide, so he could gloat. But he said nothing.

What did that mean?

There'd been no sound of an engine, had there? How would she even know? She could barely hear anything over her own panic. What if it wasn't Mark? What if it was someone who could help?

"Hello?" she called, louder this time. "Can you hear me? I need help. Please let me out."

A throat cleared and a man's strained voice answered. "Hold on."

Bang. Bang. Her rescuer swung some heavy object against the lock. *Bang. Bang.*

It took a half dozen more blows before she heard the wood splinter. He wrenched the door open, and Autumn narrowed her eyes against the sudden flood of light. A tall, thin figure filled the doorway, backlit by the sunset shining through the window. Definitely not Mark.

Autumn went weak with relief. She was saved. "Oh my God, thank you."

But the man in the doorway didn't move.

"You're hurt." His voice was low, barely above a whisper, but something in the tone sounded familiar.

"My shoulder's dislocated. If you could just untie me. Please. We need to get out of here before he comes back."

He ducked down, gripping both sides of the chair and dragging her into the light. She almost sobbed with relief, as her rescuer shifted behind her and began working at the knots. After what felt like an eternity, the ropes loosened. With gentle hands, he eased them off the rest of the way.

Autumn couldn't stop the cry of pain as her shoulders released and the dislocated arm fell limply to her side. With her free hand, she reached up, exploring the swollen tissue. It had been too long out of joint. The swelling was too bad to pop it back into place without medical intervention.

As her silent rescuer removed the ropes from her feet, she looked up. The thanks died on her lips when she saw his face.

Her father.

"No," she breathed, jerking back so hard, she nearly fell out of the chair. Only his quick motion saved her from crashing to the floor.

"Stop it, girl." There was the voice she remembered from her childhood.

Old fear hooked its claws into her spine and dug deep. Memories of beatings layered one over another, stripes of scar tissue in her mind.

But his hold on her wasn't bruising.

"I'm not here to hurt you. I'm here to help." It was her father's face, her father's voice, but the words didn't compute.

"Why would you do that?"

"You're my daughter."

That was the most ludicrous excuse he could offer. "You never gave a damn about me."

Something that might've been regret passed over his face. "I know I was hard on you. Harder than I should've been. You were a willful child."

"You did your best to beat that out of me."

"Didn't succeed. You're still willful. Still

reckless. But you don't deserve this. Let me get you out of here. Let me do something right." The desperation in his tone was unfamiliar. She couldn't believe in it.

"How did you even know I was here?"

"I made a guess. Took me a while to place the one in glasses. Knew I'd seen him somewhere before. He had a beard when he came to the prison."

"Mark visited you at Parchman?"

"Yeah. Asked endless questions about what happened here. Claiming he wanted to tell my side of the story. Mostly he wanted to know about you."

"I'm sure you had plenty to say."

Jebediah narrowed his eyes. "You really want to be a chatterbox now? The point is, I'm here now. And if you want to get out of here before the other one comes back, you need to come with me now. I don't know how much longer he'll be gone." He held out his hand.

Could she really trust him? Had he really

come to save her or was this all some kind of ruse?

"Autumn, I was a shitty father, and I ain't got much time to make up for that. Let me help you."

It came down to going with the devil she knew or staying with the devil she didn't. When push came to shove, her father was old, ill, and didn't seem to be armed. Even with her injuries, she could probably overpower him, if necessary. Right now she just needed out of this house.

She put her hand in his. His fingers curled around hers, bony but still strong as they hauled her to her feet. Her legs were all pins and needles and nearly buckled, but her father's arm snaked around her waist, keeping her upright.

"Why didn't you call the police?"

"I didn't much think that boy would believe a thing I had to say. But I went to them anyway. Told what I saw. He went haring off to the guy's house and let me go. Once I figured out who he was, I remembered how obsessed he'd seemed with what happened and thought I'd come here to see." They staggered down the hall together, toward the front door.

"Why didn't you let me out sooner?"

"I parked a ways off and walked in. Didn't want to announce I was here. It took a while. I ain't in good shape. Dying takes a lot out of you."

Was she supposed to feel sympathy about that?

The door was ajar. As he pulled her through it, out into the light, she realized at least a few hours had passed since her abduction. The sun rode just below the tree line.

"My car is about a mile out. There was no good place to leave it nearby."

Autumn remembered. Only one way in, one way out for vehicles to access the property and wide open spaces around all the roads. The woods behind had been too thick for any kind of truck or ATV. That defensive position had suited her father's paranoia growing up.

The idea of hiking that far with her battered body had nausea roiling. The idea of still being here when Mark got back was worse.

"Let's get the hell out of here."

The unmistakable metallic slide and ratchet of a rifle had them both freezing in place.

"Step away from her or I'll drop you where you stand."

"Blue Explorer just behind the house. Do you want us to approach? Over." The report from the unmarked Wachoxee County deputy's SUV was exactly what Judd had been waiting for.

He grabbed the radio. "Negative. If he's in there, we don't want to spook him. I want units in place at either end of Cedarwood Road, blocking egress. Standby." Turning to the motley crew of law enforcement assembled at the staging point, he tapped the map currently spread across the hood of his police cruiser. "We split up into three teams. One led by me, one by Sheriff Riggs, one by Marshal Greer. We'll approach from north, east, and west. As soon as we're within fifty yards of the place, we all go radio silent. I don't want anything tipping this guy off. If he's holed up in there, it could rapidly turn into a hostage situation, and we don't need that. I'll exit first to assess the situation, and the rest of you will converge on my signal."

"Are you sure you're the best one for that?" Bill asked.

"I spent my entire childhood and teenage years sneaking through these woods and around that house. I know how to do it without being seen."

The sheriff angled his head in acknowledgment.

Judd met the gaze of every man gathered. "Let's bring her home."

They split into their teams and moved through the woods that wrapped around the old Buchanan homestead. Daylight was fading fast, but Judd knew these woods, knew this trail like the back of his hand, though he hadn't walked it in years. This had been his and Autumn's place, where they'd met to play and talk and dream. When he got her out of this mess, he was going to spend the rest of his life giving her every single one of those dreams.

Soon.

Autumn was here. He could feel it.

Judd closed in on the west side of the clearing and caught sight of Caulfield's Explorer parked out beside the garage. He lifted his fist, signaling the other teams to wait. Behind him, Nash went still. The back door was closed, windows dark. He couldn't see the front door from here. Even as he braced to creep closer for a better look, Judd heard the ratcheting of a rifle.

"Step away from her or I'll drop you where you stand."

Caulfield. He wasn't inside. Who the hell was he talking to?

Reassessing, he looked across the weedy backyard toward Ethan, communicating in hand gestures that he was going to try to get closer, using the SUV for cover. Ethan nodded and melted back into the trees with his team. Signaling to Nash for cover, Judd made his silent way through the grass, to the Explorer. Rising up from his crouch, he peered through the windows and saw the man himself in front of the house, rifle at his shoulder. Beyond him, about ten yards from the edge of the woods, flame red hair glinted in the lowering sun.

Autumn.

The swift rush of relief at seeing her alive morphed to something hot and dangerous as he noted one arm dangling by her side, her shoulder misshapen. Another man had his arm around her waist, obviously helping to keep her on her feet. Judd couldn't see much to identify him in the lowering sun.

"Turn around. Slowly," Caulfield ordered.

Hands lifted in the air, Autumn and the other man turned.

Jebediah?

Shock held Judd immobile for long, humming

seconds. He'd expected to see her father here. But in collusion with Caulfield, not at the other end of a gun. Was this some kind of a double cross?

"I said step away from her." Caulfield gestured with the barrel of the rifle.

Jebediah sneered. "You think I'm afraid of you?"

"I'm the one with the gun."

He continued as if Caulfield hadn't spoken. "You're going to let my daughter go."

Was Jebediah trying to stage a *rescue?* What kind of parallel universe had they strayed into?

"She came with me of her own volition."

"That so? That why you had her locked in the closet?"

The dark. The bastard had kept Autumn in the dark. Cold rage cut through the questions still swirling through Judd's head.

"Just keeping her safe."

"Only one she needs to be kept safe from is you."

Beyond them, Judd saw Ethan and his team

in position on the east side. Catching his eye, Ethan gestured north. Sheriff Riggs and his team were closing in. All of them were just inside the treeline, waiting for the signal.

"Get away from her," Caulfield grated out. "You don't touch her. You don't deserve to be near her after what you did."

"It was a mistake, and I've paid for it." But Jebediah did as he said and moved away from Autumn, toward the sheriff's team.

Judd breathed a quick sigh of relief because the barrel of the gun followed Jebediah, away from Autumn. She shifted, favoring the obviously dislocated shoulder, but managed to stay on her feet.

Caulfield narrowed his eyes. "You really think prison was a sufficient punishment? You *tried to kill her*!" He clutched the rifle tighter against his shoulder, and Judd tensed, prepared to fire.

Autumn spoke, voice level, the same tone Judd remembered her using to placate her father. "Put the gun down, Mark. There's no need for that."

Jebediah continued to edge away from her, drawing Caulfield's aim, bringing the pair of them closer to Judd. "I was drunk, stupid, and in a blind rage because her mother left me."

"That's no excuse."

"No," Jebediah agreed. "But it's the reason."

"And what was the reason for all those years before that? The beatings, the abuse? I'm not going to let you hurt her anymore." He dropped his head to sight down the barrel.

"Mark, stop! If you do this, it's murder. Leave him to the police."

"The police? They fucking let this animal out of his cage with no regard for you. You think they're going to get you justice?"

"An error I intend to rectify," Judd called. "Drop the gun. This is the police, and you're surrounded."

Ethan and Bill's teams emerged from the trees, weapons at the ready. Autumn's head whipped in his direction. Her eyes closed, and her mouth moved in what might have been a prayer of thanks. But they weren't out of this yet. None of his men were close enough yet to get between Autumn and Caulfield.

A muscle ticked in Caulfield's jaw. "Hamilton," he spat. "Always fucking Hamilton."

Judd signaled for the others to stay put and stepped out from behind the SUV, keeping his focus and his gun on Caulfield. "You okay, Firefly?"

"No permanent damage." The rasp of her voice told him she'd been screaming. It was yet another crime this son of a bitch was going to pay for.

"How long have you been out there?" Caulfield asked.

"Long enough."

"It doesn't matter. This isn't about you. It's about her and who can protect her best. I can do what you never could. I can take him out of this world, where he can never hurt her again."

"You think I haven't thought about that a thousand times over the years? You think the thought didn't cross my mind when I got notice he was being released?"

"And yet he's still standing here. Still breathing. I think he's gotten to do that long enough."

"Don't do it, Caulfield. Don't add murder to your list of crimes today. That's a mistake you can't come back from."

Caulfield turned to look at him then, eyes full of hatred. "Like you're going to let me walk away from this?"

That's right. Look at me.

Beyond him, Ethan and his team slowly edged closer, spreading out in front of Autumn in a fan.

"So far everything you've done has been to protect her. A jury will go lenient on you for that." It was bullshit, but he'd say whatever he had to in order to keep Caulfield's attention on him. "But murder—even understandable murder—is a whole other ball game."

"How does this end, Hamilton? You think you're gonna arrest me, take me in, throw me in a cell. And you're just going to take her home, make her your little fuck toy? She deserves better than that."

"You're right. She does. But she's not gonna be getting it from you."

"Fuck you, Hamilton." The rifle snapped up and Caulfield fired.

CHAPTER 20

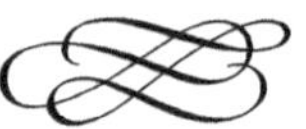

All around Autumn, gunfire exploded. She didn't even have time to scream before someone tackled her to the ground, covering her body. Terror ripped through her, a rabid animal stronger than the screaming agony of her shoulder. No, no. Not again. Not now.

Judd.

She needed up, needed to see, needed to breathe.

In the booming silence, she struggled against the man shielding her. "Judd," she gasped. The weight above her shifted, and she sucked in a breath. "Judd!"

"I'm all right!"

At the sound of his voice from behind her, somewhere closer to the house, she went limp with relief, pressing her face against the ground as her chest loosened for the first time in hours. He was safe. She hadn't lost him.

"Ethan, keep her over there."

"Got it."

The man—Ethan—sat up, keeping himself solidly between her and whatever was behind him. Death. She knew that much. Could smell the blood in the air. Her stomach roiled from it.

"You okay?" Ethan asked. "Did I hurt anything when I tackled you?"

Her wounded shoulder screamed, but what did that matter? Judd was safe. "Nothing that wasn't already hurt."

Ethan helped her into a sitting position. "Shit, that shoulder looks bad. Here." He whipped off his belt and fashioned a sort of sling to keep that arm close to her body.

Past him, she saw a single, jeans-clad leg outstretched, unmoving. Mark. He'd tried to fire his weapon at a cop. She knew protocol. Knew there was no possible way he'd survived. It was over. Really, truly over.

Judd rose from a crouch, murmured some orders, and then he was coming for her, long legs eating up the ground. He dropped to his knees and, at last—*at last*—his hands were on her. He cupped her face, his own expression caught between rage and a fierce tenderness. "He hit you."

"I backtalked him." The corner of her mouth twitched as she tried for some shadow of her usual levity and failed. "Apparently I didn't learn my lesson." The last words came out on a hiccupping sob. She couldn't stop the tears, didn't even try as she let loose all the worry and fear of the past hours.

Mindful of her shoulder, Judd pulled her into his arms, rocking them both, while the other officers went about the business of processing the crime scene.

"You came."

"Always."

"How did you find me?"

"Your father reported your abduction and Livia helped us figure out it was Mark. He had quite the shrine to you at his house."

"What?"

"He's been following you for a long time. He had articles, transcripts from the trial, pictures. There was even a box of stuff from your apartment. Some of the memories you thought had burned."

An odd sort of relief and gratitude mixed in with the crashing adrenaline. "Will I get them back?"

"Yeah. Yeah once everything is over."

That was something. She'd be grateful for it later. "But how did you get from there to here?"

"I knew he had to go to ground with you somewhere, and given his obsession, this seemed a viable location."

She turned her bruised head into his shoulder. "He was coming after you. When I rejected him, he was going to finish what my father started."

He brushed a kiss to the top of her head. "I thought they were working together."

"No. Jebediah was trying to save me when Mark got back. We might have made it if I hadn't fought him about it. I owe him thanks for that."

Judd went still, and she understood that Mark hadn't been the only casualty. "How?" she asked softly. "Did he get caught in the crossfire?"

"He jumped in front of Mark's gun."

Stunned, Autumn stared at him. "What?"

"He took the bullet meant for me. I was wearing a vest, but he maybe didn't know that."

"Why would he…?" She tried to wrap her brain around the idea, but it made no sense. Nothing about his actions today fit with the man who'd terrorized and haunted her all of her life.

"Maybe it was his way of making amends. And going out on his own terms."

Autumn had no idea how to feel. She'd hated her father most of her life, been terrified of him, terrorized by him. He'd been the source of the worst memories of her past. And he'd just sacrificed himself for the man she loved. There was a kind of circularity to that. Closure.

"We're free," she whispered.

"Yeah. Yeah we are."

"Judd?"

They both looked up as Sheriff Riggs strode over. "Listen, we've got all this taken care of if you want to get her out of here."

"Not your jurisdiction."

"We've got Officers Brewer and Blanchard from WPD. I think we can get it sorted. Go take care of your woman." He flashed a smile at Autumn. "Glad we got you back."

"Thank you." She raised her voice. "Thank all of you."

There was a chorus of acknowledgments around her.

Judd got to his feet, then scooped her up. "Hospital. You're getting a full workup."

"Want a ride?" Ethan stood, car keys in hand. "Since I'm not exactly here in an official capacity, I'm not real helpful at this stage."

"I'm sorry, who are you exactly?" Autumn asked.

"Ethan Greer, U.S. Marshal Service, ma'am."

She looked to Judd. "You called in the Marshals?"

"Actually no. Ethan's interviewing for the position as Chief, and he volunteered to help." The look Judd shot him was full of respect. "Thank you. And a ride would be much appreciated."

Autumn insisted they run on silent into town. "I don't want to draw any more attention than absolutely necessary. I was kidnapped under the noses of the press. They'll want to be all over the fact that I've been rescued."

But apparently it was too late. News vans were all over the hospital parking lot and a crowd of reporters were mobbed around the entrance to the Emergency Department.

She stared. "How?"

"Somebody probably had a police scanner. Pull on around to the ambulance bays. We're going in the back."

As soon as Ethan pulled the car inside, people were coming toward them. A familiar blonde was leading the pack, the white tails of her coat flapping.

"You can't be back here! This is for ambulances only!"

Ethan slid out of the driver's seat, not batting an eye. "We've got a dislocated shoulder, probable concussion and possible orbital fracture here, and the ER entrance is currently mobbed by reporters. We figured you could make an exception."

Standing toe to toe with him, Doctor Miranda Campbell's brows drew together before she hunched down to look into the backseat. "Oh, Jesus. Get me a gurney!" She yanked open the back door. "Autumn?"

"Hey, Miranda. Didn't know you were on duty tonight."

She hissed through the pain as Miranda helped Judd ease her out of the car.

"Shit. I know you want the inside scoop on the pool about our new Doctor McHottie, but this was not the way to get it."

Autumn barked a laugh that instantly turned to a groan. "I promise, I'm not that desperate."

They settled her on the gurney a couple of orderlies wheeled out.

Face grim, Miranda looked to Judd. "You get who did this to her?"

"Yeah."

"Good. Get her inside." She pointed at Ethan. "You, Cowboy, get that car out of my ambulance bay."

The stoic marshal's mouth twitched and he lifted a hand to his brow, as if tipping an imaginary hat. "Yes, ma'am."

Miranda blinked once, and even through the haze of pain, Autumn noted the crackle of energy between them. If Ethan took the job as chief of police, Dr. McHottie wouldn't be the only pool she'd be betting in.

With a sudden flurry of motion, Miranda was on the go again, snapping more orders, and Autumn was rushed inside.

Later—much, much later—Autumn was resting in a quiet back room of the Emergency Department. Judd perched on the edge of the bed, one hand stroking her hair, the other holding tight to her hand. They hadn't talked much. She'd been too exhausted for that. But he warned her that, while she was having her CT scan, he'd had to call the family to give them the update. Apparently a full Hamilton clan reunion was being planned in honor of her survival, just as soon as she was healed up, whenever that was.

Miranda finally returned. "Well, you are remarkably lucky." She pulled up the scan on a screen mounted to the wall and started pointing at things. "The orbital socket isn't fractured, which is a freaking miracle. You sustained a mild concussion, assorted minor lacerations and contusions. That shiner's gonna be with you a while, too. But the shoulder is the worst of it. Now that it's been reset, you'll need to wear a sling for the next few days. Light activity after a couple of weeks. It'll be about three months before you'll be cleared for any heavy lifting."

"I'm not letting her lift more than a finger to point any time soon," Judd assured her.

"I mean…you might want to be careful," Autumn warned. "A girl could get used to that."

"Well deserved," Miranda declared. "Also, congratulations on all this." She waved a hand between them. "Finally. Even if you did screw my bracket. I had January in the pool."

"Seriously?" Judd groaned.

"I told you no one would be surprised."

He pressed a kiss to her uninjured temple. "You realize I'm just going to take that as a challenge, right?"

Resting her head against his shoulder, she closed her eyes. "Can't wait."

"No, I appreciate the offer. I'll give it some thought." Autumn's hand stroked a lazy path down Boudreaux's side where he sprawled beside her Adirondack chair.

They made a picture, Judd decided as he stepped out onto the pier. The woman and the dog whose heart she owned. They both held his.

"Mmm hmmm. I'll let you know. Bye bye." She ended the call and smiled up at him. "Hey you."

"Hey yourself."

The bruising on her face had hit that worse before better stage that resembled an Impressionist blend of purples, blues, and yellows, but the swelling was nearly gone and she was out of the sling. Best of all, there were no longer shadows in her eyes. He stepped around Boudreaux, scooped her out of the Adirondack chair, and settled in it himself with her across his lap.

She snuggled in, resting her head against his shoulder. "You'll never guess who that was."

"Another agent offering you representation?" Once their story had hit mainstream media, her book sales had exploded and several major players had taken an interest in her.

"Not just any agent. Dinah McClure's agent. She's, like, huge. I mean, everybody in the romance world wants to *be* her."

"Didn't she do a signing here sometime last year?"

"Yeah, and I missed it because it was a surprise thing and I was out of town." Her lip rolled out into a pout Judd couldn't help kissing.

"So are you going to take this one or keep on trucking on your own?"

"I'm considering it. I don't want to mess with traditional publishing, but Katerina isn't pushing that. She'd be there to help handle audio, media, and foreign rights, which is all stuff way out of my wheelhouse. It would be pretty awesome to have someone experienced handling those things."

"Media? So when Lifetime shows up and wants to make us into a movie, she's the person who'd deal with that?"

Autumn clapped a hand over his mouth. "Oh God, don't even put that into the universe."

Laughing, he tugged her hand down. "You can laugh in their faces. Or get Katerina to, if you decide to hire her. You get to drive this train, Firefly, wherever you want to take it."

"It's pretty crazy to think about."

"Will you stick with this pen name? There's a lot of notoriety attached to it now, and it's certainly no secret."

"I've realized that the whole notion of a truly secret pen name is a thing of the past. Modern technology pretty well ensures that anybody determined enough can figure it out. The fact is, scandal sells. My name, Harper's name, is making a splash in the media right now. It's certainly not how I'd prefer to build a brand, but it's there. I'm not going to give up that platform out of fear. Because I can use it. I *want* to use it to write fiction that will empower women. That's been the absolute best part of this whole crazy ride—all the messages and emails from women who took that away from my work and used it to better their lives. I didn't set out to do that deliberately when I wrote it, but I want to, moving forward, because I think it's a meaningful use of my abilities."

Judd kissed her brow. "I'm proud of you. For finding your passion and following it. For making it a part of your plan for the future."

"The future's a long way off, but it's nice to have a destination in mind."

The future Judd wanted was right now.

"What about you?" she asked. "The threat is past. You aren't bound to the path you've been on for all these years."

"That's actually why I came out here. I need to run into town and take care of some things."

She leaned back and studied his face. "You're going to talk to Sandra."

"I'm going to talk to Sandra," he confirmed, though that certainly wasn't his only business in town.

"Good. It's the right decision. Do you mind if I stay here? I think I'm ready to dive in and finally get back to actually writing."

The non-job-related part of his errands were much better accomplished solo.

"You sure you'll be okay on your own?" It had taken several days to deal with all the formalities. The Sheriff's Department and Wishful PD had done their best to leave Judd out of it so he could be home with Autumn, while she recovered. He hadn't left her completely alone since her rescue.

"Yeah, I think so. Boudreaux and I were going to set up on the porch. He has some hard-core napping to do, and I'm hoping to knock out a couple of chapters by dinner."

"If you're going that head-down in the work, I'll grab take out. What do you want?"

"Surprise me."

Oh, I intend to.

Judd started his parade of errands with City Hall. How much had changed since he last climbed these steps. What a difference a week made.

He knocked on Sandra's open door.

She looked up, instantly rising behind her desk as she saw him. "Judd, please, come in. Sit down."

"Mayor Crawford." Judd took a seat in one of the visitor's chairs, feeling too big for the space and eager to get this conversation over with. "Thank you for seeing me."

"Of course. I wanted to speak with you, too. How's Autumn?"

The first couple of days home had been rough. But the nightmares had already stopped, and she seemed to be at peace with her father's death. Once his body was released, he'd be cremated. She was, as she'd already demonstrated, focused on the future instead of the past.

"She's a remarkably resilient woman."

Sandra came around the desk and sat in the other visitor's chair, facing him. "I owe you an apology. On behalf of the entire City Council. I'm sorry we questioned you. You were right and Autumn was hurt. When I think about what could've happened—"

"Don't," he said. "It didn't."

"It didn't because you did your job, and you did it well, despite or maybe because of your personal connection to the situation. You're an excellent cop and a good man, Judd, and you've done a good job as Chief of Police. We'd like you to keep the job permanently."

"I appreciate the apology and the offer, but that's not why I'm here. I'm tendering my resignation."

"As Chief?"

"From Wishful PD entirely."

Distress flickered over her face. "Judd, no. I know you took the job under stressful conditions, and you've had to cope with things that no one ought to have to cope with, but don't let that drive you away."

"I'm not. The fact is, y'all accused me of using departmental resources for personal reasons. And I absolutely did. My entire career as a cop has been for one purpose, and one purpose alone: To keep Autumn safe whenever Jebediah got released. Now, I stand by my use of those resources because she was legitimately in danger, albeit not from the quarter I expected. But the fact is, my reason for being here doesn't exist anymore."

"But you're so good at it."

"I'm good at being a cop. I'm good at investigation. And that's why I've accepted a position as Investigator with the Wachoxee County Sheriff's Department. So I'm here to officially resign and give my full support to Ethan Greer's candidacy for Chief of Police."

"Why him?"

"Because he offered up his help to find Autumn when he didn't have to. He used the resources he had to assist in the investigation. He's got a good mind, a good head on his shoulders, and a willingness to sacrifice himself for the good of this town. And he's better at all the liaising and politicking than I'd ever be. I don't know who your other candidates are, but he's my pick, for whatever that's worth."

"It's worth a lot. And much as I hate to lose you, I can see your mind is made up, so I'll wish you well in your new job."

Judd left her office feeling lighter than he had in years, no longer burdened by the specter of what might happen. The worst had come to pass and they'd survived it. He could let go of the duty that had driven him for so many years and turn his attention to granting Autumn all of those dreams. It would take a lifetime, and he couldn't wait.

As he hit the sidewalk outside City Hall, there was a spring in his step and a smile on his face. Everything was falling into place, and he had work to do to make sure the pieces landed exactly right. The family reunion was less than a month away. If he was going to move forward on the first of those big dreams of hers, he had about a million details to sort out. Time to get busy.

EPILOGUE

For all she'd been in and out of the Hamilton household all her life, Autumn wasn't sure she'd ever truly known how many of them there were. It was one thing to objectively know how many cousins Judd had. It was entirely another to see them all in one place. Owen was one of Pop and Nanna's three children. Each of them had also had three children. And that didn't even begin to cover the extended family brought in by Pop's brother and sister and their progeny.

Picnic tables and camp chairs covered the

lawn outside the back of Pop and Nanna's house, and there were people at all of them. Pop and his brother were manning the grill, arguing over the right ratio of charcoal. Nanna was inside with several of the other Hamilton women, finishing up enough cobbler to feed the army. The counters in her kitchen were covered with more casseroles than Autumn had ever seen in one place outside a church potluck. She sat at a corner of the back deck and absorbed the sounds and scents of life.

"What are you smiling about?" Judd asked, dropping onto the glider beside her.

Autumn automatically snuggled into the curve of his arm. "Just because I'm happy."

"You don't mind all the crazy?"

"It's the best kind of crazy."

"Spoken like a true Hamilton," Leo announced in a voice so loud, Autumn wondered how many beers he'd had already.

Everybody's attention shot their way.

Judd lifted a brow. "Nice, little bro."

Leo just shrugged and grinned.

Definitely at least two too many beers for this early.

Judd shifted to face her. "The thing is, you've been an unofficial part of this family for twenty-five years. I think it's time we change that."

The sudden quiet sparked Autumn's nerves, as did the look in Judd's eyes as he slid off the seat.

"What are you doing?" she hissed.

"Catching up," he said, and sank to one knee.

Someone—Patty?—squeaked, but Autumn couldn't take her eyes off Judd to check.

"When you came to us in high school, my parents could've adopted you. They didn't. And it had nothing to do with them not wanting you as part of the family. You were always meant to be a Hamilton, it just wasn't through them. They knew that, maybe before I acknowledged it myself. But the truth is, I've loved you since I was six years old. I'll love you until I'm a hundred and six. So—" He pulled a box out of his pocket. "I'm asking you, Autumn Elizabeth, in front of literally the entire Hamilton clan, to marry me." He flicked the box open.

Autumn dimly registered the ring, but she couldn't take her eyes off his. Her heart felt so full, for long moments, she couldn't speak. Here was everything she'd always wanted. Family. Friendship. And more love than a body could contain.

She reached out, cupping his face between her palms. "It's been yes since we were seventeen."

The twins whooped and everybody cheered, as Judd scooped her up and kissed her until they were both out of breath.

"Mom," he said, "you may now hit number seven on your speed dial."

"Oh boy!" Patty whipped out her phone and hit the number.

From somewhere around the corner, a tinny version of "Here comes the bride" began to play. Patty's jaw dropped open as an older gentleman stepped up on the porch. "Reverend Prescott?"

"She said yes," Judd announced.

"Got that. Congratulations!" Then the minister stuck two fingers in his mouth and let loose an ear-splitting whistle.

From across the yard, the barn door opened and people began to spill out like clowns from a tiny car.

"What is going on?" Autumn asked.

Judd lifted her hand, pressing a kiss to her knuckles. "We're getting married."

"Here? *Now?*"

"Well, as soon as you and Babette decide on a dress." He nodded toward the Brides and Belles van pulling out from behind the barn.

Autumn stared at him. "You…organized our wedding?"

"I wasted years being an idiot. I'm not wasting another day." When she said nothing, for the first time, uncertainty flickered over his face. "If this isn't what you want, we can wait and do it later. I just thought, everybody's here and—"

She cut him off with a fierce kiss. "Whatever you did, it's absolutely perfect."

"Then go find your dress, while we finish setting up."

Patty and Nanna spirited her to the back of the house. Babette brought in a full rack of dresses in her size, in every style imaginable. But like Autumn's choice in men, the first one was exactly right. Ivory satin, with clean lines and a sweep of skirt to her ballet slipper clad toes, it suited her and the simple, perfect wedding she'd been gifted. Judd's cousin, Emma, whipped out some hot rollers, while his other cousin, Amelia, started in on Autumn's makeup. It was a bit like being put through bridal boot camp. But an hour later, she was ready to walk down the aisle and marry her best friend in front of his entire family.

"They're ready!" Nanna announced. "Oh my lord, don't you look beautiful."

"So beautiful," Patty sniffed and waved a hand at her face. She was already a weepy mess.

"Don't mind me, I'm just so happy. I can't believe he did this."

Autumn smiled and linked her arm through her future mother-in-law's. "I think it was as much a surprise for you as for me. And hey, you did get to use your speed dial."

"I did." She gave a teary grin. "So I'll forgive him for depriving me of getting to plan the wedding."

"Cheer up. You still have Eli and Leo."

"True, but a daughter's wedding is extra special."

Autumn felt her throat go tight. "Oh hell, is this mascara waterproof?"

"Well, clean yourself up right quick, Patty," Nanna ordered. "The photographer's already snapping pictures."

"Oh, there's a photographer?" Autumn asked.

"And flowers, and chairs, and music. He covered everything. All your friends just showed up in a caravan."

He'd made sure there were people here for

her. "Just when I thought I couldn't love him any more," Autumn murmured.

By the time she came out of the house, the long slope of front lawn had been transformed. Rows of white chairs, filled with guests—Hamiltons and friends and even the senior center book club—had been set up in a neat rectangle, bisected by a long white runner. Little arrangements of greenery and deep blue ribbon accented the end of each row. At the front of the aisle, beneath an arbor twined with climbing roses, the minister stood, Bible in hand. Eli and Leo, both dressed in tuxes, flanked Reverend Prescott on one side and Boudreaux in a matching bowtie on the other.

"Oh my God, you're gorgeous!" Livia gushed.

Autumn turned to find her friend in a blue dress that matched the ribbon, a bouquet of flowers in her hand. Riley stood beaming right behind in a matching dress.

"Oh God, *now* I'm going to cry. He even made sure you were both bridesmaids?"

Riley flapped a hand toward Autumn's stinging eyes. "No, no crying until this and all the pictures are done. It's the rule." She handed over an enormous bouquet of lilies. Autumn's favorite.

Livia grinned. "Married now. Hugs later. Let's get this show on the road."

As if waiting for her signal, music rolled out of speakers from…somewhere. Riley began making her way down the aisle to Pachelbel's Canon in D.

But wait. Judd wasn't up front. They couldn't start the wedding without him. Autumn started to call out, but refrained. Maybe he was going to come out after the wedding party was in place? Didn't some weddings work like that? So she held her tongue as the processional continued. Livia took her position beside Riley.

Everybody stood up and turned around, looking at her. The music shifted into the bridal march and still no Judd. Cameras flashed. Autumn didn't move. How could she? Her groom was MIA.

A warm hand slipped into hers. Autumn looked up. And there he was, breathtaking in his tux, as she'd known he'd be. He smiled at her, and she smiled back, her moment of doubt washed away by joy. Judd tipped his head toward the crowd.

Ready for this?

Autumn nodded.

Judd tucked her hand through his arm and they walked the aisle, between family and friends, as they'd done everything else for most of their lifetime.

Together.

Choose Your Next Romance

In the wake of Judd's resignation, changes are coming to Wishful PD! *Watch Over Me* is a neighbor/hot guy next door romance between Reserve Officer Nash Brewer and Rowan Beale, niece of former Wishful police chief Robert Curry. Nash is another of those big-hearted, caretaking heroes you love.

Or maybe you're feeling bad about what happened to Mary Alice. I don't blame you. So did I. Judd did her pretty wrong in all his self-denial, so I had to make it up to her by introducing her to her TRUE match—Wishful's favorite Dr. Hottie, Chad Phillips. You can read all about their romance in *The Christmas Fountain,* Book 9 in my Wishful Romance series.

OTHER BOOKS BY KAIT NOLAN

A complete and up-to-date list of all my books can be found at https://kaitnolan.com.

THE MISFIT INN SERIES
SMALL TOWN FAMILY ROMANCE

- *When You Got A Good Thing* (Kennedy and Xander)
- *Til There Was You* (Misty and Denver)

- *Those Sweet Words* (Pru and Flynn)
- *Stay A Little Longer* (Athena and Logan)
- *Bring It On Home* (Maggie and Porter)

RESCUE MY HEART SERIES
SMALL TOWN MILITARY ROMANCE

- *Baby It's Cold Outside* (Ivy and Harrison)
- *What I Like About You* (Laurel and Sebastian)
- *Bad Case of Loving You* (Paisley and Ty prequel)
- *Made For Loving You* (Paisley and Ty)

MEN OF THE MISFIT INN
SMALL TOWN SOUTHERN ROMANCE

- *Let It Be Me* (Emerson and Caleb)
- *Our Kind of Love* (Abbey and Kyle)

WISHFUL SERIES

SMALL TOWN SOUTHERN ROMANCE

- *Once Upon A Coffee* (Avery and Dillon)
- *To Get Me To You* (Cam and Norah)
- *Know Me Well* (Liam and Riley)
- *Be Careful, It's My Heart* (Brody and Tyler)
- *Just For This Moment* (Myles and Piper)
- *Wish I Might* (Reed and Cecily)
- *Turn My World Around* (Tucker and Corinne)
- *Dance Me A Dream* (Jace and Tara)
- *See You Again* (Trey and Sandy)
- *The Christmas Fountain* (Chad and Mary Alice)
- *You Were Meant For Me* (Mitch and Tess)
- *A Lot Like Christmas* (Ryan and Hannah)
- *Dancing Away With My Heart* (Zach and Lexi)

WISHING FOR A HERO SERIES (A WISHFUL SPINOFF SERIES)
SMALL TOWN ROMANTIC SUSPENSE

- *Make You Feel My Love* (Judd and Autumn)
- *Watch Over Me* (Nash and Rowan)
- *Can't Take My Eyes Off You* (Ethan and Miranda)
- *Burn For You* (Sean and Delaney)

MEET CUTE ROMANCE
SMALL TOWN SHORT ROMANCE

- *Once Upon A Snow Day*
- *Once Upon A New Year's Eve*
- *Once Upon An Heirloom*
- *Once Upon A Coffee*
- *Once Upon A Campfire*
- *Once Upon A Rescue*

SUMMER CAMP
CONTEMPORARY ROMANCE

- *Once Upon A Campfire*
- *Second Chance Summer*

Kait is a Mississippi native, who often swears like a sailor, calls everyone sugar, honey, or dar-lin', and can wield a bless your heart like a saber or a Snuggie, depending on requirements.

You can find more information on this

RITA ® Award-winning author and her books on her website http://kaitnolan.com. While you're there, sign up for her newsletter so you don't miss out on news about new releases!